A POWERFUL SECRET

THE WORTHINGTON DESTINY ▪ BOOK 2

A POWERFUL SECRET

A NOVEL

DR. KEVIN LEMAN
AND JEFF NESBIT

Published by Revell
a division of Baker Publishing Group
P.O. Box 6287, Grand Rapids, MI 49516-6287
www.revellbooks.com

Printed in the United States of America

Library of Congress Cataloging-in-Publication Data
Names: Leman, Kevin, author. | Nesbit, Jeffrey Asher.
Title: A powerful secret : a novel / Dr. Kevin Leman and Jeff Nesbit.
Description: Grand Rapids, MI : Revell, a division of Baker Publishing Group, [2016] | Series: The Worthington destiny ; book 2
Identifiers: LCCN 2015040486 | ISBN 9780800723316 (pbk.)
Subjects: LCSH: First-born children—Fiction. | Ambition—Fiction. | Choice (Psychology)—Fiction. | GSAFD: Christian fiction.
Classification: LCC PS3612.E4455 P69 2016 | DDC 813/.6—dc23 LC record available at http://lccn.loc.gov/2015040486

"To those who are given much, much is required" is a paraphrase of Luke 12:48.

"It is when you are weak that true strength comes" is a paraphrase of 2 Corinthians 12:10.

Edited by Ramona Cramer Tucker

16 17 18 19 20 21 22 7 6 5 4 3 2 1

To all those curious enough
to seek, question, and forge their own path in life.

And to those who choose to do the right thing,
no matter the consequences.

Glossary

AF: American Frontier
AG: Attorney General
API: American Petroleum Institute
DA: District Attorney
DHS: Department of Homeland Security
DOJ: Department of Justice
DSCC: Democratic Senatorial Campaign Committee
EPA: Environmental Protection Agency
FBI: Federal Bureau of Investigation
GJ: Green Justice
GOP: Grand Old Party (Republican Party)
IPO: Initial Public Offering
NGO: Nongovernmental organization
NYPD: New York Police Department

1

New York City

"I don't get you. I don't get you at all."

Sean Thomas Worthington hurled the words at his brother, Will. The two faced off outside the door of Will's three-bedroom suite on 71st, overlooking Central Park's west side.

Sean thought he knew his brother. William Jennings Worthington VI always identified his goal with laser-like clarity and then relentlessly pursued it, never letting anything or anyone stand in his way. But that very day, just when Will had been prepared to launch his bid to represent New York in the US Senate, he'd disappeared from their campaign headquarters. He hadn't answered Sean's texts either.

Then, with only a minute to spare before the scheduled start of the campaign launch and media briefing, Will had reappeared. He strode briskly past Sean and the other members of their family in attendance and mounted the platform.

The speech he'd given wasn't the one he and Sean had polished for hours until it was a pristine masterpiece. Instead Will said with little preamble, "I've decided not to run for the United States Senate seat in New York."

Shock skittered down Sean's spine.

"I've made this decision for personal reasons," Will added with the steely calm that was his trademark. "I don't intend to discuss those reasons now or in the future." Then he exited the stage while the media whipped into a feeding frenzy.

For the past several hours, Sean, Will's campaign manager, had handled the unanswerable questions from reporters with professional but vague responses. He had no answers himself as to why Will had suddenly backed out of the race. Will hadn't confided in him.

Now Sean was beyond furious. Evidently it showed, for one glimpse of his face at the door of Will's home, and Laura, his sister-in-law, had held up a hand.

"Look," she warned, "you two have to work this out. But don't do it in front of the kids. I'll tell Will you're here."

Then she closed the door firmly and left Sean in the hallway. Laura didn't care that he was a Worthington. Her first priority, always, was to make sure that their home was a safe and loving place for their children. There would be no war of words in their home.

Two minutes later, with Sean pacing all the while, Will opened the door, slipped out, and closed it carefully behind him. Instead of his impeccable Giorgio Armani suit, he was dressed in his usual running clothes for his daily miles through Central Park.

"You drop out of the race now, after all our work?" Sean's anger flared even hotter. Their mom's Irish heritage was showing, but he honestly didn't care. What had gotten into his brother?

Will didn't reply. He merely took a step back—away from Sean, away from the fight. An indiscernible emotion flashed into his dark eyes. For a second, it looked like pain . . . pity . . . sadness . . . or fear.

Fear? Sean frowned. His brother had never been afraid of anything. As Worthingtons, they'd learned early to face down bullies and not only hold their own but win. Their father said it was good practice for when they'd assume their roles in the family business, Worthington Shares.

"So, are you going to tell me why?" Sean demanded.

Will raised his chin. "I said publicly that I didn't intend to discuss the reasons now or in the future."

Sean crossed his arms. "And that goes for me too? Your brother? Your campaign manager? You just walk away into the sunset and leave me to pick up your mess?"

Will tilted his head. Sean felt his brother's piercing gaze sweep across him—the one that had intimidated Sean and their sister, Sarah, in childhood, making them acquiesce to whatever Will wanted.

But instead of the final brief words that usually ended any fight in his favor, Will relaxed his stance. "I did what I needed to do," he said stoically. "For me, for you, for our family. That's all I can say."

At that moment Sean knew what he'd hoped for was over—the opportunity to work arm in arm with his older brother on a venture where Will actually needed Sean's well-honed networking talents. He shook his head. He'd mistakenly thought that this time he could make their father, William Jennings Worthington V, proud. That instead of bypassing Sean to zero in on Will as the one the Worthington name depended on, Bill might give Sean the long-awaited "well done, son" he longed for.

It was not meant to be.

"So that's it," Sean huffed.

"That's it."

With those few words, Will walked toward the elevator.

More than anything, Sean wanted his brother to do something normal, like force him into a headlock or tell him to shut up, like he used to when they were growing up. Instead Will was strangely calm, distant, like he was in a business meeting.

But what bothered Sean even more than the eerie detachment was that indiscernible emotion in Will's eyes. That frankly terrified him.

What could invoke that kind of emotion in his brother, who wasn't afraid of anything?

2

As soon as the elevator doors shut, Will was alone with the clamoring voices in his thoughts. He heard his mother's plea: *"Family first. Promise me."*

He heard his father: *"Always do the right thing. But know when it's time to fight and when it's time to back away. Listen to that still small voice."*

So Will had listened and done what he knew was right. Eric Sandstrom, the CEO of American Frontier, the most powerful oil company in the world, had played his dark trump card in the sunshine of Washington Square Park and thought he had Will trapped. Will had acquiesced to the demands of Sandstrom's lawyer lackey, for now.

Will had no explanation for what he'd seen in the photo Jason Carson showed him—Sean sitting with a shady character in a bar. A man now identified as the Polar Bear Bomber. But Will knew what that photo, if released, would mean to the public. Sean Worthington, billionaire trust-fund playboy who usually sported the latest up-and-coming model on his arm at black-tie events, was somehow involved with the bombing of the American Frontier building—the biggest domestic terrorist incident of the past 20 years.

The timing couldn't be worse—right in the middle of the oil spill fracas, with Sean center stage in chartering a boat that had taken him, Green Justice's Kirk Baldwin, and *New York Times* reporter Jon Gillibrand into the icy Arctic waters as firsthand observers. Green Justice had pulled gutsy maneuvers before, but never something colossally stupid and life-threatening, like bombing a building.

Sure, Sean colored outside the lines at times, but Will had never known his younger brother to step outside any moral or ethical boundaries. Still, there was a first time for everything, and maybe Sean's departure from the norm had been caught on camera. The photo—or, most likely, photos—going viral would not only ruin Sean in the business world, tarnish the reputation of Green Justice, and put Jon in the hot seat with his feisty boss, but it would bring the entire Worthington family under scrutiny. Will couldn't let that happen. He'd been playing the role of his brother's and sister's protector for as long as he could remember. With their father traveling and in meetings as they grew up, his siblings had turned to Will, as much as they hated to admit it. He'd gotten them out of more trouble than he ever wanted their parents to know about. So he'd done what he'd needed to do to keep that photo from going viral. At Carson's "request," Will had stepped out of the Senate race to protect his family—most of all Sean.

Drew Simons, the Worthington family's financial advisor, had been right as usual. He'd reported that Sandstrom was worried Will would use every opportunity to beat up on American Frontier during his Senate campaign. So the hot-under-the-collar Sandstrom had pinpointed the three billionaire sibling heirs as the key to solving his dilemmas, Drew said. After all, Sarah was calling the shots on the Department of Justice's criminal negligence case and had investigators actively digging for dirt on AF. Add to that her friend Darcy Wiggins, a Department of Homeland Security agent, coming to conclusions that would blow AF sky-high as a company, and Sarah was a formidable opponent. Sean was too. Not only was he an eyewitness to the oil spill, but his ecological biodiversity NGO was talking about billions in damages if they could prove how much oil was gushing from the bottom of the ocean and the toppled AF platform. Then there was Will, former board member, who had crippled AF by selling the Worthington shares and then joining the shareholder lawsuit.

"Knock out the Worthington kids, and he thinks his problems are solved," Drew had warned. "He told Jason Carson he wanted to tie up loose ends for good . . . kill three birds with one stone."

Unfortunately, Drew hadn't been able to uncover any specifics of Sandstrom's plan before that day in Washington Square Park.

Will now knew about the plan firsthand. But he also wasn't going down without a fight. He hated bullies, and Carson was a bully. Worse, he was an underhanded slimeball who didn't care how dirty his hands got. He'd been rewarded for it throughout his career. Will wasn't about to go on record as one of the good people Carson brought down, nor would he allow his family to be thrust into the harsh limelight Carson was capable of generating.

His wife, Laura, understood his last-minute decision. That he knew from their brief exchange of glances when she and their oldest child, Andrew, had arrived home from the Senate launch event. Approval glimmered in her eyes, as well as a challenge. *So what's next, Will?* she seemed to be saying.

Yes, Laura knew him well. She grasped the stakes of why

he'd backed down—the secret he was trying to keep under wraps. She understood his love for his family, his fierce protectiveness of his brother, and his steely determination that they not be hurt by what his mother, Ava, had revealed to him on the shores of Lake Chautauqua outside their family summer home. A stunning, devastating truth that only Will, his mother, and Laura now knew.

But Laura doesn't know the rest of it, Will thought wryly. *When she hears what Carson pulled today* . . . A chuckle escaped, the first in his intense day, as he pictured the scene. His slender, hazel-eyed wife was a straight shooter and called things as she saw them. She was a force to be reckoned with in her own right when her loved ones were in someone's sights.

Will sobered, recalling the confusion on his son's face. No words had been exchanged. Andrew, who had Laura's dark brown hair, lean frame, and hazel eyes, studied Will a minute, then embraced him a trifle longer than usual before padding up the stairs toward his room. Somehow the solemn Andrew, almost 13, understood a momentous event had played out. He was so like Will—serious, hardworking, hard on himself, and learning too early the high price of wealth and fame—that Will worried at times. Yet someday Andrew would assume the mantle of Worthington firstborn heir, and he needed to be prepared.

As the elevator doors opened, Will adjusted his focus. The Jason Carsons and Eric Sandstroms of the world would not win—not on Will's watch. He had plans to make, and a run would clear his head.

Will had never walked away from any challenge. But now he was a quitter in the eyes of the world. That was a very difficult pill to swallow. But only his wife and mother could ever know the truth of why he'd walked away from the Senate run and national politics. He needed to protect his younger brother, both to preserve his mother's secret and to shield Sean from the searing scrutiny of any potential connection to the domestic terrorist action against American Frontier. One secret—Sean's birth father—could never emerge. And the other—the picture of Sean sharing a drink with the man who would become the AF bomber—must likewise remain in the shadows forever.

But Will couldn't escape the feeling that with two startling revelations surfacing so recently, more were certain to follow.

3

Sean knew what his brother did to strategize any difficult quandary. He ran. Will's drive to increase his endurance, to best his own time, was what had made him an undefeatable force in high school in long-distance track. The same competitive edge had earned him captain of the lacrosse team while at Harvard.

Sean had a lifetime of practice in keeping up with his brother, trying to beat him in a race, but this time he didn't follow. He didn't even try. Anything he could say would be pointless. Once Will made up his mind, it was a done deal. Sean had learned that, or thought he had, until his brother short-circuited the Senate race and an almost certain first step toward an even bigger prize in national politics.

Sean paused outside Will's front door to rein in his anger. It was bad enough that he had put his own life on hold, including many of his own NGO travels on behalf of Worthington Shares start-ups, to assist his brother with a fast-track campaign. With Worthington money, power, and connections, Will had been a shoo-in as candidate. So much so that Kiki Estrada, the executive director of the Democratic Senatorial Campaign Committee, had clearly focused her first-tier choice on the Worthington family, Will in particular. She'd pestered Will nonstop until he had agreed to run.

Now Kiki was fit to be tied. She'd already called Sean four times, and he knew she wouldn't give up until she got an answer that made sense.

Sean had nothing to tell her. In addition, he'd used every networking connection he had, tapping into his far-reaching social media circle to ensure Will would get that Senate seat and it would be an easy run. Now Sean was embarrassed. True, Worthington money had financed the campaign up to the launch event, so they hadn't needed to go after outside donors. Still, Sean had cashed in a lot of long-standing favors with his colleagues. How could he explain Will walking away—with nothing to show for it?

The media circus would be bad for a while, but Sean could deal with that. Hardly a day passed where one of the Worthingtons, particularly Sean and his social butterfly sister, was not emblazoned somewhere. So even though this was the rich and famous Worthington family that all of New York liked to watch, Will's withdrawal from the race would play in the headlines for only a short while. Then the press would be back to wringing what they could out of the oil spill and the mystery of the Polar Bear Bomber. When that failed to offer public titillation, they'd be on to the next hot story.

Sean could understand Will leaving the mess at American Frontier. Who on earth would want to remain a board member, much less take on a role as the new CEO of an oil company in the midst of a colossal oil spill that would affect every ocean system on the entire planet? Well, other than Will, who thrived on challenges that appeared impossible to overcome.

A snippet of their childhood flashed into Sean's mind.

Whenever the two brothers played, Will cast himself in the role of the Caped Crusader, complete with their mother's tablecloth draped for effect. Sean was the villain.

I guess nothing's changed in Dad's eyes, Sean thought.

Will would forever be the perfect son, groomed for the helm of the family company. He managed the stable end of Worthington Shares—the big, established, blue-chip companies.

Sean fell into the "we might as well see if we can make any money here" role. Entrepreneurial ventures, launched with Worthington capital—the risky side of the business, where big money was won and lost—had ended up a natural fit for Sean. They allowed him to stay at the forefront of world events. Jet-setting across the globe, connecting with people, and kicking off dreams energized him. Seeing a few of those dreams fly whetted his appetite for more. Ten or so of his more than 100 start-ups were now poised to break out in big ways.

Bill Worthington understood both sides of the business but, like Will, was more comfortable with the blue-chip companies. However, it had been Will and Drew Simons who had maneuvered for Sean to take over the expansion of Worthington Shares in the start-ups. The job perfectly fit him and his entrepreneurial ways, they said, and Bill had agreed to give Sean the opportunity.

Sean had more than delivered—nearly a billion dollars in value in the last five years. Why then did he feel like he didn't belong around the family dinner table? Or that no matter how much he did, he could never fully please his father? Maybe it was because, when they were growing up, he was the least likely one to be missed if he was MIA. With the spotlight on either his older brother or his charming baby sister, Sean felt stuck in the middle, which is exactly where he was.

Just like he was again, right now. Stuck between his family and those who had expected more out of a Worthington.

Sean sighed. Bill Worthington would find a way to cast Will in the role of Caped Crusader even in this situation. And that left Sean with the role of . . .

Some things never changed.

Will picked up his pace in Central Park. Once his breathing steadied and he'd fallen into a natural rhythm, he kicked into brainstorming mode again. It was a given that he needed to get more information about that photo of Sean and the Polar Bear Bomber, but how exactly could he go after it without tipping his hand?

The easiest solution in the short-term was to ask Sean what he was doing in the bar with the Polar Bear Bomber. But asking that question would spark further tension between the brothers when tension was already high. Still, Will played out the scenario in his head.

"You think I had something to do with that?" Sean would say. "Are you crazy? Do you think I'm crazy?" His mysterious brother, who drifted in and out of their lives, disappearing occasionally for days or even weeks at a time without telling them where he was going, would be incensed. "You don't trust me. You never trust me."

The conversation would turn and head downhill fast, and Will would learn nothing. Worse, if Sean was unaware of who the soon-to-be bomber was—if he'd been set up—he would be driven to vindicate himself. He'd pursue the original source of the photo. He might be hotheaded enough to start asking the wrong parties questions. And he would run squarely into people like Jason Carson, who played the lowest kind of hardball.

Will's protectiveness kicked in. *No, that's not the way to go.*

His processing switched gears. *What about Sarah? Or Darcy?*

The answer came swiftly. *A no-go on both fronts.* Yes, Sarah was a Worthington, but in the case of the Polar Bear Bomber, she was spearheading the lawsuit on behalf of the DOJ. If she had information on a possible link or suspect, even if it was her brother, she'd have to follow it to the hilt. Ditto with Darcy, who was like a dog with a prize bone. The agent would never back down.

No, the only thing he could do with Sarah was insert an occasional question about how the search for the Polar Bear Bomber was going. Carson had assured him the news story would hit soon. Then the world would know that the man in the polar bear suit had committed suicide by jumping from the top of a building near Times Square. He'd even left a signed note in a flat in Brooklyn, explaining why.

He could already hear Sarah's response: "Well, isn't that a little too tidy."

The news would only add to his sister's and Darcy's suspicions about the timing of the bombing. It had morphed the public ire against the oil spill and the dying whales into empathy for the poor, beleaguered oil company that now had to battle ecological crazies.

Will had come to his own conclusions—that Eric Sandstrom, CEO of AF, had ordered the bombing of his own building to turn the tide of opinion in AF's favor. Only a storehouse section had been damaged by the backpack bomb.

As Will slowed his pace to wind down, he decided that as soon as his parents left, he would tell Laura about the photo. There were never any secrets between the two of them. She was the only one who knew everything of import that happened in his world, so of course he would tell her about Jason Carson. Because she also knew about Ava's revelation, she could help put the pieces together of what moves to make next.

Drew? The man always knew more than anyone gave him credit for. He hadn't texted or phoned Will since Will stepped out of the race, and his silence spoke volumes. Likely Drew was already on the trail, connecting the dots. It was only a matter of hours before Will would have to come clean with him. But how much should he tell? Only about the photo of Sean and the Polar Bear Bomber? Or about Ava's surprise too?

4

Sean poised his hand to knock again on Will's penthouse suite door and then jumped back, startled, as it opened. Laura ushered their three children—Andrew, ten-year-old Patricia, and eight-year-old Davy—out the door.

"Uncle Sean!" Patricia shouted, her pink, blingy phone in one hand as she threw her other arm around him.

Davy grabbed him in a waist hug.

Andrew stood solemnly in the doorway.

Laura eyed Sean. "Robyn is taking the kids, plus Emily and Eliza, on an outing. She'll be here any minute."

In any other situation, Sean would have chuckled. Laura's mama-bear drive was still in full swing. Anyone who chose to do anything except nod in response would be stupid indeed.

Good ol' Drew and Jean, Sean thought. They'd sent their nanny and two girls over to get the Worthington kids out of the line of fire so the adults could process.

The elevator dinged right on schedule, and in less than a minute, the door opened and the three Worthington kids were off on their adventure.

Laura put her hands on her hips. "We're all going to be civil about this, right?" It really wasn't a question. It was a command.

Sean gave another simple nod.

"Your mother and father are both here, and Ava is pretty upset. Don't upset her further," she warned. Then her tone softened. "I'm sorry, Sean. None of us knew. We still don't know why. Will's tight-lipped. Come on in. I've got coffee brewing, and I'll get you a cup."

His anger calmed. At least he wasn't the only one on the outside.

And then he stepped into the lions' den.

When Will had made his announcement, Sarah Katherine Worthington had for once been stunned into silence. She'd sat in a shocked stupor until the media, recognizing her, had converged, jostling to get a comment. She did the only thing she could in her confusion. She fled in the first yellow cab she could flag down and had the cabbie drop her at Washington Square Park.

No way was she heading to Will's, where World War III would erupt as soon as the three males in her family stepped into the same location. She couldn't face her volumes of work at the DOJ either. Instead she'd spent the last couple of hours strolling and pondering.

What had happened to her usually predictable brother? Will had been so certain of his trajectory in politics after he'd given up his position as a board member at American Frontier. She'd never forget how happy he looked the day he moved into the campaign office. He was sure, he'd told her. And it had made sense. For years, the Worthingtons had talked about getting into national politics—taking their place alongside the dynastic political families like the Bushes and Clintons and Kennedys. The siblings joked about it, while their father pushed Will to take the Worthington name into the national political arena, with the constant refrain that Will was "a natural leader."

Sarah and Sean had exchanged rolled eyes at the worn-out litany. *Like we aren't in everything we do too*. Leadership was in the Worthingtons' DNA. But a long time ago, she'd come to accept that Bill Worthington would treat his firstborn son differently. And honestly, she wouldn't want to be Will, with so much expectation and responsibility heaped on his shoulders and most of his time spent in stuffy boardrooms. Nor would she want to be continually under the microscopic lens of their exacting father. Without Laura, who balanced him and added zest to his life, Will would be too serious—all work, no play, and a little boring.

She chuckled. That was certainly not true of Sean, an icon of New York's hottest social scene. His curly red hair, sea-green eyes, and slightly scruffy, rakish good looks had garnered him national and international front-cover magazine profiles on more occasions than she could count.

Her connection with Sean was even closer than the one she had with Will, perhaps because their father obviously favored Will. Or maybe it was because with Sean, Sarah could simply be a sister. With Will more than five years older and acting even older than that as they grew up, he'd played both older brother and father roles in her life.

Bill Worthington had worked hard to ensure that his children had opportunities to match their emerging gifts. But only Will had fallen directly in line with his father's wishes—accepting the helm of Worthington Shares when his father announced his partial retirement. It was no surprise. They'd all expected things to go that way, and neither she nor Sean wanted the position.

Sean was doing what he loved, running solo. He worked even harder to evade family events.

As for Sarah, she had surprised the family by removing her legal obligations to Worthington Shares when she took a career government position shortly after turning 28. Now she'd settled in at the Department of Justice and more than had her hands full with the American Frontier shareholder lawsuit and the criminal negligence suit—perhaps the highest-profile action against a massive corporate giant since the days of the antitrust actions against Ma Bell and Microsoft.

Did she want to remain the deputy assistant attorney general all her life? No, she had other plans—plans only she was privy to. Someday she would take an unexpected turn. She believed passionately in the ability of individuals to make needed changes for the greater good—whether it was reining in the excesses of carnivorous, monopolistic corporations or holding national leaders accountable for their actions on behalf of their constituents and the unique political experiment known as American democracy. But for now, she was satisfied with prosecuting big companies like American Frontier, who had taken too many risks unchecked, and had put both people and the planet in jeopardy.

She checked the time. Exactly 40 minutes before her next meeting. She needed to refocus, but she couldn't escape the prickling at the back of her neck that something was very wrong.

Just yesterday she'd talked to Will, and he'd been all business, focused on the Senate race launch. What had happened in between?

If this had been Sean, she would have understood. Sean was changeable. He went with the flow. That was why he was so good at what he did, including hopping on a private jet with only an hour's notice to a remote location half a world away. Sometimes she wondered if he ever truly unpacked.

But this was Will, who lined up his shoes exactly an inch apart in his closet. Why would he change his mind . . . and especially so suddenly?

Sarah knew she wouldn't be able to focus fully on her DOJ work until she got to the bottom of that question. The only one who might be able to shed some light was Sean.

Trying to get an answer out of Will right now would be like chiseling granite with a spoon.

It wouldn't make a dent.

5

Sean sipped coffee at Will and Laura's kitchen table, but the piping hot brew did nothing to warm his insides. Across from him sat Laura, and next to him was his mother. Ava, whose eyes lit up whenever she saw one of her children, barely greeted him. Her regal posture was slumped, her eyes downcast. Silence descended as they waited for Bill Worthington to reappear after taking a call.

Then, as the quietness lay far too heavy, his sister's cheerful ringtone sounded on his cell. Sarah had timing. He had to give her that.

"What on earth happened?" she blurted out.

"I have no idea," Sean replied, "but I aim to find out. I'm at Will's right now."

"Right. Fill me in later then." Then, in usual fashion, she abruptly ended the call.

Bill Worthington strode into the kitchen and poured himself a cup of coffee. He set it on the counter and leaned his tall frame against the wall nearby. "Seems like William has a few things to think about."

Their father was the only one in the family who called Will "William," and his simple pronouncement rankled.

"*He* has a few things to think about," Sean spouted, getting up from his chair and nearly toppling it. "What about me? I'm the one who has to clean up the mess. Return all the angry calls. He'll just hide in the boardroom until things settle down."

Bill Worthington's dark eyes intensified. He straightened to an intimidating height. Within a second Sean felt the heat of his father's glare—the one that immediately halted sibling bickering, as well as any corporate directions Bill didn't agree with.

"Bill," Ava begged.

"It's all right, Ava. Let the boy speak," he said in the same calm, steely tone Will had adopted.

"The boy," Sean thought. *Not "my son" or "our son." Not even an adult. Just "the boy."* Suddenly he had nothing else to say. Why was he fooling himself, thinking he might get answers here that could help him understand? Thinking he might find empathy?

"Don't be so hard on your brother," his father continued. "William thinks things through before he acts. There must have been a reason. When he's ready, he'll tell us."

"Hard on him? What about hard on me?" Sean seethed. "Will's side, again. You never see mine."

"Maybe there's good reason for that."

"Bill!" Ava looked up again. "Stop." Tears streaked her cheeks.

"See—you've made your mother cry." Bill exhaled in disgust. "Let's get something straight. I love both you and William. But I can trust that William will do what's right, even when he can't tell us why. Eventually the truth will come out."

Ava gasped and trembled. Laura reached a hand across the table and clasped her mother-in-law's.

Sean stiffened. "So you can trust Will. But you can't trust me. That's what you're saying, right?"

Bill tilted his head. "Let's face it, Sean. You've always been a wild card, off doing your own thing. But yes, I think I can trust you."

"You think, but you don't know, do you? You're not sure of that?" The ache in Sean's throat threatened to push to the surface.

Laura got up from her chair. "Okay, you two. You're worse than my kids. Enough duking it out for the day, or I'll put you in separate corners. Neither of you are too old for a time-out."

Sean lifted his chin, strengthening his resolve. "You won't have to, because I'm leaving."

"Son," Ava pleaded.

"No, Mom, I need to go."

The instant he said the words, he realized how true they were. He'd spent so many years feeling like an outsider in his own family—the middleborn who marched to the beat of a different drummer, the one his father said he could never understand. Sean hated it but put up with it because he truly loved his family. When push came to shove, he'd do anything for them. Traveling globally was a good excuse, though, to not have to show up often in the same locale as his father, who either grilled him or ignored him. There was no middle ground.

But that middle ground is what Sean longed for. The lack of it now—no understanding and compassion from his own father—crushed him. He had to flee before he broke down.

Without saying good-bye, he strode out of the kitchen, out the front door, and to the elevator. The penthouse suite door opened, and his mom rushed out, calling his name. But for the first time ever, he didn't stop, turn, and embrace her. He stepped onto the elevator as soon as the doors opened.

Yes, he knew he would fulfill his duties as a Worthington son by remaining at the helm of the risky side of the business. That was his gift. But it was also time to make his own way in the universe . . . even if it meant cutting himself off for a while from those he loved most in the world.

Once in the lobby, he didn't wait for the concierge. He stalked through the doors, grabbed a yellow cab outside, and barked, "Get me to One Madison fast."

Sean was done with waiting. He'd done more than enough of it lately.

The yellow flag that had been waving in the back of Sarah's mind morphed to a bright red as her cab pulled up in front of the Department of Justice building.

Sarah twirled her right index finger in a circle as the cabbie peered in the rearview mirror. "Go around the block a couple of times," she directed.

He raised a brow but did as she asked. People in New York City did crazy things. It was probably the least crazy thing he'd been asked to do today, and there was more money in it for him, so what did it matter?

Sarah settled back against the seat and pinpointed what had been bothering her. Jason Carson, Sandstrom's underhanded attorney, had been at Will's Senate launch. In fact, Carson had lingered right by the side of the stage. What was he doing there?

Something's up. Something dirty. Why else would Carson be there?

With the man's reputation, his presence couldn't be a good omen. Still, he'd managed to evade being caught on the wrong side of the law for years.

She closed her eyes and zeroed in on the scene, trying to

recall every detail. It was a technique she'd learned from her older brother.

After Will had walked offstage, he'd paused for a few seconds at the side of the stage.

He stopped to say something to Carson, she realized.

Sarah focused, remembering seeing her brother lean in toward the attorney. When Will straightened, there was a stiffness in his march down the aisle that showed determination but also duress. Sarah recognized it now. And when he'd passed her, his expression was granite-like, as if he'd been forced to do something he wasn't happy about. She'd seen it many times.

So, Sarah thought, *it's Carson. Or something to do with Carson.*

But what could he have on her brother that would cause Will to change his path?

Will was a straight arrow. Yet even that wouldn't stop Carson, who had been known to create dirt on good people out of thin air. With Sean's support of ecological causes, Will voting for Worthington Shares to join the shareholder lawsuit against American Frontier, and Sarah's role with the DOJ in the lawsuit, Carson had plenty of material to work with and probable cause.

So now he's targeting the Worthington family. Sarah crossed her arms. *Well, we'll just see about that.*

6

Sean arrived at the renowned One Madison building and tossed a Jackson over the front seat at the cabbie. Within minutes, he'd entered his apartment and collapsed on the off-white uncomfortable couch, still attired in the suit he'd worn to the Senate launch. Exhausted, he didn't take his shoes off but propped his feet up on the coffee table. A second later, he could hear his mother in his head: *"Take your feet off that table. You know better than that."*

The irony struck. Even when his family wasn't there, they still controlled him.

Anger, embarrassment, and the futility of trying to please his father built to a crescendo as a text arrived on his phone. For the first time ever, he didn't check the message. Just muted his cell, then slung it down the hallway.

After kicking his shoes off so his good breeding wouldn't go to pot, he propped his sock feet back on the table. While waiting for his stress headache to subside, he scanned the room. Stark off-white walls, off-white furniture, with only a single large painting of birch trees and a weird sculpture crafted from branches that he'd allowed the extraordinarily expensive New York designer to talk him into. It was cold, sterile . . . like his life. Just when he'd thought things were about to change for the better, they'd leaped into the worst category.

When the AF board had swung in the direction of the old CEO, Will had walked out and arranged for an immediate sale of the Worthington family's shares. Sean had applauded that decision. When Will decided to make a Senate run in New York, Sean not only supported him but agreed to be his campaign manager.

Sean loved Will—always had, always would. His older brother could walk on water. He was powerful, in control of his world. Sean admired Will far more than he'd admit to anyone, even himself. The problem was in the comparison. Sean came up lacking time after time. Knowing he could never measure up to Will as a standard, Sean had pushed ahead in his own accomplishments—in the opposite direction.

While at Harvard, Will had pursued the highest academic achievements and captained an NCAA national championship lacrosse team. Whenever Sean called him, though, Will was hunkered down in his room or in the library, studying. It was rare for Will to be found in a social setting, even on a Friday night. Sean never asked him why. It was Will's pattern and had been since childhood.

Sean had chosen Stanford—as far from Harvard in location as he could get and still receive the satisfied nod from Bill Worthington—and had nearly achieved a 4.0 GPA. But his education lay more in the friendships and loyalties gained there and the discovered bridges that connected him with a wide world. He also garnered significant firsthand perspective by traveling and interning in far-flung locations that needed what a Worthington could provide. By his junior year, he was building wells in remote parts of Africa, improving the drinking water in parts of India, refitting old corporate cell phones so disadvantaged areas could access health services in China, and much more.

As a Worthington, he had nearly bottomless resources. He wrote six-figure checks often to launch start-ups. But more and more, pursuing NGOs with the sole purpose of increasing Worthington Shares wealth bothered him. What good was it to build an empire if it couldn't bring a better life for those who were disadvantaged?

He could hear his father's response already: "Without the empire and the resources it creates, we wouldn't even have the opportunity to do good." Such answers were so expected that years ago Sean had given up asking aloud the questions on his heart and his mind. Yet his longing to do all he could to make life better for others multiplied.

And there it was, the quandary he found himself in every day. The Sean Worthington on the front pages of *GQ* and the tabloids—the smiling, handsome playboy—wasn't the real Sean Worthington. The real Sean felt more at home saving marine species on the high seas with Green Justice, stooping in the dirt with a Malawi villager to locate the best spot to dig a well, or assessing a remote mountain settlement in China to evaluate its medical needs. The real Sean didn't sleep for 36 hours straight when he identified an emerging NGO that could financially sustain villagers for a 100-mile radius.

The people who knew the truth about Sean were disconnected—disparate groups who welcomed his help, flourished, and gave their loyalty, time, and talents in return. Even if an NGO wasn't "successful" in the eyes of Worthington Shares, if the enterprise increased the standard of living of an area, Sean was satisfied.

Yet, in his wide social network, only two contacts had completely gained his trust and confidence—Dr. Elizabeth Shapiro and Jon Gillibrand, who had both been on the Russian-flagged ship with him in the Arctic.

The three had met some years back at an environmental symposium. Elizabeth was the quirky, brilliant daughter of a world-renowned marine biologist. She wanted to earn her own PhD in ecology and biology at UCLA. Jon, already a veteran reporter for the *Times*, was more informed about a wide variety of relevant issues than anyone Sean had met. They all cared passionately about ecological issues and disadvantaged groups.

Since that meeting over a cafeteria lunch table, the three had formed a deep friendship as they traversed the globe. Sometimes they couldn't communicate for months when Elizabeth was undertaking a remote scientific expedition with her father, Jon was buried in a high-profile assignment, or Sean barely had time to switch out the clothes in his carry-on before he was on to the next potential NGO. However, in the ever-changing social scene of the wealthy and powerful, where dirty deals and betrayal abounded, two facts were a given—the three friends would reconnect, and if something big came up, they'd have each other's backs.

Sean knew his family would also support him. However, the baggage that came along with that support—the expectations—he sometimes had to flee from. His father, never satisfied with anything Sean did and pushing him to do more. His mother, with her perennial questions about when he was going to find a nice girl and settle down. His sister, who nagged him to show up more often at family events and routinely shot down his excuses. Lately she'd even started calling him an hour before, then a half hour, to make sure he was on the way.

Will? He didn't pester Sean. When a bottom line on the start-ups was particularly good, Sean could feel Will's approval. At times his brother verbalized it.

But Worthington Shares and the unspoken comparisons by their father continued to be the thorns that kept the brothers apart.

7

The minute Sarah walked into her penthouse on 66 East 111th Street in Greenwich Village, her cell rang. She ignored it. It had been a long enough day already. Whoever that was could wait until tomorrow.

But her cell continued to ring as she perused the FreshDirect soups and salads in her fridge for dinner potential. She was more than grateful for the housekeeper who came three times a week to tidy up her place, do laundry, and stock her fridge. Not that she couldn't do it herself, but she was rarely home enough to do it. And when she finally got there, all she could manage was a ready-made meal in the microwave. But knowing she was eating healthy made her mother happy, which meant less pestering about Sarah's coffee-drinking habits.

The caller was certainly persistent. Finally, she checked the caller ID. Darcy.

"Hey, what's up?"

"About time you answered," Darcy huffed. "We got the guy."

"The Polar Bear Bomber? Seriously?"

"He did a Peter Pan off the top of a building near Times

Square. NYPD got an anonymous tip about a jumper. He was tracked to an apartment in Brooklyn." But Darcy didn't sound satisfied like she did when a case came to a close.

"I'm hearing a 'but' coming," Sarah prompted.

"When they got to the apartment, there was plenty of DNA to match to his body. He was definitely staying there. Even found a suicide note," Darcy added. "Identified him as an eco-terrorist, an activist with Green Justice. That's when NYPD called DHS."

Sarah's mind flashed to Sean and his buddy Kirk Baldwin. "You sure about the Green Justice connection? There's no mistake?"

Darcy snorted. "Clear as day to anybody who can read. The guy was a whack job. Had it in for AF and big oil companies in general. The Arctic spill pushed him over the edge into crazy. At least that's the theory."

"But you're not buying it."

"The top dogs at DHS are so sure it's wrapped up that they already released to the press that the Polar Bear Bomber is dead. It'll be a news headline by tomorrow morning." There was a pause. "They won't release his name yet, until they do the customary search for closest relative to notify first."

"I know what you're thinking," Sarah said. "It's too neat and tidy."

"Yeah. Too easy. The guy didn't show up and handcuff himself to my desk but conveniently showed up dead. End of story."

"And you can't ask him any questions."

"Like I said, too convenient. Especially with that bear suit showing up behind the radical environmentalist group's office. Paints a trail wide enough a kindergartener could follow it."

Sarah agreed with Darcy. The NYPD and DHS might think the case was wrapped up, but it was looking even more like a setup.

Langley, Virginia

The photos were spread on the mahogany desk in his study. They'd been funneled to him through the usual channels. He'd been staring at them for the past several hours.

His eyes narrowed as he studied the men again, looking for any details he might have missed. The photos had been taken at an upscale bar near 20th and Madison, his source said. Both men were sitting on bar stools next to each other and seemed to be conversing in a friendly manner.

One man, with his slightly mussed red hair and well-known profile, was easily identified—Sean Worthington. He appeared to be laughing at something the other man had said.

The man at his desk frowned. He'd been told plenty of high rollers stopped at that bar after work, but it wasn't the typical kind of place someone high-profile, like a Worthington, would frequent. Then again, Sean wasn't known for doing what was typical.

The other person in the photo had been a mystery until an hour or so ago, when he was identified as the Polar Bear Bomber. He'd been found splattered on the pavement in downtown New York City.

The man reached for the most prominent photo and held it up. After studying it again, he sat back, concentrating on the task at hand. He wasn't going to let the person responsible get away with this.

8

New York City

Something wasn't right, and that something kept Sean awake most of the night, thrashing in the bedcovers. Finally, sweating in the new silk sheets and vowing to tell his housekeeper to go back to the 100 percent Egyptian cotton ones, Sean threw the sheets and covers off. He padded in bare feet to the fridge, opened it, and grabbed a carton of orange juice. Just as he tipped it back to chug it, he heard his mother's voice in his head.

"Sean Thomas Worthington, pour that into a glass first!"

He chuckled. Why did mothers always use a child's full name when chiding them?

Then what had been bothering him struck home. When he was sitting at the table with his mom and Laura, more than one unusual glance passed between the two women. At the time he'd been agitated enough to pass it off as women sharing empathy in a difficult situation. But the more he thought about it, he recalled that their gazes had often flickered to him and then back to each other.

Laura had said none of them knew before Will made his

announcement. She had never been known to tell a lie. *But they do know something*, he realized. *And they're being as tight-lipped as Will.*

Once again, Sean felt like an outsider in his own family. Perhaps that was why, as time passed growing up, he had become more comfortable relating to those who weren't Worthingtons. The two exceptions were Drew and his wife, Jean. Sean considered them both family and friends. In fact, it had been Drew and Ava who had escorted Sean to his first day of kindergarten. His father had been in India.

Since then Sean had never doubted two things—Drew would shoot straight with him, and he would be in Sean's court. In the swirl of wealth and fame, loyalty was a priceless commodity. Perhaps that was why, when Drew had phoned to get the Worthington siblings together for dinner awhile back, Sean had gone, even though he'd been late due to a business commitment at a bar near 20th and Madison.

That night Sean had nursed a drink for nearly an hour, waiting for the executive from the start-up company to show. The man never did. Instead Sean had chatted with a talkative guy who seemed slightly drunk or maybe a bit off his meds.

Later that evening Drew had given Sean, Will, and Sarah the longest speech of his life, warning them that the oil spill would shape each of their destinies. "I will fight with every ounce of my being to protect the Worthington business. But what I most care about is how this will affect you—each of you," he had said.

That was one of many qualities that distinguished Drew from anyone else in the Wall Street high-roller circuit of America's wealthiest individuals. Drew didn't care just about the business. He cared about each of the Worthington kids personally.

That was why it had been Drew and Jean who had sent their nanny, Robyn, over to take Laura and Will's kids away for a while. It was also why, Sean surmised, Drew was conspicuously MIA. He still hadn't texted Sean to check in, which was highly unusual for the man who kept tabs on everything Worthington. That meant Drew was on the trail of figuring out what had happened.

For now, that was enough. That security would allow Sean to go back to sleep.

He squinted at the kitchen clock. It was 4:00. So he'd have a short sleep. That was nothing new. With his globe-hopping, he was used to pulling all-nighters.

But even when he settled back in bed, he was haunted by Will's strange expression—the sadness, the pity, the fear. It was downright weird. Will was normally the high-strung one, needing every detail to be perfect. Instead he was calm, as though his emotions had been wrung out.

Sean couldn't shake the impression that something was deeply wrong with his brother.

Will and Laura were still awake, drinking decaf at their kitchen table. It was after 4:00 a.m. In another three hours, their youngest, Davy, would bounce in, demanding breakfast.

Laura's brow furrowed in thought. "So Carson and Sandstrom think they won." The green in her hazel eyes won out over the brown. That happened only when she was spunky or really angry, and both emotions now vied for precedence.

"Yep," Will said.

She tilted her head. "But you're not going to let them win."

He smiled. "Of course not."

9

Sarah was already on her third cup of coffee at 9:00 a.m. The hours she'd pondered in the park yesterday gave her even more to catch up on at the office. Ever since Harvard Law School, she'd given up on any real breakfast or lunch and adopted the dark brew as the catchall for any meal missed. She'd long ago dismissed the guilt for not eating "balanced meals," as her mother would say, and had become a master at evading Ava's questions about what she ate and when.

The DOJ offices buzzed with activity. Her lead investigators on the criminal negligence suit against American Frontier continued to dig. They were cross-checking information as it came in with the red-haired CNN field producer, Catherine Englewood. She had inadvertently shot footage of the Polar Bear Bomber and had given both Sarah and Darcy their first real leads in tracking him down. For now, the trail seemed to end with the bomber's suicide in Times Square.

Still, Sarah and Darcy believed that the timing was too perfect, as if it had been planned to sidetrack the public from the much bigger, real issue—a disastrous oil leak that was wreaking ecological havoc in the Arctic but would spread to all the earth's ocean systems. No one had been injured in the bomb's blast. The only part of the building damaged was a storehouse. And the Polar Bear Bomber had been walking around in Catherine's footage calling attention to himself, like he was a street actor and it was his job to be noticed.

Darcy strode into Sarah's office and plunked a newspaper on her desk. "And there we have it," she stated with her usual flair. "Sews it up nice and tidy, doesn't it?"

Sarah followed Darcy's pointed finger to the large-print headline: POLAR BEAR BOMBER DEAD. She skimmed the article. No surprises there. And no, they didn't yet list his name. "Well, as my father says, if something stinks like a dead fish, it probably is one."

"You got that right." Darcy waved the coffee in her hand. "Speaking of Bill, how did he take Will stepping away from the campaign? Can't imagine that went over too well."

Sarah frowned. "Now that you mention it, Dad has been pretty hard to reach. Maybe he's as confused as the rest of us. He's been pushing as long as I can remember for one of us—well, the demigod in particular—to get into politics. Save the country from the mess it's in, as Dad would say."

Darcy sat on Sarah's desk. "Ouch. Do I detect a little disgruntlement in paradise?"

Darcy was one of the rare straight shooters Sarah could confide in. Yes, she was rough around the edges, but Sarah had seen her friend's kind heart over the years. Darcy didn't see Sarah as just a member of the privileged upper class. Both were extremely hardworking and determined to make America a better place. Plus Darcy had an older, "perfect" brother, at least in the eyes of her father.

Furthermore, tell Darcy a secret and it wouldn't go anywhere, unless that secret had to do with anything illegal. Then she'd go after it with guns blazing, like an Old West gunfighter. For all her brassy exterior, Darcy Wiggins was an honest, moral soul who had seen the worst of humankind's ugliness. It had morphed her into a rocket-powered agent who upheld justice and never allowed a perpetrator to walk away. Investigative experience had also given her a sharp instinct for when even small things weren't right.

Now Darcy cocked her head, waiting.

"Sometimes I get a little tired of Dad not taking me seriously. Of him only considering Will"—Sarah paused to put air quotes around her next words—"'leadership material.' Especially when his two other kids could just as easily run things on a national scope."

"You? At the White House?" Darcy laughed. "I'd pay to see that."

"Don't hold your breath."

"Wouldn't you have to figure out which party you were in?" Darcy teased. "I mean, they're generally friendly to Christians in the Republican Party, so you're fine on that score. But they're also the party of big business, and you're now in charge of the federal office that's beating the daylights out of that wing of the party."

"Well, maybe it's time the Republican Party stopped allowing corporate America to lead it around by the nose," Sarah said guardedly. She rarely discussed her own political views—even with a trusted someone like Darcy. She especially didn't talk about her own politics around the family dinner table. "They could use a bit of populism and corporate reform. We need more Main Street and a whole lot less Wall Street."

"So you're a Republican, then?"

"I didn't say that," Sarah answered.

"A Democrat?"

"I didn't say that either. But Daddy's a Democrat. So is Will, sort of. Maybe I'm . . . something else. I am working for a Republican president, even if it is a career appointment."

Darcy laughed. "Well, well. Daddy's little girl doesn't want to be so little anymore. I get it. Been there. Still there." Then she added, "But you're tough. Resilient. What you're doing now matters. What you'll do tomorrow matters. And what you'll do someday . . . well, you'll blow 'em all out of the water."

"Okay then, pity party over. Back to work, huh?" Sarah reached over and nudged her friend.

"You got it. We've tightened the noose around Sandstrom, so now we need to squeeze a bit harder."

"We both know he's dirty. But, as Jon said, we have to prove it. Real proof, not guesswork."

Since Sean's return from the Arctic, he had connected Sarah again with his friend Jon Gillibrand. The intelligent reporter wasn't one you'd pick out of a crowd at a party, but Jon continued to impress Sarah with the way he assembled complicated pieces in any puzzle and handled confidential information with sensitivity. Like Darcy, he was completely trustworthy. The three were now sharing whatever information they could legally with the common goal of connecting Sandstrom to the bombing of his own building.

Sarah enjoyed getting together for coffee at a mom-and-pop hole-in-the-wall with Jon and Darcy when they could carve a minute out of the whirl of New York. The shop, like Jon, had its own unique charm. Nothing chain or run-of-the-mill there.

Darcy waved a hand in front of Sarah's face. "Ruminating, were we? Couldn't have anything to do with a certain reporter, could it?" she teased.

Sarah blinked. "What? You mean Jon?"

Darcy lifted a brow.

"Yeah, I think he's interesting." Sarah shrugged. "Not for me, but interesting."

"Not for you, why?"

Sarah waved away the question. "Enough of that. We've got to get to work. Trace the PB Bomber back to Sandstrom."

She narrowed her eyes. *And maybe in the process I'll uncover something on Jason Carson that explains Will's expression right after his announcement . . . and his phone silence now.*

10

Sean's best ideas came when he was on the move. So, with Will's Senate race off, there was nothing to hold him back. After his restless night, it had taken only a couple of hours and a few well-placed calls to book a visit to a new NGO in Nepal that had sprung up after the earthquake to handle health care delivery. If all panned out, he was prepared to offer the company's executives up to three million dollars to expand their emergency response platform.

He'd booked his usual first-class seat on a commercial flight from JFK. He easily could have chartered a plane, but he preferred having lots of people around him when he was on an airplane. It helped pass the time, especially on cross-Atlantic flights.

His flight wouldn't depart until evening. Sleeping on planes was no fun. Sean didn't know anyone who did it well. But he didn't want to burn any more time. He certainly didn't want to sit around his apartment, which was more a landing place in between trips than a home. He'd much rather people-watch at the airport and engage a few characters in interesting conversation. Within 10 minutes, he'd gain a new contact or two.

He and Jon Gillibrand kept up a healthy competition in comparing their social networking skills. Thus far, Sean had the contest nailed with Facebook and LinkedIn and his more than 1,700 mobile contacts, but Jon towered above him on Twitter.

With several hours to spare before his flight, Sean grabbed one of his well-stocked travel bags that the housekeeper kept ready for him, strode out the door of the building to the limo, and was off to JFK.

Will knew he was living on borrowed time. It had been over 24 hours since his aborted campaign announcement. It wouldn't be long before his father, Drew, or both contacted him. When Will's cell rang, he was surprised either had waited this long.

His father was first. "So what's next, if not the Senate race?"

Will halted, stunned, in the corridor outside his office at Worthington Shares. *He doesn't want to know why I pulled out? Just what's next?* "I'm evaluating my options. First, though, I want to make sure I'm up to speed on Worthington Shares."

Will was certain he'd stay at the helm of Worthington Shares, but he was also open for an additional challenge. He didn't know what that might be, but he was confident there was a next step. He simply needed to uncover it.

"That's good, William. Okay then." His father paused. "Give your mother a call sometime, would you? She's taking this little fork in the road hard." Bill cleared his throat. "I think she needs to know you're all right."

"I'll call her. Very soon," he promised.

For any other father-son relationship, it might have been a traditional checkup call. But it was so unlike Bill that Will was unnerved. His father had pushed for what was next—nothing different there. But he didn't address Will pulling out of the campaign or ask why. Instead concern and gentleness had colored his father's tone.

When Will walked into his office, Drew was sitting in one of the leather chairs opposite his desk. *Guess it's a two-for-one event*, Will thought.

Drew didn't say a word, only studied Will with his keen blue-gray eyes. Will knew that unsettling gaze. Whenever it landed on him, since childhood, he'd had no choice but to confess either what he'd done or what was on his mind. He had no choice now either. Likely the man who seemed to know everything about everyone already had some of the information Will was withholding. But how much? Which of the two secrets, or both, should Will reveal?

At that moment, Will decided to choose the easier one, if either revelation could be considered easier. "You're wondering why I pulled out of the race?"

Drew gave one short nod.

"It had to do with a visit in the park with Jason Carson." Will stared at Drew, trying to judge by his response how much he knew.

Drew didn't even flinch.

"He showed me a photo of Sean chatting up a guy at a bar. A guy now identified as the Polar Bear Bomber."

Still no flicker in Drew's expression. *So he does know*, Will realized. *That's why I haven't heard from him. He's been busy with his contacts.* In that regard, Drew and Sean were quite similar.

Will drew a deep breath. "You know what that means—for Sean, for our family. Carson assured me the photos wouldn't go viral as part of the investigation if I stepped out of the race."

At last Drew spoke. "You know Sean's not connected, right? He would never do that."

"I know, or at least I think I know. But Sean has seemed awfully different of late, more unsettled. What if . . . ?"

Drew frowned. "It's a setup, and you know it. Your sister's on edge too."

"My sister? Sarah knows about the photos?" Will sank onto his desk chair.

"No, but she called me. Saw Jason Carson in the shadows by the stage and you getting in his face afterward. Sooner or later she's going to follow that rabbit trail. With Sandstrom and AF already in her sights, I believe she just added Carson to that list. She knows something's up, but not exactly what."

Will jumped to his feet and started to pace. "So we target him in our sights too." He eyed Drew. "Just like in the old Westerns."

The normally solemn Drew cracked a smile. "I'd hate to go up against this posse of gunfighters."

Will smiled back. "Exactly."

11

En Route to Nepal

"If there's anything I can do to help you during the flight, or afterward, let me know." The flight attendant's gaze lingered on Sean. "We'll be landing soon. I'm free for a couple of days before I have to service a flight back to the States."

Sean nodded, then closed his eyes, ending the conversation. He didn't open them until he heard her move down the aisle.

Sean knew what she was offering, but he didn't want any part of it. He was used to the attention, though. Flight attendants flocked around him often, many suggesting services that weren't on the airline's menu. So did some models and other social climbers who would be more than happy to drape themselves over his arm for photographs at black-tie affairs.

His sister ribbed him about it. "It's your Irish charm and swashbuckling good looks. 'Course, it doesn't hurt that you're a recognizable billionaire," she'd told him once when they were on a flight to Dubai. The siblings had been sitting next to each other, and Sarah had been amused at the harem that gathered.

Some men would have been flattered, but Sean wasn't one of

them. He wasn't interested in a one-night fling or any meaningless relationship. That's why he was still single, though he easily acquired dates for media events when he needed them. He admired Will and Laura's deep connection and wanted that same kind of intimacy in his life partner. Also on his "most wanted" list was someone who had a lively intellect, who cared deeply about the world and its people, and who had a natural beauty that shone through because of who she was on the inside.

Someone like Elizabeth. The thought leapt as naturally as breathing to Sean. It wasn't the first time he'd entertained the idea of following the direction his heart nudged him—toward his good friend. What would it be like to live a simpler existence, out of the Worthington spotlight, as a "regular guy"? To travel with Elizabeth and her father, exploring the world and its oceans, pursuing solutions for the planet's environmental concerns?

It ticked him off that now, with the Polar Bear Bomber's suicide note discovered, the public was focused on environmentalist nuts. That meant stalwart, good-hearted Green Justicers, like his buddy Kirk Baldwin, were once again insects under the media's microscope.

Sean closed his eyes again as the brunette flight attendant made her way back up the aisle in first class. Since he couldn't be a regular guy for now, he determined once again to use his wealth, power, and trust fund to do good in the world.

No matter where he traveled, he couldn't get away from the mantra "To those who are given much, much is required" that his father had implanted in his head since childhood. Nor would he want to.

But now he had to try to sleep on the flight.

New York City

Will was tired. He'd had 11 meetings in one day at Worthington Shares. All he could think about was going home, putting on his favorite T-shirt and sweats, and enjoying a brain rinse in front of the television.

Then he received a call from Laura. "Okay, I set it up," she said.

"Set what up?"

"Your visit to your mother. Why don't you go by their place before you come home?"

It wasn't a suggestion.

"All right. But then I may not make it home before Davy goes to bed."

Laura's next words were softer. "I know. But Will, this is important. I've never seen your mom like this. She thinks you backing out of the Senate race is all her fault and that she's ruining your career because she was weak one day in her life. She has no clue that there are other issues at play."

"Understood."

"And Will? You'll be . . ."

"Gentle. Sensitive." He laughed. "I knew what you were going to say."

"I guess that's what happens to old married people." She chuckled.

Within 20 minutes, he knocked on the door of his parents' penthouse suite. Although they were now living full-time at the family's summer home in Chautauqua Institution, they maintained their New York City residence so they could pop in and out whenever they wished. Tonight Bill was at dinner with a business colleague.

Ava flung open the door and hugged him as soon as he stepped inside. "Will! Are you okay?"

"Of course, Mom."

She looked him in the eye, still holding his forearms. "Son, you did the right thing."

He stiffened. "Maybe. Maybe not. But I did the necessary thing, for now."

She dropped her hands to her sides and assumed her usual regal posture. "What are you not telling me? Is there more I don't know? I assumed you got out of the race to protect your brother . . . and us."

He switched the subject with a blunt question. "I never asked you—does Dad know that Sean is not his biological son?"

His mother sank onto the cushion of the nearest chair. "No." She covered her face with her hands. "No," she said, words muffled, "we've never talked about it."

Will's brain kicked into overdrive on potential scenarios, as it did in business situations. He sat on the chair opposite her.

When she raised her head, her pale skin was flushed. "As far as I know, and because your father and I were . . . intimate . . . shortly after my return from Camp David, he wouldn't have any reason to think Sean is not his child. He has curly hair, like Bill." She wrung her hands. "Bill just commented at his birth that he favored the Irish side of the family more than the Worthington side."

Thomas, Sean's birth father, had curly, dark auburn hair when he was younger. To Will's recollection, it was nearly a match for Sean's now. "Do you think Dad suspects?"

Tears glimmered. "At times I've wondered. I mean, he loves all three of you, but he seems toughest on Sean."

Will had to agree. Snippets surfaced of the times his father had commented on how different Sean was from his sister and brother.

"At Chautauqua, you said you think Thomas may have guessed

when he saw Sean as a child and learned what his middle name is."

Will put the pieces together. Nothing like learning that Thomas Spencer Rich II, president of the United States, had fathered a child out of wedlock with a dear old Harvard friend at Camp David. Even more, that she was the wife of his best friend.

Silence hung as Will waited for information. At last he prompted, "And Sarah? Does she know?"

Fear flashed across Ava's face. "No, and you can't tell her. I don't know how she'd respond. What she'd think of me, or how it would change her relationship with Sean."

But the truth will come out sometime, and when it does . . .

"And Sean? Has he guessed?" Will asked.

"No," she whispered. "I always told him he favored my side of the family. That you and Sarah got your father's curly chestnut hair, but he got my family's auburn, with his father's curls."

Will tilted his head. "Did he ever ask why you'd given him Thomas as a middle name?"

"I told him Thomas was a good, solid name I'd always loved and that I'd wanted his first name to be Irish because of my heritage. Sean has no idea he is Irish through and through, on both sides." She sighed. "Or that the restlessness I see in him is very much like the way Thomas was when we were at Harvard."

"How so?"

"Thomas told me once that he felt displaced, with his family stipulating his path in life. After all, he was the firstborn son of a prominent family who'd long ago made their mark in presidential politics. He didn't want to follow that path merely because it was expected of him. But once he realized that he really did want it, the stormy restlessness I saw in his eyes changed to passionate purpose."

"So that's when he went after presidential politics." Will nodded.

Ava leaned forward. "I see that passionate purpose in Sean's eyes when he talks about his NGOs. But for him, building Worthington Shares isn't enough. I've talked with Bill about the restlessness I see. But because Bill has always known what he wants to do, he never understood that part of Thomas, and he doesn't understand that part of Sean. He thinks Sean's role at Worthington Shares should be enough for him. You?" She lifted a hand in question. "You're different. He thinks you should run Worthington Shares *and* do something else to make your mark on the planet."

Will shook his head. "I'm still working on that. I thought I knew where I was headed, but twice now recently that's changed."

Her expression turned sad. "Son." She clasped both his hands in hers. "I am so sorry for the role I played in you having to turn down the Senate race. I know you did that to protect Sean, to protect me, to protect our family. I will be forever grateful to you."

"Mom—"

"No, let me finish. I'm also sorry for the way in which Sean arrived in our family, and the impact it will have on the Worthington name and the Rich name if the truth is ever revealed. But I am not sorry Sean did arrive. Someday he will blaze his own path, maybe even find a woman who will love him for him, like Laura does you. Then he will become a shooting star for the world to see, even more than he is now." Her chin lifted. "I'm sure of it. That's why I called him Sean, which means 'God has favored' in Gaelic. I knew that someday the truth might be revealed, and I wanted his very name to show him how much I loved him from the beginning, in spite of the circumstances in which he was conceived."

As she sat there, looking so blue-blood regal yet simultaneously fragile, his caretaking side and his problem-solving skills warred for control. “Somehow we’ll figure this out,” he told her.

But when he walked away, he felt weighed down. *Too many secrets. I hold too many secrets.* How could he ever tell his mother that her son might be implicated in a domestic terrorist bombing?

12

Kathmandu, Nepal

Sean strode through the Kathmandu airport with his carry-on. He had 15 minutes before his meeting with the young CEO of GlobalHealth SMS, who had been on the ground the day after a long-anticipated mega-earthquake had devastated the country and killed thousands. GlobalHealth had gotten its start in Haiti after an equally devastating earthquake had destroyed that country's information infrastructure. The organization had been instrumental in delivering timely emergency information in Nepal based on lessons learned in the Haiti disaster.

With his plans and questions stirring, Sean hadn't been able to sleep on the overnight flight. He headed for a local coffee shop. A quick cup or two of coffee would give him the zip he needed to combat the jet lag and sleepless night, and then the adrenaline of meeting his contacts would take over.

One idea had surfaced about 2:00 a.m. as his first-class seat neighbor snored. Sean had just started to hit his stride in the political arena in Will's campaign when the rug was pulled out from under him. *Maybe I should consider taking a run myself at the governor of New York.*

The brainstorm seemed tenable. The press often compared the Worthingtons to the Kennedys, Bushes, and Clintons. All three families were like royalty in national political circles. Siblings, wives, and husbands from all three families had made runs at political offices, even the presidency. Sean too had deep financial pockets and was already a well-known figure.

Maybe that was his next move. *Make Dad proud. Be the Worthington to break in.*

He chuckled. *Wouldn't that be ironic, if it were me instead of Will?*

New York City

Sarah met Jon Gillibrand this time for dinner at the Four Seasons. Tucked into a corner where they wouldn't be overheard, they kept their conversation mutually light until the waiter had placed their entrées and stepped away.

Then Sarah asked Jon, "Are you heading back to the Arctic anytime soon?"

He shook his head. "No point in it. Can't get anywhere near the AF platform. The site's locked up tight with Sandstrom and President Rich controlling what information goes out to the media."

Sarah caught the glint in his eye. "But you're on to something?"

"I just talked to Elizabeth. I'm going to be in Seattle for a few days working on a story and thought we might be able to finagle a dinner. She updated me on the research. As you might already know from Sean, before Elizabeth and her father were booted from the USS *Cantor*, they dropped a buoy and infrared camera right in the middle of the oil mess."

Sarah nodded.

"The Shapiros and their colleagues have been tracking the data from the geosciences department at the University of Washington ever since." His intelligent eyes intensified. "They can prove scientifically there's more oil beneath the ocean than anyone knows about."

"Which makes an uncapped geyser shooting up from the bottom of the ocean even worse. Will was against drilling in the Arctic without AF doing a lot more research first. But Sandstrom and the rest of the AF board vote went against him. Will said it was foolhardy to jump in with so many unknowns in a fragile ecosystem. He doesn't often get heated." She shook her head. "In fact, he's often so calm it drives me crazy. But that situation really bothered him."

"Sean told me."

"We're well on our way to proving fraud and criminal negligence. Sandstrom is named repeatedly in the documents we've filed. We've made President Rich nervous."

"Good. The media release that Mark Chalmers obviously crafted makes the White House look stupid—or inept."

She narrowed her eyes. "Or reveals them as downright liars."

It had been Jon's *New York Times* firsthand account that had blown the White House and Chalmers, the president's chief of staff, out of the water. Chalmers had thus far rescued the White House by claiming they were going on information filtered through AF's media officers.

"Or all of the above," Jon said. "Chalmers is really in Rich's line of fire now. He's running laps around the White House to put out new Fact Sheets, saying they've received updated information from AF."

"Hoping to cover up the cover-up. But we've got to prove all the connections."

"Exactly. I managed to blow two of the White House's four main points—that the oil was only leaking, not gushing, and that the platform wasn't toppled." He toyed with his water glass. "Hopefully soon I'll have enough from Elizabeth and Leo's research to blow another of their points out of the water—that there is no evidence the oil is moving beyond the Arctic."

"And point four of the media brief—that AF is cooperating fully with the White House to resolve the problem ASAP—looks like it's on the rocks too." Sarah grinned. "Now President Rich is backtracking a bit in his support of AF. Sandstrom has made some pretty heated comments about fair-weather colleagues in AF's time of need, though he hasn't mentioned the president in particular."

Jon raised a brow. "I know. Especially with all the money Sandstrom and AF funneled Rich's way for his presidential campaign. The two aren't happy bedfellows right now."

"No, and it's about to get worse for each of them. Between you, me, Darcy, and the wide net we've cast, we're going to find that elusive piece that will connect Sandstrom and the Polar Bear Bomber."

Jon chuckled. "Stated like a stubborn Worthington."

She winked. "No, a *determined* Worthington."

Langley, Virginia

It was late evening. At last he was alone.

He unlocked his right desk drawer. After removing an envelope, he opened it and shuffled through the photos of Sean

Worthington snapped from around the globe—in Dubai, in Malawi, in London.

At that moment a strident female voice interrupted. It grew louder as the woman progressed down the hallway. Right before she opened his study door, he stuffed the pictures back into the drawer and quickly locked it.

He couldn't let her know his intentions. Everything about this had to remain a secret, even from his wife. Far too much was at stake.

13

Kathmandu, Nepal

It had been months since a 7.9 magnitude earthquake had struck Nepal, killing thousands in different parts of the mountainous region, but the country was still suffering terribly from its aftermath. Aftershock tremors had continued to topple buildings. Food, water, and medical supplies had been sparse for months. Aid workers had struggled to bring stability to the region.

Sean had visited Nepal several times in his life. He was constantly drawn to the beautiful country. Its people were colorful and friendly. Even now, despite the destruction wrought by the earthquake that officials had long anticipated and dreaded, Kathmandu was still jammed with more than a million people. Its narrow lanes were lined with numerous brittle brick buildings. Some of those structures had managed to remain standing during the earthquake. Most had collapsed.

The countryside was slightly better, Sean observed. Many of the humble stone and mud-walled homes of farm families had likewise suffered some form of damage. These homes were more easily rebuilt, though not without some pain and toil. Sean marveled at the resilience of the Nepali people.

In such a place, surrounded simultaneously by majesty and tragedy, Sean imagined what life for Homo sapiens might have been like 12,000 years earlier—when they clung to parts of the earth where the ice allowed them to hunt and gather their food. Then the ice receded, and water flooded in from surrounding oceans. Humans had to fight once again for survival—much as the Nepali people did here, encircled by towering mountains and forced to provide for themselves from the land however they could.

From the moment Sean landed at Kathmandu airport, as often happened when he journeyed outside the confines of America, his troubles receded as he focused on the immediate task at hand—to provide aid and comfort to people who thought that all Americans had wealth and resources at their disposal like the Worthington family.

Sean sometimes felt he should just give away all of his money—literally empty his bank accounts—and spread his vast wealth across the landscape to every family and person he met. The Nepali people expected so very little. They were happy to share their homes and their dinner with Sean and his entourage. They asked for nothing in return.

And what do I offer? Sean wondered. *A few million dollars of a wealth that is incomprehensible to every single person I will meet in this country. It makes no sense. I have so much. They have so little. How can I possibly justify what I've been given—even if it carries with it a burden that so very much is also expected?*

At times like this Sean felt humbled in the presence of the indomitable spirit of the human species. There was something wholly other about human beings. Even in the midst of their pain and chaos, the Nepali people were still able to give, care, love, and offer a kind, generous word to a stranger who wanted nothing more than to help them in any capacity he could.

Sean could see that infinite spirit in the faces and the lives of the Nepali people, who were surviving and moving forward in the face of a devastating earthquake that had literally shaken the entire countryside to its foundations. *Who am I? What can I do as just one person in the face of all this?* Sean thought over and over as he made his way throughout the city with the aid workers from GlobalHealth at his side.

It made the life of American wealth, privilege, and politics seem so small, so inconsequential 10 time zones away. And so, as he often did when confronted with the realities of need in a place such as this, Sean determined that he simply had to do more, to give more. He decided that three million wasn't enough to make a difference. He resolved that he would give ten times that amount to GlobalHealth in ways that would matter. The cares and worries of his life in America could remain on hold for the time being. There was work to be done here.

After dinner with GlobalHealth's team at one of the few restaurants in Kathmandu that had managed to come back to serve foreign aid workers, Sean was glad to go back to his room at the lone hotel also still serving the aid workers. Since his arrival more than two days ago, he had packed in as many meetings and trips as he could. He wanted to see everything, because it would help him understand where the greatest need was. He was satisfied, in the end, that GlobalHealth was more than worthy of his investment. They were relentless and seemingly everywhere. They networked with every group. They were known as *the* organization most willing to do whatever it took to make things work, to bring normalcy back to a land that seemed anything but normal.

He kicked off his shoes and collapsed on the bed. It was also at times like this, when Sean was alone with his thoughts about his place on earth and what was expected of him, that he wished for a companion who would understand what he needed to do, what was expected of him in a family like the Worthingtons that had been given so much. He wished for a bit more connection to another life beside his own. He wished for . . . *Elizabeth*.

He sat up. Why did Dr. Elizabeth Shapiro always come to mind? After their Arctic expedition, she was back at the University of Washington with her dad. Dr. Leo Shapiro, chair of the geosciences department, was on the hot seat with both the university and the US government. Wondering how that was going, he shot her a text.

Sean

How's the heat?

Elizabeth

University's ticked again. Says our protocol wasn't to collect oil samples. Not like they haven't told us that before, but the heat had died down. Then the White House got embarrassed with their dirty laundry aired. Chalmers was all over the university president for having a rogue scientist who can't follow the rules. Dad said we were there to study marine life, which includes collecting water samples to test their habitat. "How exactly can you collect water samples without oil in them, if there's oil gushing into the water from the bottom of the ocean and that's part of the water?" he asked.

Good one.

They're threatening to pull gov't funding for the new science lab if Dad doesn't back off his research and shut up. You know Dad never will. He's an old goat, he says. Since he has tenure, he's hard to let go.

How are you doing with all this?

They don't have any control over me. I don't work for U of WA, only Dad does.

Sean chuckled. The world was much richer in flavor with people like the Shapiros in it.

Nobody will ever tell you what to do, that's for sure.

You're darn right.

He laughed again, imagining her face. The last time he'd seen her was on board the ship in the Arctic. Her anger over the dying marine life because of the oil and the lack of research that had gone into the drilling had made her normally pale skin glow with intensity. *Simply beautiful.* The thought arose, unbidden.

Elizabeth Shapiro was the real deal.

Like Laura.

Like Jean.

Like Sarah, whom their father underestimated.

Elizabeth cared about the planet—the environment, the animals, the people. She had committed her life to making her mark wherever she could. Her tenacity and arrow-like trajectory were admirable. But there was something else about Elizabeth that he couldn't put his finger on. Was it simply because she was so different from the social climbers who loved to be seen with him?

His phone dinged again.

Jon will be in Seattle for a couple of days soon, and we're going to do dinner. Wish you could be here too.

Sean flinched as if he'd been stabbed. *What's wrong with me?*

Suddenly he knew. For the first time ever, he felt jealous. Jealous because he wanted to be the one spending time with her. She stirred his mind, yes, but also his heart. *Have I finally found the right woman for me?*

Maybe it was time to make a move, to put the rumors swirling about him—about why he was still single in his mid-30s—to rest. Make his mom happy.

He needed to give that angle a little more thought once he was back in the States. For now, he texted Elizabeth one last time.

Enjoy that dinner.

But he knew he wouldn't relish the thought of even his best friend spending time alone with the woman he might be in love with.

LANGLEY, VIRGINIA

The call was quick, to the point, and on a secure line. "Jason Carson just walked into the White House and demanded a private audience with President Rich." There was a slight pause, then the caller continued, "At least Carson thought the conversation was private."

"Go on," the man behind the mahogany desk said.

"Carson basically told the president that if he doesn't tell the DOJ to save him when Sandstrom is taken down, he's going viral. He'll not only embarrass the White House but make it highly unlikely that Spencer will stay in his cushy job."

"Any specifics?"

"Carson knows about the $25 million quid pro quo."

"How?"

"Don't know, but I can guess. Sandstrom probably told him. When Sandstrom is hot under the collar, anything can fly out of that mouth. Now Carson wants to cut a deal to save his own neck. Says he's not taking the fall. He's not going to prison. That prison orange isn't his color."

The man leaned back in his chair, phone in hand. He knew people like Jason Carson. They had no scruples. Didn't care about anyone or anything but themselves and climbing up the financial ladder. If they thought they might go down, they'd come out swinging. And if they went down, they'd take everyone they could with them. That included the president of the United States, who couldn't afford the scandal of the public finding out that his reelection campaign included a $25 million quid pro quo—funds donated by Eric Sandstrom of American Frontier in exchange for exclusive drilling rights in the Arctic. Especially now, with the mess in the Arctic. It wouldn't take long to track any special favors the Rich presidency had done for AF to get them into the Arctic in the first place.

"So what is Spencer going to do?" the man asked.

"You mean, other than throw a few things around the Oval Office in a fit? Don't know." The caller sobered. "Just know that he's far from happy, and Carson strolled out looking confident and in the driver's seat."

That could only mean one thing. Thomas Spencer Rich III, president of the United States, had just made an unholy alliance between himself and one of the dirtiest men on the planet.

It didn't bode well for either of them . . . or for anyone in their way.

14

Kathmandu, Nepal

Sean lay awake in his hotel room. As much as he traveled, he still always felt a little out of sync for a few days in the new time zone. Then, by the time he got adjusted, it was time to head back to New York. He knew all the tricks—drinking plenty of fluids to avoid dehydration, taking only a two-hour nap to adjust to the time zone, and resetting his internal clock by a brisk one-hour walk when he got up. But he still often felt sluggish.

Tonight, however, he was wide awake, as if a lightning bolt had struck him. Indeed, it had. *Why not take a stab at running for governor of New York?* His thoughts kept circling back to that possibility.

He threw the idea out to his social network, and the responses were massive and nearly instantaneous.

"Makes perfect sense."

"It's about time, buddy."

"You already know the ropes."

"You've got what it takes."

"Go, Sean!"

"You're a Worthington, for heaven's sake. Of course it'll work."

Within minutes, he scrolled through the responses. Not a single negative one. Everyone in his loyal circle encouraged him, even pushed him, into pursuing that possibility.

Why not give it a go? He didn't have anything to lose.

Sean knew exactly where to start with an exploratory commitment—Kiki Estrada, the executive director of the Democratic Senatorial Campaign Committee. He'd gotten to know her well while working on Will's campaign, and he owed her a phone call. He'd been ducking her insistent calls about Will for days. Kiki knew politics better than anyone on the planet, especially New York politics, and she'd be able to advise him on a bid for governor. While it wasn't the Senate, her current bailiwick, all political roads in New York intersected in some capacity with DC politics.

Why not consider exchanging one Worthington running for a Senate race for another equally important political office? Both races were on the ballot at the same time. Sean had the same financial resources Will did, and a lot of the work they'd already done could still be put into play. It wouldn't take long to change the paperwork and kick off an announcement in the press.

With that idea settled, he turned over and, within minutes, was asleep.

"It's about time," Kiki Estrada exclaimed when Sean phoned her the next day.

"Before you get on a roll," he said, "let me tell you confidentially that I didn't have a clue that Will was going to back out. No one did."

A memory of his mother's and Laura's exchanged glances flashed into his brain. *But you have no real proof*, Sean argued with himself.

"But what on earth—" Kiki began.

"What's done is done. Will won't change his mind. He's not saying why. I can't pry it out of him, and you won't be able to either."

"Isn't that the truth," the feisty Latina replied. "He isn't even returning my calls. He owes me at least that much. I mean—"

"I know," Sean soothed. "In time, I'm sure things will come to light, and everything will be explained. But you know Will. He doesn't go off half-cocked about anything. He had a reason. He just can't share it yet. Maybe he needs to think it through."

"Well, he better think fast, because I'm holding the press off with a bunch of mumbo jumbo, and that isn't easy." The words were heated, but her tone was calmer.

"I really appreciate that, Kiki, and you know that Will and I appreciate all you've done and are doing." He took a breath. "But I'm calling because I may have something else to offer."

"Like what? An instant candidate as prominent as Will?" she joked.

"Well, what would you say if I told you I was thinking about getting into politics as well? I obviously can't run for the Senate. That would be too awkward. But the governor's race is on the ballot at the same time."

There was a resounding silence on Kiki's end of the line, then an unbelieving, "You'd do that? Be willing to step into the line of fire?"

"Maybe. You could—"

But Kiki was already up and running. While she had no immediate dog in the New York governor's race, she was a longtime political operative who knew that all things eventually come around in politics. Governors from New York actually had a better shot at the White House than senators.

"I can help with your exploratory commitment," she said. "Once the paperwork is settled, maybe we tell the press that through you and Will working together on his campaign, Will decided that politics wasn't for him, and you realized it was more for you, but you hadn't done the exploratory commitment for yourself yet, so he wasn't able to say anything except that he was stepping out of the race . . ." And Kiki was off, her excited ideas and the possibilities jumbling together into a stream-of-consciousness soliloquy.

Sean smiled. *Nothing like taking care of a phone call you don't want to return and jumping into a new career path all at once.* If there was one thing he'd learned growing up in a house with a rock-headed older brother and an outspoken little sister, it was how to be an outstanding mediator. In fact, he'd earned his PhD in it by now.

He hadn't said for sure he'd do it. He'd merely dangled the bait as a possibility.

Diplomacy worked every time. It was also a great stall technique.

It didn't fail him now.

15

JFK International Airport

Sean exited the commercial airline and made his way down the ramp to JFK International Airport. He was relaxed, happy he'd delayed his return flight 24 hours in order to tell the Global-Health team that he was increasing his commitment to their work in Nepal tenfold. They were literally speechless at the news. That sort of gift, while not unprecedented, was nearly unimaginable on the spur of the moment. They were apprecia-tive beyond words and had already begun to email preliminary plans for what the expanded gift could do for their critical work on the ground in Nepal.

Sean decompressed in a Starbucks at the airport. As much as he loved the adventure of traveling to distant places where his philanthropic wealth could make a difference, there was some-thing grounding about sitting quietly in a brightly lit, familiar place, slowly drinking coffee. It was one of his favorite things to do after closing a deal on financially backing an NGO, but he sometimes didn't have the time before his next flight.

Somehow traveling to new locales and connecting with an

intriguing variety of people also kept his restlessness at bay, at least for a while.

When his cell rang, Sean didn't check caller ID. He picked up his cup of coffee, exited Starbucks, and answered out of habit.

"You certain this is what you want to do?" Drew's tone was unruffled.

It never ceased to amaze Sean how much information Drew knew quickly. The man had connections Sean could only guess at. Drew was a master networker, and he'd taught Sean well.

But Sean hated questions. To him, asking a question was like waving a red flag in front of a bull. Questions implied, "Hey, I don't think you're smart enough to think for yourself, so make sure you've considered all the angles." Of course Sean had considered the angles. He just did it more swiftly than Will.

Sean blinked. His competition with his brother was so ingrained it naturally rose to the surface and irked him, especially at times like this. "You worried I'll smear the Worthington name if it ends badly?" he shot back.

There was a pause, then a quiet, "You know better than that. I only want to make sure you're not taking on your brother's fight as your own."

"Why? Because you think I can't do it, but Will could? That his shoes are too big for me to fill?"

"Maybe it's time to stop trying to be your brother and just be yourself. The man I know you are. The man I know you can be."

Then, for the first time ever, Drew was the one who ended the call.

Sean stopped and stared at his cell as the maze of people in JFK parted around him like rivers running in two opposite directions.

New York City

There was a first for everything, and Will had experienced more than enough of them lately. Firsts were always surprises, and Will didn't like surprises. He liked the highways of life to be smooth, with signposts marking each mile of the journey to his destination. Lately, the signs posted along the way to his destiny had either given him incorrect information or taken him on detours. Now they were entirely missing. That was disturbing indeed.

He'd been groomed from babyhood to assume the helm of Worthington Shares. In that role, he was confident.

He'd also been groomed by his father to take American Frontier, the world's most powerful oil company, to even greater heights. Developments in clean energy would literally save the planet, ensuring the healthiest possible future for generations to come. But when the board was swayed in their vote, Will had walked away without looking back. He had felt lighter, no longer sullied by his tie to a company that had lost its integrity in the midst of a push to expand horizons and pursue the almighty dollar.

Why then did he still keep an eye on every AF development in the news? Only because he was used to doing so?

Will had thought Frank Stapleton, the longtime CEO of City Capital who was also on the AF board, would be in his court. But Stapleton had gotten in bed with Sandstrom to take Will down the instant his political aspirations became known. The betrayal stung, Will had to admit. But it was a good reminder to choose alliances carefully. He could count on two hands the people he could trust, other than his family. The number was shrinking, but Drew and Jean remained among the loyal few.

Then there was Sean. Will hoped that photo Carson had

shown him wasn't another first—a lapse in his brother's ethical judgment. But until Will could be sure, he had to be cautious.

Another first was happening right now. Drew had phoned the previous night, asking Will to meet him for breakfast at the restaurant on the ground floor of the Trump International Hotel at Columbus Circle. It was their usual pre-meeting spot, but today wasn't a regular meeting day. And it was Drew, instead of Will, who had called the meeting.

Will frowned as he neared the Trump Hotel. The only other time Drew had called a meeting was for the dinner at his home, when he'd requested all three Worthington siblings attend. This had to be about something big, or Drew would have discussed it with him over the phone.

Drew sat at their usual table. After the waiter had taken their orders, he asked, "Have you heard from your brother?" Concern creased his brow.

Will shook his head. "He's been skillful at avoiding me. Not that I can blame him. The last time I saw him, he was in my face about backing out of the race. I couldn't give him an answer."

"And you still can't?"

"No. If I tell him about the photo now, he'll think I don't trust him." He sighed. "It's more that I don't trust human nature."

Drew nodded. "So what's your next move?"

"I'm not sure. And it's driving me a little crazy."

"You mean regarding Sean and the bomber connection? Or what your next personal career move is?"

"I guess both."

"And that's all it is?" Drew's gaze was intense.

Suddenly Will felt like a boy again, caught with his hand in the cookie jar. So this was another first—not telling his mentor the entire truth. He wanted to reveal what he'd learned from his mother about Sean's parentage—the other factor that, combined with the photo, had caused him to turn down the Senate bid. But even Sean himself didn't know. Was it fair then to tell Drew?

Finally Will said, "For now, that's all it is."

"I see. Well then." Drew didn't look convinced, but he didn't press further.

However, outside the door of the restaurant before they parted, Drew hesitated. "Will, I know a few things. And one is that secrets always come to light . . . sometimes not in the way you'd like them to."

As Will rode the subway toward his home, his conscience was troubled. He was caught in a great moral dilemma—protecting his brother from emotional pain that was certain to follow or telling him the truth about one or both revelations.

If he did tell his brother, he might be able to filter the details. Then Sean would realize that who his birth father was didn't change his value in Will's eyes. Will could report that Carson had approached him with a photo and then say, "It was a photo of you chatting with some guy in a bar. Do you remember anybody taking a photo with you?" He could then describe the photo, gather any details from Sean, and judge his brother's body language before he revealed that the guy had been identified as the Polar Bear Bomber.

Will continued to play out the scenarios in his head. Should he or shouldn't he?

Wait, the still small voice whispered.

But waiting had never been harder.

16

Gravity Canyon, New Zealand

Air currents rushed around Sean's body as he plummeted at a speed of over 150 miles per hour. His friends were right. This was the ultimate rush—free-falling 50 meters into the Mokai Canyon above the Rangitikei River. Even better than zip-lining over the Great Wall of China in Simatai at nearly 100 miles per hour last year.

"Woo-ahh!" was all he could say with the breath nearly knocked out of him. So he simply grinned and gave his other three adrenaline-seeking friends a thumbs-up.

Ian Jones, CEO of Overland Adventures, grinned back. "Told you. Major rush!"

The Rangitikei District was south of the Ruapehu, Tongariro, and Ngauruhoe volcanoes on the central North Island of New Zealand. Sean and his friends had crammed into a Jeep, driven State Highway 1, and gone off-roading for a couple of days to explore the area. This afternoon the weather had been perfect for zip-lining.

Sean was ready to put his feet up at the River Valley Lodge.

He even loved its nickname: the Adventure Lodge. He and his friends planned to thoroughly enjoy the hot tub and then the farm-style dinner.

Tomorrow they'd enjoy one of the supposed best Grade 5 white-water rafting trips in the world—down the Rangitikei River.

Sean had been in overdrive mode the past several weeks visiting potential start-ups. Now that he'd decided to set his sights on the governor's mansion in Albany, he had a sudden urge to visit as many far-flung places as he could and pay closer attention to several of the critical start-ups in his portfolio. He had to do it now, because the campaign would suck all the oxygen out of the room soon enough.

He'd put his travels with friends on the back burner during Will's campaign. That had included the trip to New Zealand they'd discussed for over a year. For Sean, travel—whether for the start-ups or with friends—was a good thing. It energized him, connected him more deeply with his ever-widening social circle, and helped him duck his family's phone calls when he didn't want to answer.

Ever since the end of the Senate race, he'd felt disenfranchised from Will in particular, and his father as usual. Bill's backing of Will and disregard for Sean picking up the pieces made Sean even more determined to show his father what he could do. He was tired of playing second fiddle in the family orchestra.

He texted Sarah often but was reticent to pick up his mother's calls. The strong woman he'd grown up with had become pensive, worried, and often tearful. He was weary of her asking him if he was all right and encouraging him to come for dinner. Instead he hit the road.

But as he headed back in the Jeep to the River Valley Lodge, restlessness stirred again. He shook his head to clear it. He was on an exotic adventure many would only dream of, with great friends who had become family to him. So why was it in the midst of the fun he still struggled with the uncomfortable notion that there was a piece missing in his life? That no matter where he went, he longed for a more permanent connection, a place for his heart to land?

He knew what his sister would say—that only God could fill that hole. In the past couple of years, Sarah had turned more religious than he was comfortable with. She'd even given him a compact Bible for Christmas last year and pestered him to read it for himself.

"How can you dismiss something you've never even read?" she'd challenged him once. "Maybe you're not as smart as I give you credit for."

Sean hadn't even cracked the book open once. Maybe because he disliked anyone telling him what to do, especially a family member. Or maybe because only in places like Nepal was it natural for him to reflect on a God who otherwise seemed elusive and disconnected from his life. Ironically, he carried that small book in his luggage wherever he went. It comforted him like the ragged blanket he used to sleep with and drag around with him when he was a toddler.

Funny how, when he was born, his mom had insisted he be called *Sean*. He felt anything but "favored by God." In fact, in the midst of wealth, privilege, and traveling the world, he felt . . . lost. That was the only way to describe the ache inside that descended upon him in the quiet moments.

For now, that restlessness would keep him globe-trotting, searching for adventure.

Eventually, though, he'd have to settle somewhere. What then?

///

Langley, Virginia

It was finally quiet in the house at 11:00 p.m. The man shut the large double doors to his study and waited for the 11:30 call. He answered the instant it rang.

"The DOJ noose is tightening around Sandstrom," his contact told him. "And he's highly nervous. He's trying to rein in Carson. I think he suspects Carson's got a side deal going on. Everybody knows Carson is Sandstrom's bagman for dirty work. Just never have been able to prove it. But word is, Carson has made himself a little 'unavailable' for Sandstrom lately."

The information was exactly how the man liked it—condensed and straightforward. He narrowed his eyes. *So let's see how much hardball Carson will play.*

Aloud he told his contact, "Keep eyes on Sandstrom, Carson, and the White House. We need to know their next moves even while they're thinking about them."

"Will do."

The man behind the mahogany desk knew it would be a long time before he would sleep.

///

Gravity Canyon, New Zealand

As Sean's eyes drifted shut at 3:00 a.m., his cell rang. It was Elizabeth. He hadn't heard from her in several weeks. Likely she was in the midst of a big research project.

"Hey, Mr. Night Owl," she teased, "you sound a little sleepy. Where are you, and what are you up to?"

"Gravity Canyon," he replied.

"So you did it—the ultimate rush. And?"

"It was everything they said it would be and more."

"Don't think I'd ever be that brave . . . or that stupid."

He laughed. Yes, Elizabeth was rooted—rooted to the ground and perfectly at home on the ocean. But plummeting to earth was not her idea of a good time. She'd been clear about that when he'd asked her to accompany him once.

"Jon said something similar."

"He told me that too. But he added another word—*crazy*."

"Yeah, well . . ." He couldn't help it. He had to ask. "Were you able to see Jon while he was in town?"

"Don't know how, but we finagled a whole afternoon and evening. Even did the touristy thing—visited the Space Needle and had dinner at the SkyCity Restaurant."

Again Sean was stabbed with jealousy. Why hadn't he scheduled to join them? He could have carved the time out of his start-up trips. *Get a grip, buddy*, he told himself. *You weren't there. And why shouldn't two friends get together?*

Still, he decided he needed to swing by the University of Washington soon.

"And Sean . . . ," Elizabeth hedged, "you sure you want to get into politics for yourself?"

"Why? Do you find that so hard to believe?" Annoyance crept into his tone.

"Whoa. Don't get feisty with me," she shot back. "I'm only asking because it's never been something on your grid. At least that you've talked with me or Jon about."

So they discussed me and my next move. Sean hated that. It felt like betrayal.

"Neither of you know everything about me," he said.

"Evidently not," she replied quietly. "When you want to discuss and be civil, call me. Otherwise, have a good day." Elizabeth ended the call.

Have a good day? Elizabeth was the last person on earth to throw out something as banal as that. Nor was she the type of person to hang up on anyone. That meant she was really angry.

Well, he wasn't happy himself . . . or with himself.

Maybe that U of WA trip needed to wait awhile until he wrestled with his feelings and made a definite decision, one way or another, about Dr. Elizabeth Shapiro.

17

NEW YORK CITY

Will couldn't help it. Now that the media frenzy over his aborted Senate race was over, his eyes and ears were attuned to American Frontier news. At last he gave in and did what he was good at—assessing a massive amount of information at lightning speed.

The announcement of the Polar Bear Bomber's death had mostly played out in the press now. People didn't care that they didn't know his name. Knowing he was mentally unstable sealed the deal and provided a reasonable intent to bomb a building.

The lack of interest in the bomber was both good and bad for AF. Some people were still sympathetic since a supposed eco-crazy had blown a chunk out of AF's building. But now the media attention was back on the oil-coated animals and the shorelines where the oil was migrating, generating anger. A worldwide audience was bending toward Green Justice's cause, no longer viewing the organization as a wacko environmentalist one.

In complete transparency, Green Justice had opened their records to the DOJ and DHS, and the search of activist rosters revealed no trace of the man who became the Polar Bear

Bomber. All three organizations had released statements from their offices to that effect.

Sean's friend Kirk Baldwin had been in the news frequently and had done a lot of good for Green Justice's cause. "If the man who bombed the American Frontier building was truly connected with environmental causes, he stepped over a line that no one I know in the environmentalist circles would," Kirk stated. "We are about saving lives, not destroying them. One look at the history of what Green Justice has done makes that abundantly clear." His even-keeled manner and well-seasoned words took the fire out of the opposition.

That the public's opinion had changed direction was clear from the fact that in the past week, Green Justice had received a surge of funds—37 percent more than their average. Will expected to see that percentage inch upward in the weeks to come.

He hadn't talked to Sarah lately about the criminal negligence lawsuit, but he knew she was still neck-deep. He rarely heard from her. Others might underestimate his sister, but Will knew better. When Sarah set her direction to do something, she was unstoppable.

Sean was the same way.

And so am I, Will thought. *Except when my family is threatened.*

What Sean was doing now—exploring running for governor of New York—made absolutely no sense. Then again, Sean was impulsive. His methods were often the opposite of Will's, but he got results.

Will shook his head. *Who knows? Maybe Sean will be the first Worthington to get to the White House. Wouldn't that be something?*

Sarah's attorney instincts were in overdrive. Her mother had been too enigmatic, too unavailable for phone conversations. So Sarah took the first day off of work that she had since the siblings' Chautauqua trip to announce the launch of Will's campaign. She didn't tell her mother she was coming. After a stop by their favorite bagel shop, Sarah simply showed up at her parents' penthouse in the city at 8:30 a.m.

Ava was an early riser, but she never ate breakfast before 9:00. Her children teased her about it. She claimed that she had to allow her morning tea to settle and prepare her stomach for breakfast. They all rolled their eyes about it. Ava was the only Worthington who didn't survive on multiple cups of coffee in the morning.

The minute her mother opened the door, Sarah's heart sank. Ava's light auburn hair was messy, and she was still in her robe. Sarah offered the bag. "Thought I'd bring you breakfast since Dad's out of town."

Her mother gathered her robe about her. "I didn't know you were coming by."

"You feeling sick?" Sarah stepped inside the foyer.

"No, just didn't sleep well."

Once in the kitchen, Sarah scanned the shelf by the coffeepot. No Irish tea. Something indeed was wrong. She swiveled to face her mother. "So, what gives? Clearly you're not yourself. I'd like to help, if I can."

Ava slumped. "I'm worried about your brothers."

"Will? He gave us a shock, but he'll be okay. And Sean? Why Sean? Other than the fact that he's had to deal with a lot of heat over the aborted campaign?" She paused. "Are you concerned because he's exploring stepping into politics himself?"

Ava placed the bagel bag on the table and sank into a chair. "Will had to give up his dream. And Sean . . ."

Sarah sat next to her mom. "Will has given up two dreams. But he'll find another one. He's probably already strategizing his next move. After all, he's a Worthington, and we're tough cookies. I don't think one of us has ever crumbled."

"Yes, but I'm afraid he did it because of me."

Sarah frowned. "What do you mean?"

Her mother looked down. "I told him I was worried about him campaigning—about what it might mean to our family."

Sarah shrugged. "So we take a little heat. That's nothing unusual. Anything we do is in the news or the gossip pages. Doesn't matter whether it's truth or lies. It's easy for the media to sell either one." She studied her mother. "So you were worried about Will getting hammered by the media, and now you're worried about Sean because of the same thing? Because it will catapult us as a family even more into the spotlight? Seriously, when has that stopped any of us?"

When tears brimmed in Ava's eyes, Sarah backed off her attorney mode. "I'm sorry. I'm not listening very well. Guess I'm doing a good job of preaching at you." She chuckled. "I think that's usually your role and I'm the one sitting in the pew."

At that, her mom looked up. A smile flickered before her brow scrunched. "The last time I called Sean, he was in New Zealand. It sounded like a party was in full swing. And it was 3:00 a.m. his time. Since then he hasn't picked up when I've called."

Sarah opened the bagel bag. "So? That's Sean. Has been for years. What's different this time?"

"Ever since the aborted campaign, he's been living faster than he ever has. He's been on double the normal amount of start-up trips—and those are only the ones your father knows about."

"I know, Mom, but you can't stop him. None of us can. Sean will do whatever he wants to do, and he won't fill us in sometimes. He was like that as a kid too. Besides, he's probably trying to make up for the time he lost helping Will with the campaign, and cramming in as many trips as he possibly can before he knuckles down to the campaign in New York." Sarah offered the bagel bag, and Ava absentmindedly took a cinnamon crunch one.

There really was something wrong. Ava hated sweet bagels, preferring the healthy whole-grain variety. Sarah had picked up the cinnamon one for herself.

"And then there's the campaign." Ava straightened in the chair, still holding the bagel. "Since when did Sean want to go into politics? He's trying so hard to be someone he's not."

"Will, you mean." Sarah's jaw tensed. She was used to favoritism from her father, but it was disconcerting coming from her mother.

"Yes." Ava's eyes clouded. "To please your father. Earn his love."

Recognition dawned. So she wasn't the only sibling who felt that way. Sean had joked with her over the years about how Will was their dad's favorite. But maybe it had hurt Sean as much as it hurt her. Maybe that was why he was shutting them out, to shut out the pain.

"What Sean needs most," her mother murmured, "is a father's acceptance. That's what he's missing."

"I know he and Dad haven't seen eye to eye. I admit that. But Dad's been there for us over the years. Sean too," Sarah countered.

Ava's gaze turned distant. "Maybe." She took a bite of her bagel.

Is something going on with Mom and Dad? Sarah wondered. *Are they having trouble? Why else would Mom say that?* A sliver of fear inserted itself into her heart.

But no matter how much Sarah tried her attorney logic and

tactics from that point on, she couldn't get another word out of her mother on the subject. Ava simply continued to eat the cinnamon crunch bagel without even slicing or toasting it. She brushed off the walk in the park Sarah wanted to take with her and said she was a little under the weather and needed to go back to bed.

Sarah finally gave up. As she exited the elevator on the main floor of her parents' building, her thoughts tumbled.

"Will had to give up his dream . . ."

Ava's statement leaped into Sarah's recall, and she halted by the large umbrella plant in the lobby. *Why didn't Mom say Will* gave *up his dream? Why did she say he* had *to give it up?*

Her attorney instincts on full alert, she strode from the building.

18

Paris, France

Sean had been in Paris many times. While it wasn't as exotic as places like Nepal, it was nevertheless a place where the old-world ways of business now collided with the new global economy. Sean had Worthington Shares investments in several new businesses involved in the world's new energy economy, all based out of Paris. This time he'd come to tend to an exceptionally high-flying solar tech company, which was on the cusp of disrupting the utility sector with a new home storage battery capable of holding enough of the sun's stored energy to power a small home for up to a week at a time. The start-up had utility companies all across the planet worried.

Sean had been at the company's headquarters for two days when he got a call from Jon, who said he was working on a couple of big stories, plus continuing his work with Sarah and Darcy.

"Your sister's really something," Jon said. "A sharp attorney with a sense of humor—now there's an unusual combo. Plus she can charm anyone, including the old coot at the table next to us who let anyone who came near him have it. She even got him joking with her."

Sean chuckled. "Yeah, that's Sarah."

"Don't know if it's the Worthington side—raised with a silver spoon in your mouth, able to maneuver nearly anything or anyone your way. Not like some of us, who have to work extra hard to make a living," Jon teased. "Or if it's Sarah in particular."

The two friends often bantered back and forth about the pros and cons of Worthington money. But this time, for some reason, Sean had to fight back his irritation.

Jon could have had it easier in life, if he chose. His older sister had gone to an Ivy League school paid for by their parents, but he'd refused. Instead he had gone to an in-state school on a cross-country scholarship. He'd only allowed his parents to pay for some room and board. Then, after a couple of years, he'd worked odd jobs to pay his own way. Jon said he never wanted to rest on anyone else's laurels, or their money. He wanted to make his own destiny.

Maybe that was why the comment bothered Sean so much this time. He felt trapped. *What would I be doing right now if I wasn't a Worthington?*

Jon continued. "All I know is that Sarah's impressive. Not many could hold their own against her. Now, Elizabeth? Two peas in a pod. Those two could be good friends—or die-hard enemies. Neither ever backs down."

Sean decided to bite the bullet. He had to know. Was his gut right, that Jon might be interested in Elizabeth? "How was Elizabeth when you saw her?"

"Fabulous. She's quite a woman."

Sean flinched.

"You remember a year or so ago, when we talked about the kind of woman we might give up bachelorhood for?" Jon asked.

Sure he did. It was the longest discussion they'd ever had. Both agreed on similar qualities they'd go for—strong-minded women who weren't pushovers, loyal, family-oriented, globally knowledgeable, passionate about making their own mark on the planet in some way.

"I think Elizabeth is that kind of woman . . . if I was looking, that is," Jon said.

Sean drew in a breath. "Well, are you? Looking, I mean?"

"Possibly," Jon admitted. "You wouldn't mind me pursuing that idea, would you? I mean, all three of us are friends . . ."

"Of course not. You'd be good together," Sean said.

But he did mind. He minded very much. Sean was used to winning and losing in the business world. He played with high stakes every day. Somehow, though, this seemed like the biggest loss of all.

In spite of her testiness the last time they'd talked, he'd been able to think of no one else but Dr. Elizabeth Shapiro. But maybe Sean wasn't right for her. Maybe Jon—who was more even-keeled and seemed comfortable with himself—was who Elizabeth needed. She deserved the best the world had to offer, Sean was sure of that. Jon, with his quick intellect and stellar character, was the best of the best.

Why, then, when the phone call ended, did a heaviness descend over Sean?

He shook off his suddenly dark mood. For now, he must turn his mind to other things. Though running for governor was mere speculation at this point, bantered around Sean's social circle, word had somehow gotten out that he'd had an exploratory conversation with Kiki and other political advisors. His cell was inundated with queries from the *New York Times*, the *Washington Post*, the *Guardian*, and others.

Funny how Jon hadn't mentioned it, even when he and Elizabeth discussed it. Especially since Jon was a *New York Times* reporter, for heaven's sake.

Sean's stubborn streak kicked in. He might as well let the rumor reign for a while until he decided for himself whether or not politics was for him.

At least it would give the press something to gossip about other than his single status.

New York City

As soon as Will walked into his three-bedroom suite, Laura handed him the phone. He already knew what it was about. That morning the *New York Times* had had yet another post:

> Rumors fly about the upcoming New York governor's race. Will Sean Worthington finally take the family name into politics? And if so, will he stay the course, unlike his brother?

"Can't you stop him?" Ava pleaded with Will over the phone.

He sighed. "Mom, I've never been able to control Sean—maybe only stop him momentarily when we were kids—and neither have you. He'll do what he's going to do. Whether the speculations are true, Sean will keep that to himself for a while. But for now, I can guarantee he's enjoying letting the press have their field day on a new subject."

That seemed to calm his mother for the time being.

19

Lights from media cameras flashed around Sean like stars as he climbed the steps to the Metropolitan Museum of Art. Tonight was the opening of the Van Gogh exhibit, which the Worthington family had funded. Ava Worthington had long been a patron of the arts, and it was rare for her to miss an opening. However, she'd left a message on Sean's cell, asking if he would represent the family tonight instead, since he was in town.

The darling of the press, in contrast to his more reclusive, executive brother, Sean put on a good show of loving the limelight. In truth, he was tired of being photographed, interviewed, and stalked by paparazzi. He also detested the artistic style of Van Gogh's people portraits, which were the main focus of this exhibit. He only found the landscapes and flowers palatable. But he could talk and act a good game when he needed to.

However, when microphones were thrust in his face right before he entered the impressive stone building, the reporters didn't ask about his love for art. Instead, most asked the same question: "Are you going to run for governor of New York?"

Sean flashed his most charismatic and enigmatic smile. "We'll see, won't we?" Then he proceeded to usher Renee, the beautiful model accompanying him for the evening, inside.

Why not let the speculation swirl? No one was going to trap Sean into revealing anything he didn't want to. He loved leaving things in a rather mysterious light.

After the exhibit, he ushered Renee home. She made an offer for him to come upstairs. He declined, claiming jet lag after flying halfway across the world, to avoid hurting her feelings. Then, to avoid the paparazzi, he sneaked out the back door of the building.

Let them think what they want. They wouldn't believe the truth.

The truth? His apartment was empty when he arrived there and sank onto the decorator couch he hated. He didn't want a vapid woman to fill it for a night. He wanted a woman with a lively intellect and a quirky smile. He wanted . . . Elizabeth.

But what was he thinking? His best friend had declared interest in her. She was off-limits now.

Or is she? He sat up as a spark of competition more fierce than he'd ever felt in the business world blazed into being.

Maybe he would have to make that trip to the state of Washington after all.

"You can't let go, can you?" Drew strolled into Will's office.

"Would you?" Will fired back.

Drew didn't have to answer. The two knew each other too well.

"Okay, I admit I keep track of American Frontier. But I can't get it out of my mind."

Drew studied him. "So no new challenge has reared its head?"

"No."

Will had continued to listen for the still small voice but hadn't heard any definitive direction. Only the whisper, *Wait*. Now he switched the subject. "So is our plan progressing? To keep tabs on Carson and dig more deeply into his dirty dealings and background?"

Drew nodded. "I've got people on it. Good people. They'll turn up something."

The Polar Bear bombing case still haunted Will. Maybe it was because he had seen the bomber with his own eyes and had been in the area right before the bomb went off. Sure, a guy in a polar bear suit was a little weird, but nothing in the guy's eyes or behavior had flagged him as a terrorist.

"That's all I need to know at this juncture," Will said. "I'm going to give Sarah a call to see if anything's new with the criminal negligence case. At least anything she can tell me officially."

"Got it." With those two cryptic words, Drew headed back out of the office.

When the large double wood doors swung shut, Will placed the call to Sarah.

"Things are progressing, but much too slowly. There are too many loose ends. No way can we go into court like this. But we'll prove it—we'll get Sandstrom," his sister declared. "Darcy and Jon are helping with some details officially and on the side." She chuckled. "You know how it goes. And both Darcy and I have teams of investigators on it."

"Great. I always liked those two—honest, straightforward people with integrity."

"Yeah, Jon's like a Dad clone, only younger and with a reporter's voyeuristic edge and instinctual snoopiness. Mostly quiet but a good listener." She laughed. "You know what Mom says about still waters running deep."

The words sounded like his sister but didn't have her usual

sassiness. They were tempered with what sounded like admiration.

Sarah? Who swore off dating after that TV producer jerk?

Will couldn't even remember the guy's name, just that he and their parents couldn't stand him. One dinner together with him and his pompous manner had sealed the deal. Sean had said the guy was a jerk from the first time Sarah mentioned his name. He'd refused to give specifics, but he'd insisted that Sarah deserved far more. But he'd also told Will that their sister was too headstrong to listen. She had to learn for herself—and she had, the hard way.

Was she intrigued by Jon Gillibrand? Will smiled, considering the possibility. He'd have to mention it to Laura and get her take, even if he knew what she would say.

"Stay out of your sister's love life," she'd chide. Laura had hated it when her parents and brother finagled dates for her when she came home from college. "As if I couldn't find one for myself," she'd told Will in a heated moment, when they were getting to know each other that first summer in Chautauqua Institution. Sure enough, Laura had found the right match. Will was thankful every day it was him.

But then he knew what Laura would do next. She'd take his arm and whisper, "So, what's he like? Would I like him? Would Ava like him?"

In spite of her repeated vocalization against trashy romance novels, which ended predictably with the woman finding the perfect match, Laura was a romantic at heart. She and Ava would love it if Sarah at last found her match. Ditto for Sean.

Only time would tell, but it would be interesting to watch . . . even if his wife did make him stay out of it.

20

LANGLEY, VIRGINIA

The call came in at 11:30 p.m. His source was prompt and to the point. "Carson went to cut a deal with Spencer, but the president didn't act fast enough for him. So Carson leaked something to the press to protect himself. Don't know the details, but I can guess. It'll run tomorrow in the *Washington Post*, the *New York Times*, and the *Guardian*. Those three at least."

The man could already see the story in his mind's eye: "President Rich has secret rendezvous with unknown source. Does he know more than he is willing to say about the bombing and the Arctic oil fiasco?" It would send Spencer's ratings into a major nosedive if it looked like he was lying. It also set Carson up for the role of good guy, driven by his conscience to tell the truth about what was happening behind the scenes in high-powered circles.

"Any sources we can tap at one of the papers?" the man asked.

"Working on it as we speak. But it doesn't seem like anybody knows much more than the basic info."

Enough for the media to dangle out there to whet people's

appetites, but not enough details to make a full meal. It was what the man had expected—a well-worn technique to manipulate national and international events in the direction those in the know wished them to go.

When the man didn't respond, his source went on. "Speculation has already kicked in. A media firestorm will soon explode. Spencer will have to act."

That was a given. The president couldn't let speculation like that go on for too long, especially when he was kicking off his reelection campaign.

"So, any movement?" the man asked.

His contact hesitated. "There's a rumor, not yet confirmed, that Spencer has gone to the DOJ with a deal that's to go into place for Jason Carson."

"So when Sandstrom goes down, Carson doesn't, is that it?"

"You got it. At least, that's the hope."

Politics was often like a shell game, with the shells shuffled until it was hard to tell who did what or which shell the item was under. The only thing that mattered was who was left holding that item when the game was over. Mark Chalmers was a pro at that.

"Stay on it," the man directed.

"You know I will." His source ended the call.

The man knew how the game would be played next. Spencer would make the deal with the Department of Justice to protect Carson—in order to keep any prying eyes away from the quid pro quo of $25 million from American Frontier. Then the rationale for the deal would be handed out as the truth to the national media and fed to an easily believing public. Carson would shine like the good guy telling the truth for the cause of life, liberty, and justice.

Spencer would stand behind American Frontier as a company.

He'd explain his recent dip in backing as due to his discovery of recent details about the bombing, AF's potential involvement, and who in the company might be involved with the cover-up. He would disavow any prior knowledge of Sandstrom's actions regarding hiring the Polar Bear Bomber in order to turn sentiment to sympathy for the beleaguered oil company. He'd then say sadly that the events in the Arctic were a result of the greed of the CEO, who did not allow the proper time for research to be completed regarding safety of drilling in a fragile ecosystem before plowing ahead. He would promise that a full investigation into the matter had already been launched. As a result, his ratings would rise right before his reelection campaign. His honesty and drive to secure justice in a difficult situation would be heralded by the press.

Jason Carson? He'd get a hand slap—at the most—for following Sandstrom's orders and be applauded for coming forward. The details surrounding what Carson did exactly for Sandstrom would be fuzzy and gray enough that he couldn't be prosecuted. No, he might not hold a high position in government or business circles ever again, but neither would he be in prison. With the nest egg he had stashed away, he could live obscurely and more than comfortably in a country that didn't have extradition, should things go south.

Sandstrom? He'd be the scapegoat, fed to the media pack. It was as simple as that.

It wasn't that Sandstrom didn't deserve it. The man behind the mahogany desk had been watching him for some time. Sandstrom played it fast and loose in many areas. This was the first time he might be caught.

However, Carson deserved his share of payback. The man had spent a majority of his career dealing with people like Jason Carson who had no conscience. People who were masters in manipulating others with fear and lies and then introducing to the press whatever speculation served them best.

The man hated it in every fiber of his being when the manipulators won. This time, he vowed, Carson wouldn't.

But Spencer? That was a different matter entirely. It would keep the man awake the rest of the night.

New York City

At 11:45 p.m. Sarah was in wind-down mode, curled up on her couch, eating takeout brick-oven pizza. Other than the gala donor affairs she attended on behalf of the Worthington family that went late into the night, she now liked to settle in at home before midnight. It didn't often happen that way, with her packed schedule, but she relished the evenings it did. Such desire was a far cry from her undergraduate days at Cambridge, where her social circles had kept her so booked she slept for no more than four or five hours straight.

Then, at Harvard Law, she'd discovered her passion for justice—to speak for those who couldn't speak for themselves and to go after those who treated others as prey. The last seven years she'd spent in the DOJ had been fast-paced and hard but also ultimately satisfying. There was nothing like defending the country against high-roller low-life types who thought their wealth and position made them untouchable.

Like Carson and Sandstrom, Sarah thought. She frowned as she took another bite of pizza. She couldn't help it—sometimes her work followed her home. It happened even more for this case because of her family's long connection with American Frontier. It still bothered her that Jason Carson had been skulking around in the shadows when Will walked off the podium.

Especially since she hadn't been able to get anywhere with her quiet queries of what he was doing there—only that Sandstrom had been worried that Will would use the campaign to make things difficult for AF.

Just then her cell rang. Startled, she grabbed it, knowing it had to be Sean. Of course he'd call right before midnight, when she was likely to be at home, eating junk food to take the edge off her stressful day. He loved to wind her back up. It was a running joke between them.

"Hey, good lookin', right on time," she teased as she picked up the call.

The other end of the line was silent for a moment. Then a masculine voice said wryly, "I'm glad to know that. The compliment is much appreciated, but I don't know what I'm on time for."

"Jon! Oops. Thought it was Sean. He's the only one who calls this late."

"Ah, got it. Sorry it's so late, but there's something you need to know." His tone morphed to all business.

She snapped upright on the couch and muted the sound on her TV.

"The *Times* office is still awake and buzzing over an anonymous tip."

"Tip? What tip?" she asked, now as alert as if she'd drunk two cups of coffee.

"That a secret meeting took place between President Rich and a confidential source regarding the Polar Bear bombing."

"And?"

"Chalmers must be running loops at the White House with the president, trying to figure out next steps. That's all I have right now. The anonymous tip seemed a bit too convenient, so I took a pass on writing the story. But it's going to run. Not all journalists are discerning. Especially if they're too eager to get their name in print on a breaking story. Anything 'conspiracy theory' sells papers and gets a byline that people pay attention to, at least temporarily." She heard his disgust, tempered with realism. "Some journalists have made their careers on what turns out later to be lies, but I don't want to be one of them."

His integrity and his on-target gut were only two of the qualities she admired about Jon Lucas Gillibrand.

"I wanted you to know," Jon added. "I'm contacting Darcy too."

"That will be an interesting call." Sarah could imagine Darcy's fiery response, especially if DHS hadn't already been notified. "I'll make some inquiries myself and let you know if I find out anything."

"Sarah," Jon asked hesitantly, "have you heard from Sean?"

She thought hard before she answered. "No, not for a while. That's why I thought your call had to be him. But you know that's not unusual for Sean—social with everybody except for his family."

"I know, but this time feels different. I'm . . ."

Sarah took advantage of the pause to slide the pizza box off her lap and onto the coffee table. Her mother would have been horrified she was eating it out of the box without putting it on a proper plate. "You're what?" she asked, scooting the phone to her other ear.

"I hope I didn't offend him."

"Offend him how?"

"By telling him I might want to spend some more time with Elizabeth."

His words were sparse, but Sarah got it. "So you're worried that you're stepping on Sean's toes? Did he tell you he was interested in her in that way?"

Sean had never said anything like that to Sarah. Sure, he talked about how much he admired Elizabeth . . . but Sean, romance on the brain? She couldn't picture it. Sean had tons of dates but said he liked it that way—a date for a night, nothing deeper.

"No. I asked him if he would mind me pursuing that idea, since the three of us are good friends. He said, 'Of course not,' and that's where our discussion ended. But I haven't heard from him since."

"Maybe he's just busy catching up on the start-ups," she suggested.

"Maybe." But Jon didn't sound convinced.

By the time the call ended, her favorite pizza felt like lead in her stomach. She wasn't sure why, but she did know she had an immediate call to make.

Minutes later, she was drumming her fingers in frustration as she was stonewalled by Chalmers's executive assistant, who refused to send a message to her boss this late at night. Twenty minutes later, she'd had enough. "Look," she announced, "I am well aware that an anonymous tip was passed to the *Times*. My guess is that it's gone to other papers as well. I'm certain they're all busy, trying to outdo each other with breaking the story. If the president had a meeting with a confidential source about the bombing, why wasn't the DOJ notified? It is, after all, our case. So why wasn't I informed before it got to the press? Explain that, will you?"

She was determined not to back off in her pursuit of the truth.

21

Drew arrived at Will's front door at 6:30 a.m. with a paper copy of the *New York Times* under his arm. With Will's kids and Laura still sleeping, the men entered the kitchen, where coffee was brewing.

"So?" Will pointed to the article.

"I assume you already read it online?" Drew asked.

Will nodded. He'd done that immediately after Sarah's feisty call at 5:30 a.m. that had awakened him from a deep sleep. "Sarah said Jon had alerted her about it but had refused to write the story himself. He was suspicious of the source. Thought the leak was too convenient. But he wanted Sarah to know and said she could pass the info to me. Jon had tried to call Sean but didn't reach him."

Concern flickered in Drew's eyes before his typical thoughtful expression returned.

Will laughed. "You know Sarah. Unstoppable when she's on the warpath. Called the White House at midnight and demanded an audience with Chalmers."

A chuckle escaped from Drew. "Underneath that belle-of-the-ball exterior is a woman of steel who won't take no for an answer. She was always good at manipulating you boys and your father to do her bidding with one crook of her finger. Did she get any information that wasn't in the article?"

"Nothing, and that infuriates her. Where do you think this rumor came from?"

"I could guess." Drew pursed his lips. "But I could be wrong."

"Come on, Drew." Will waved his coffee cup. "Your gut?"

"Carson is the leak. Word is, he's feeling the heat now that the DOJ and DHS are turning it up. Would make sense for him to go straight to the president to try to cut a deal. Especially since the president has a lot to lose if all of AF goes south." He shrugged. "But you know Carson. No scruples. No patience."

Will lifted a brow. "So you're saying when he didn't get what he wanted fast enough, he thought he'd get some fire insurance to protect himself?"

"That's what I'm saying."

Will straightened. It made sense. "Then Sarah's poised in the middle with the Polar Bear bombing case. And Darcy's right there with her."

"Those two will never give up a prizefight like this until there's a knockout."

"So he's desperate." Will narrowed his eyes. "Trying to save his own hide."

Drew nodded. "And he must have a pretty big get-out-of-jail-free card to play."

The idea of Jason Carson living on edge was a little bit of justice for what he'd put Will through, but it wasn't enough. He hated that Carson was still on the loose, pulling strings, and worse, that he had that photo of Sean with the Polar Bear Bomber as collateral.

Will wished he knew if there was any connection between his brother and the bomber and, if so, what kind it was. With his sister investigating, he only hoped his brother wouldn't be implicated in whatever she uncovered.

But maybe, just maybe, Will thought, *this new wrinkle for Carson will sidetrack him from thinking about taking down Sean—and the entire Worthington family.*

Then again, Will had found out the hard way that bullies usually came back for more.

Langley, Virginia

His contact was hedging, and he'd called at an unusual time—early morning. The man behind the mahogany desk knew what that meant—his source had news he wouldn't want to hear. But the man didn't care for delays of any kind. Even if the information was unpalatable, he had to know. "Out with it," he barked.

"Evidently Sarah Worthington has been calling the White House nonstop since the news leaked. She won't give up."

If she doesn't, the man thought, *she might get a lot more than she bargained for—like her brother implicated in the Polar Bear bombing.*

He couldn't let that happen. He knew what he had to do.

A simple call would take care of it.

22

NEW YORK CITY

Sarah sat scowling in her desk chair at the DOJ. *The Washington Post*'s lead story revealed Jason Carson as the good guy who blew the lid off the Polar Bear bombing—risking all by telling his story. A quote from him proclaimed:

> I have done things I'm not proud of, things I wish I could change in my desire to assist Eric Sandstrom and American Frontier with their mission to provide bountiful, economic fuel for our nation. But none of my actions were illegal. However, I became convinced now was the time to tell about the events behind the scenes. My conscience won't allow me to do anything less.

Conscience? He has a conscience? Sarah dropped the newspaper on her desk in disgust.

As far as what had really happened, no details were revealed that could be supported or rebutted. Just a bunch of general information to raise the noise level.

Furious at not being notified by the White House of these events, Sarah again phoned Chalmers's staff there. Again she was stonewalled with a song and dance: "I'm sorry. As you can imagine, Mr. Chalmers is rather busy at the moment but will return your call as soon as he is able."

She slammed down her office phone and called Darcy. "I smell rotten fish."

Darcy took over. "A whole barrel full of them. DHS wasn't informed either."

The next several hours flew by as Sarah pieced together details with the DOJ investigators and made multiple calls to the White House.

At 3:00 she was summoned to her boss's office. John Barnhill, Criminal Division chief of the Department of Justice, was a political appointee in a Republican administration. At first he wasn't keen on a blue-blood trust-fund baby working for him, but he'd grown to trust Sarah and her instincts. In fact, Sarah had served as a very useful shield for him on key cases like American Frontier. It looked good to have a member of one of the country's wealthiest families working for him and the president, especially when her family was known for supporting the opposing party in power.

Barnhill was ambitious. The current attorney general had announced months earlier that he was leaving. Sarah knew, from Drew and Jon alike, that her boss was angling for the job. It made sense, actually. Barnhill had done everything that was asked of him. While jobs like AG usually went to those who were closest to the occupant of the Oval Office, they sometimes went to deserving and talented political appointees like Barnhill. But not always. Sarah knew that as well as anyone.

She assumed that her boss had news about the White House and that he'd give her a difficult time for her relentless badgering. This time, though, when Barnhill was silent, studying her, she had a feeling she was in deep trouble. *So I'm going to be keelhauled for annoying the White House.* She steeled herself for the onslaught that usually followed silence from John Barnhill.

"I just got a call from President Rich," he announced. He

looked at some papers on his desk, then up at Sarah. There was a glint of anger in his eyes, and perhaps a bit of resentment. "He wants to vet you as a possible candidate for attorney general. When he puts it that way, who am I to say no?"

Sarah opened her mouth, closed it, then opened it again. She honestly had no idea what to say. This was totally out of left field. "I'm not qualified."

"Yes, you are," Barnhill replied. "As much as anyone is qualified for jobs like this. AGs are political appointments. They serve at the pleasure of the president."

"But you . . ."

"It doesn't matter what I might or might not want. Appointments like this often serve very specific political interests."

"And what possible interest could I serve?" Sarah was genuinely perplexed.

"I think you know," her boss said softly.

"I don't," Sarah answered honestly. "I mean, it's true that our family has the resources to support a Democrat to oppose President Rich in the next election. But that's no reason—"

"There are always reasons. And right now, the issue with American Frontier, campaign contributions, culpability—it all presents a big problem for the president."

"And my appointment as attorney general helps that?" Sarah mused out loud. But she and Barnhill both knew the answer. Of course it helped. The appointment would effectively keep Sarah from pursuing things to higher levels.

"Yes, it does." Her boss smiled wanly. "If it works, and you're confirmed, then at least I can say that I'll have a boss I genuinely respect."

Sarah blushed. "Thank you." She rose from her chair. "So that's all?"

"Isn't it enough?"

Sarah nodded and left Barnhill's office. She was still reeling as she walked back to her office. *Attorney general? Now? In the midst of the AF case?* In a daze, she headed back to her desk and dialed Darcy.

"Two times in one day?" Darcy quipped.

But when Sarah told her the news, her friend exclaimed, "Good for you! But . . ." Darcy's voice lowered. "You know I have to ask this. Why the AG job? Why now?"

Sarah almost laughed. Her friend knew her so well.

"Maybe you did more than ruffle a few feathers by pestering the White House," Darcy said.

"What do you mean?"

"Ever think somebody is anxious to take you out of the picture? What better way than to put you in a place where you have to report directly to those you're trying to investigate, and to distract you from your bombing investigation and who that somebody might be?"

The possibility and weight of that knowledge settled in. Was the president of the United States trying to buy her off?

Just how deep and high was that barrel of rotten fish?

So Carson is now a good guy in the eyes of the world. Will exhaled in frustration. *Drew was right, as always.*

Then he remembered what his father always said: "Those who are honest and stay honest will win in the long run, son. Those who aren't will be revealed for who they are someday."

Still, Will was aggravated. He wanted that someday—when Carson and Sandstrom would both be revealed for who they were—to come soon enough that he could enjoy seeing it.

And he hoped his family wouldn't be hurt in that revelation.

23

///

Geneva, Switzerland

Sean made his way to the new NGO headquartered near the World Health Organization. While his heart longed to be on the front line of where the greatest need might be—like in Nepal, helping with the aftermath of the earthquake, or in Malawi, assisting severe flooding victims—he knew that the best use of his time, wealth, and talents was to network with those who commanded the troops in the field.

GlobalHealth was now flourishing and making even more of a difference, thanks to Sean's generous gift. Now, in Geneva, he was doubling down on that gift by meeting with one of the key partners in their work, a relatively new NGO that worked closely with the pharmaceutical industry to take drugs about to expire and make them available across the world.

Prescription drugs were expensive in the West, in the developed world. But this particular NGO was run by a brilliant medical doctor who'd developed a system to move nearly expired drugs quickly. It was a bit like hedge funds that used computers to track data. The NGO, Quant Medical, used big data to find gaps in sales and approach companies about making donations. Those companies could then hedge their losses through the tax benefits. Both sides won.

GlobalHealth had introduced Sean to Quant Medical through a consultant who'd worked in some capacity for both organizations. Sean had texted back and forth with her several times prior to today.

It had been a long time since Sean had connected with his family. Even Sarah seemed to have given up trying to contact him for a while. By now she was used to his patterns.

"I figure you'll pop up on the grid when you're ready," she teased him once when he'd been out of pocket for a month. "I can't blame you for wanting to take a break from the Worthington craziness. I feel like that sometimes myself."

He could count on his sister to be honest, even if she was good at manipulating him.

Sean hadn't talked to Jon since he'd stated his interest in Elizabeth.

And Elizabeth? It had been even longer since their abruptly ended call when he'd behaved so badly. Yes, he could admit it now. But with his start-up globe-trotting he hadn't had a minute to schedule a trip to Seattle, and she hadn't responded to his texts asking how her work was going. Maybe she was neck-deep in a research project. Maybe she was still mad at him. Or maybe she was too focused on Jon now to respond.

The first two options he could handle. The third? He didn't want to go there.

Strange how being on the road so much in the last month had increased his loneliness instead of energizing him. He felt fragmented from everyone he truly loved, even while his social networking circle increased exponentially. At least the jet-setting kept him from thinking too much.

He entered the bistro in downtown Geneva to meet his new colleagues from Quant Medical for dinner. Before he knew it, the two glasses of wine he'd had with dinner were taking a fuzzier toll on his brain than he'd expected. Sean wasn't a drinker. Just a glass of wine with dinner sometimes, or the occasional beer after work with friends or in one of the suites at a New York Yankees game. That was all. He'd learned to nurse one drink for a long time.

Right as their evening was winding down, an exotic dark-haired, dark-eyed woman approached. "Hi, I'm Vanessa." She pointed a well-manicured finger playfully at him. "And you are?"

"Sean." He didn't add his last name. Tonight he didn't want to be a Worthington.

They started chatting, and he assessed her as his colleagues drifted away one by one. She was the flirtatious, looking-for-a-one-night-stand type who scoped out bars, and she seemed to be paying attention only to him.

Loneliness swept over him in the midst of the noisy crowd. *What does it matter if I give in? No one will know*, he rationalized. The woman he really wanted was quite likely gone—into the arms of his good friend, no doubt.

Suddenly his head ached from the alcohol, and he wanted the pain in his heart to go away. He found himself walking, one arm around Vanessa's shoulders, back to his room.

But just as he reached his door, he heard an irritating voice in his head. *Stay on the right path*. He couldn't brush it away. Even here, halfway across the world from New York City, he couldn't escape the morals he'd grown up with.

So he did the only thing he could. He told Vanessa, "You're beautiful. But this is not for me."

She reached out one hand and stroked his face, then his chest. Her hand glided sensuously downward. "But I can—"

He grabbed her hand. "No, you can't. I'm going inside my room. Alone. And you are going to leave."

When he dropped her hand and turned to insert his key in the lock, he felt a brush in just the right place. His body betrayed him, responding almost instantly. She moved closer behind him, one arm snaking around his neck. Her breath was warm on his left ear.

Loneliness and desire peaked, weakening his resolve. For a minute he relished the touch, the promised pleasure. The key wavered in his hand.

Then the voice spoke again. *Stay on the right path.*

He spun and gave her a little shove away from him. "No. Leave now."

With a swift movement that didn't match his dulled faculties, he inserted the key in the lock and stepped inside his room. Slamming the door shut, he double-locked it.

Then, using the door as a prop for his back, he slid to the floor.

An image of Elizabeth, her brown eyes sparking with indignation like they had the day she'd been off-loaded from the USS *Cantor* during the oil fiasco, burned into his now crystal-clear mind.

He sat on the hotel room floor, stunned. How could this be happening to him? *Talk about stupid.* Suddenly every muscle ached like he'd been running a marathon, and he held his head in both hands.

Another thought struck him. People were always looking to take the Worthington family down, and he'd almost given them a reason. *Talk about doubly stupid.*

He straightened. What if Vanessa had been sent by political enemies he didn't yet know even existed, to cause him harm? Giving in would have ended the potential of him running for governor of New York before he'd even begun. Even events that seemed secret would come to light, he knew. Drew had drilled that into his head especially in Sean's teen years, when he'd been far more prone than his brother and sister to wander down the wrong path.

As crazy as it sounded even to himself, he truly was entertaining the idea of running for governor. It would make his father proud, for starters. What were Bill Worthington's words when the family was gathered at Chautauqua? Sean searched his recall. *"It's about time for someone to turn this country around. Might as well be a Worthington."* Yes, that was it.

More than anything else in the world, Sean longed to hear from his father, "Well done, son."

But that seemed to be his dad's line to Will.

Langley, Virginia

The man flipped through the package that had just arrived by special courier. Multiple digital shots showed Sean Worthington and an unknown woman walking down a hotel hallway, then stopping outside a room door. Tilting his head, the man studied every detail in the photos. Next he'd turn to the video footage.

His contact called several minutes later. "I assume you got the package."

"Did he fall?" the man asked.

"No." There was a pause at the other end of the line. "He was tempted, as you can see—what man with a pulse wouldn't be? But he didn't fall. He made his intent clear by slamming the hotel room door. Bet it was the first time anyone rejected that woman. Did you see the clip of her face right after the door slammed?"

"I haven't watched the video footage yet."

His contact chuckled. "It was murderous. Gives a new meaning to the old adage about what a spurned woman will do."

So Sean is a good guy after all, untainted morally by wealth and position. The man nodded to himself. Bill Worthington had always been a straight-as-an-arrow kind. It would make sense he'd taught Sean to stay on the path. It was one of the many reasons the man was having Sean watched, to find out the truth behind the tabloid blarney.

"And the woman?" he asked.

"Top-of-the-line courtesan, flown in from London. Very expensive. Noted for getting the desired results."

That merely firmed the man's resolve to do what he needed to. He leaned in toward the phone. "What about that other matter?"

"Done," the contact announced. "Sarah Worthington will be named the new AG."

Ah, so the sharp young attorney can be derailed, the man thought. *But for how long?*

24

NEW YORK CITY

"Son, would you come to the penthouse today?" Ava's authoritative tone was the kind Sean knew he couldn't ignore. At least not for long.

Less than 24 hours ago, he'd been in Geneva. Between the flight time, a delay at the airport with a plane that had to be serviced, and jet lag, he hadn't been able to sleep for more than four hours at his place. Thank goodness his housekeeper had cleaned out the fridge and stocked it with fresh food. He'd been poised at the open fridge door when his mother called.

"Sean? You heard me, right?"

Of course he did, loud and clear. "Yes, Mom, I heard you. I'm in the middle of checking out my breakfast options."

"Well, come on over, and I'll make breakfast for you." Ava announced it like it was a done deal.

Sean shook his head. *Must be a mother thing—assuming your kids want you to take care of them even when they're grown up.*

But his mother was in her glory when she could cook for her family. It didn't matter that the Worthington siblings had been reared surrounded by top-notch household staff, including a world-renowned culinary artist.

"How about some Irish oatmeal? With fresh peaches?" she suggested.

Inwardly he groaned. *Not oatmeal.* He'd had too much of it over the years. Didn't matter what fruit she put in it, it was still too mushy. He liked food with texture and enough cholesterol-laden fat to give it some taste. "Okay, Mom, that's fine. But don't make me much. Jet lag, you know, so I'm a little off." He would choke down a couple of spoonfuls to please her.

"So, within the hour?" she asked.

"Give me a little over that, and I'll be there." He decided to try one last time. "Mom, I'm really tired. Just got back. Is this important, or could it wait?"

He heard an intake of breath. "Yes, it's important. And no, it can't wait. Please, Sean."

He never could hold his own against his mom's or sister's begging. He'd learned that a long time ago, so he didn't fight it now. "Okay, I'll get in the shower. See you soon."

"Thank you. And son? I love you." His mom sounded choked up when she ended the conversation.

Weird. Sean stared into the still-open fridge. When he blinked, he spotted the packet of already cooked bacon. A few minutes in a skillet would crisp it right up. He'd fry an egg to go with it. If he ate breakfast before he took a quick shower, even his mom's sensitive nose wouldn't be able to sniff out the scent of bacon on his clothes.

A short while later Sean was dining on one of his favorite breakfasts, leaving just enough room for a bite or two of his mother's oatmeal. He held up a strip of bacon and grinned. He loved the real deal. None of that turkey bacon his mom tried to feed them.

Will didn't seem to mind it. Then again, his brother didn't have much of a choice. Laura and Ava had both converted, so he got hit from both directions.

But Sarah shared his perspective and was outspoken about it. "Mom, if you're going to cook bacon, then cook bacon. I don't know what the heck this stuff is, but it's sure not bacon." As the baby of the family, Sarah could get away with anything. After that, his mom cooked regular bacon for Sarah, but the rest of them had to suffer through the turkey bacon.

Suddenly he missed his vivacious sister. After he got back from his mom's, he'd give her a call to catch up. Maybe they could even finagle a dinner.

He slid into his most comfortable zipped sweatshirt and his favorite Nike Dunk Low Pro SB "Paris" athletic shoes. They were a couple of years old now and broken in, just the way he liked them. Sarah had laughed when she'd seen them, saying they went with his wild streak.

"So you're going for attorney general? That's great news," Will told his sister.

"Yeah. Timing is everything."

He lifted a brow. This was a big next step for Sarah, but her tone was sarcastic, maybe even a bit anxious. Will had spent a lifetime reading his siblings' moods, and this one wasn't celebratory. "Well, you deserve—"

Chatter exploded in the background at the other end of the phone. "Gotta go," she blurted out and ended the call.

Will frowned. He was glad for his sister. She worked hard. But why the nervousness? Something was not right.

Sitting back in his leather executive chair, he stared out the large glass wall that overlooked Madison Avenue and tapped his pen on his right thigh. *Is this really what she wants? Or is something else bothering her?*

His chatty, enthusiastic-about-life sister had just delivered big news in a straightforward manner, without her typical dramatic embellishment.

And what was that snarky comment—"timing is everything"—about?

They had to talk again as soon as possible. Maybe Sarah didn't want the AG position but felt forced to consider it. He thought back to her undergraduate days, when his free-as-a-butterfly sister had hated to be trapped under any net of responsibility. She'd certainly come a long way since then. But what if she wasn't meant to do the AG job?

Then again, what do I want for myself? Other than his drive to see justice stick for Eric Sandstrom and Jason Carson, he still hadn't answered the question, "What's next for me?" Was it to remain CEO of Worthington Shares only? To focus like a laser on growing the company? Or would some other plan reveal itself? The answers to those questions eluded him.

Will liked his ducks quacking in a row. When one was out of line or wandering out of sight, he felt fidgety, restless, incomplete. Like the time he was nine and his favorite stuffed animal had disappeared for three days from its central place on the headboard of his bed. He'd searched everywhere for Fred and at last found him buried under his sister's covers.

Maybe if he searched hard enough, long enough, he'd find the answer to this dilemma too.

25

Sean knew the instant his mother poured tea for him that she was distracted. She intimately knew the tastes of each of the cubs from her den. Like Sarah, Sean hated tea in general and loved coffee, especially the Kopi Luwak he brought home every time he traveled to Indonesia. He only drank tea when he had to, to be polite. *I guess this is one of those times*, he thought.

"Okay, Mom, what gives? Why the song and dance? Do you want me to represent the family at another fund-raiser? If so, all you have to do is ask."

Ava got up swiftly from the kitchen table and moved to the stove to stir the oatmeal. He could hear it bubbling. "No," she said, back turned to him. "That's not it. But it is important."

"So . . . ," he prompted.

She poured a large helping of Irish oatmeal into one of her heirloom bowls. The brown crystal sugar and small pitcher of buttermilk were already on the table. Her hands trembled as she carried the bowl to the table and placed it in front of him.

Now alarmed, he asked, "Mom, are you all right? You're not sick? Dad's not sick?"

She lowered herself into the chair next to him and touched his hand. "No, I'm not sick. Your father is fine. He's golfing and catching up with Wendell Neal at the Eller College of Management at the U of Arizona. He won't be back until sometime tomorrow or the next day. You know your father. Semiretired of his own volition, but still moving at a faster clip than most 20-year-olds."

"Then why the rush meeting?"

His mother straightened to a regal height in the kitchen chair. "I needed to talk to you . . . alone."

So this is it, he thought. *She's going to hammer me about stepping into politics. Tell me it could go south and it could hurt the Worthington family name. Same concern she had about Will, now transferred to me.*

He tried to stop the onslaught. "If it's about me running for governor—"

"No, it's not," she countered, lifting her chin. "For once in your life, Sean, stop trying to smooth over situations that might come up. I need you to listen—and eat your breakfast."

It was her "listen to me, I'm your mother" tone. He knew better than to argue. "Okay, Mom, I'm eating." Reluctantly he poured a dab of buttermilk on his oatmeal and took a small bite. *No reprieve here.*

She interlaced her fingers and rested them on the tabletop, almost as if she were praying. "I need to tell you a story—a story that started almost 50 years ago, when your father and I were at Harvard." Her sea-green eyes seemed to look back over the decades. "It was only a few weeks into my freshman year that I met Bill. He was so handsome, so sure of himself. He knew his path in life, while I was only beginning to figure mine out."

Where on earth is she going with this? Sean wondered. *Is this the "I'm concerned because you haven't found your life partner yet" talk?*

Ava smiled at him. "Most of all, Bill Worthington, a sophomore, paid attention to me. It didn't take long to figure out that he too came from a long line of wealth and privilege. And if the rumors that abounded at Harvard were even halfway true about what his trust fund would be at age 21, it far exceeded what my parents and their parents and grandparents had achieved. When I mentioned I'd met a Worthington, my mother seemed quite excited." She waved a hand. "I didn't marry your father for his money, though. I admired him—his drive, his competitive nature, what he was already accomplishing at Harvard to make his mark on the world. When he invited me to dinner the spring of my freshman year, I was all aflutter—"

"Okay, I get it," Sean interjected. "Enough said."

"Anyway, your father graduated the year before I did. He jumped right into Worthington Shares work, so I didn't see him much my senior year." Her voice quivered. "I was very lonely. If it wasn't for Thomas . . ."

"Yours and Dad's friend—Thomas Rich?"

"Yes. We were like the Three Musketeers, doing things together for three of our Harvard years. It's amazing, though, how close we were as friends, especially since Bill and Thomas were so different."

Okay, he'd play along for a while, since this conversation was important to his mother. Better, it distracted her from noticing he wasn't eating her oatmeal. "How so?"

Her eyes flickered, and she exited from the past. "Bill was a blazing star, gathering people along his trajectory who believed in him—who he was—and what he might accomplish. Thomas was more on the unruly side." She laughed. "Unpredictable. Stubborn enough to want to go the opposite way his family wanted him to go. Determined to make his own way in life, not coast along on his parents' wealth and status."

Like Jon, Sean thought.

She looked at him. "He was restless—not sure what he wanted to do but knowing somehow that when he found his path, he would blaze a trail unlike anyone else's. We had many discussions about it."

Why were they talking now about Thomas, his parents' old friend, the former president of the United States? A man Sean had never met in person and their family hadn't connected with for years?

"I still miss our conversations," she added wistfully. "Thomas had a way of drawing you in, making you feel like you were the only one in the room. With Bill, I sometimes felt like one of the stars orbiting his constellation."

Sean suddenly felt cold. *Are Mom and Dad on the rocks? After all these years?*

Sarah was running flat-out. "Late to bed and early to rise" had been her mantra even more since her boss had told her she was in line for attorney general. She was determined to nail the American Frontier criminal negligence case before moving on, and her time frame for doing so was closing.

With stakes so high that the president of the United States was making a deal with Jason Carson, she knew that whoever stepped into her job would be paid off, if they could be bribed in some fashion. If not, one of two things would happen. That person or their family would be threatened, or false information that looked like truth would be manufactured and could ruin that person's reputation, even if the information was later corrected.

She narrowed her eyes. They'd decided to remove her or distract her by trying bribery. She could just hear the unknown person saying, "Offer her a promotion and see if she'll take it. No, change that. Insist she take it and don't give her any other path to walk down."

Sarah really didn't have a choice, she realized. John Barnhill, her boss, had just announced the president's intent and then waved her out of his office. Barnhill wasn't the kind of man you argued with, if you wanted a job anywhere in New York City or Washington. You simply said, "Yes, sir" and "How high do you want me to jump, sir?"

But what if she could find the missing pieces of the puzzle before her move to AG? Sarah hated to leave any stone unturned in her investigation. Somewhere the answer was hiding under one of those stones.

She frowned. All she knew was that she would not be swayed from her purpose of finding the truth, no matter who or what had to be hooked and squirm on the fishing line in the process.

It was like the worms her brothers had hooked for her when they were fishing at Chautauqua. For a long time she didn't have the heart to watch the worms wriggle on the hook, so her brothers did the dirty deed for their squeamish sister. However, after she'd finally hooked a few, it wasn't so bad. She kept imagining the plump fish they'd catch and fry for dinner.

Now her career had become hooking the worms, watching them wriggle on the hook, and seeing what catch the bait brought in.

26

Sean couldn't take another bite of the oatmeal. By now it was cold anyway. Every nerve ending was on edge as he waited for his mother to continue her story.

"After I left Harvard and got married, I lost touch with Thomas," Ava said. "Bill and I had so many social functions to attend that I had little time to myself. Adjusting to the whirlwind of Worthington affairs was rough."

He chuckled. "I can imagine. Getting thrown into our family. I've often wondered how Laura has managed it so easily."

Ava's gaze dropped for a minute. "It hasn't been easy for her either. But she's a solid rock for Will." Her eyes met his. "And I hope . . ."

Sean reached over the table and patted her hands. "I know, Mom. You want the same happiness for me."

"What I wanted most of all, though, during those years, was to be a mom," she murmured. "Finally, after five years of trying and uncountable doctor visits and tests, we conceived Will. The doctor said it wasn't likely we'd have any other kids."

He spread his arms wide and grinned. "Well, I guess I'm living proof that wasn't true, huh?"

She blinked. "More than you know."

Sean frowned. "What do you mean?"

"The doctor was right," she said. "I did have difficulty conceiving again. For nearly four years Bill and I tried. It was really stressful for both of us. Bill was traveling a lot, so when he was home—"

Sean held up both hands to block the words. "Okay, Mom, TMI. You can stop right there." Somehow the image of his parents . . . He didn't want to go there.

"After Will was born, Bill and Thomas had reconnected. Our families did a few things together, though usually Victoria found an excuse not to be there. When Will was four, I begged Bill to take a vacation. He told Thomas that he was looking for a place, and Thomas invited our family to come to Camp David."

From the tidbits Sean had gathered over the years, that summer was the last time his family had seen the Rich family. The information had never mattered much to him, though, since he'd never met Thomas, his wife, or his son in person.

Thomas was simply the smiling face of his parents' friend in an aging university scrapbook. Sure, he had become president of the United States and a household face and name, but that was where Sean's interest ended.

Thomas's wife, Victoria, was a society belle from one of the best blue-blood families. But her stint as the president's wife had either brought out the worst in her or revealed what was already there.

As for Thomas and Victoria's son, Spencer, he was the current president of the United States and a big reason the country was in the mess it was in. Sean didn't have much tolerance for President Rich.

Sean nodded. "Will told me about that trip once. He couldn't remember much about it except that Spencer was a tantrum-throwing bully." He laughed. "Guess nothing much has changed."

She ignored his jab and didn't even tell him to be nice, like she usually would.

Wow, I guess this is serious.

"I so looked forward to that vacation. I thought it would draw us—Bill and me—closer again." Her jaw tensed. "We had three hours of vacation. Then Bill got a call and felt he had to leave us to attend to it. Later the same day Victoria announced she'd had enough of 'camping,' as she called it, and left with Spencer in the presidential limo." She sighed. "I was so glad to see the limo and extra security detail drive away. Victoria is . . . a difficult person."

Leave it to his mother to choose her words sensitively about the woman everyone else called a harpy or worse.

"But I missed Bill. I was drowning in loneliness. Thomas knew that, even without me saying it. We resurrected our college friendship and caught up. I laughed again. I dreamed again. I felt hope again. And late that night . . ." She gazed directly at Sean. "I rediscovered what I thought I'd lost—the warm, passionate side of myself that I'd left behind. The fiery Irish spirit that had been buried under the weight of being a Worthington."

What was she saying? Was she saying . . . ? Pressure squeezed Sean's temples.

She stretched out both her hands to clasp his. "Nine months later, you were born."

For a second, he was numb. Then shock descended like a tsunami, blocking out logic.

His world slowed as he stared at his mother.

The truth was clear in her eyes, now a muddied, sorrowful green.

Suddenly he couldn't breathe.

She squeezed his hands. "In the long run, truth will always win out. Things that are hidden will be revealed. I wanted you to know. You deserve to know. From me."

His lungs burned. He couldn't stop holding his breath.

"Sometimes desperate, lonely people do desperate things. And even good people can get desperate," she whispered. "I wish . . ."

Sean gasped for air. Yanking his hands out of hers, he shoved away from the table, toppling his chair.

He was choking in the seismic wave of a lifetime of lies.

He had to get away before he drowned.

27

It had been a full day, with three key company decisions to make. As Worthington Shares expanded, Will's work grew exponentially. He juggled, streamlined, and kept an eye out for trustworthy staff he could hire to take point on various aspects of the company and then report to him. The kind of people who could absorb large amounts of information, process it efficiently with crystal clarity, and know what to consult with him about and what to handle themselves.

Even in a place as big as New York City, that description was a tall order. It was one of Drew's major responsibilities on behalf of Will and Worthington Shares. Drew searched nationally and internationally for sharp, honest stars in the making. If he recommended someone, Will knew that person's background had been thoroughly examined by confidential checks in Drew's massive social network.

Today Will had hired a new chief operating officer who could handle the day-to-day operations of Worthington Shares, while also being sensitive to the privacy of the family. It had been a long search, but he and Drew were confident this was the right person for the job. After six months or so of training, Will should be able to hand off the majority of the responsibility, just in time to take on other responsibility. For him, such roles were a constant ebb and flow.

He settled back in his black leather chair with a satisfied sigh. He gazed out the window facing Madison Avenue. So many people moved from place to place far below that the setting often seemed unreal, like a chess game unfolding.

Power was a strange thing, he thought. Some at the pinnacle of the buildings in New York City boasted about being in control of that game. But Will knew better. Moves were made every day behind the scenes, even above the scenes, that directed the game. That was why he listened to the quiet voice that brought clarity and long-term perspective. He simply wished that voice spoke to him directly more often.

Will took his grandfather's timepiece, made by luxury watchmaker Patek Philippe in the 1930s, out of his desk drawer. It was one of Will's idiosyncrasies—he loved old timepieces, and particularly this one, even though most would call it too old-fashioned. Will liked things that were solid and had a history behind them. It was one of the many reasons he'd slid into his role at Worthington Shares so comfortably.

He glanced at the hour. *I can get there if I hustle.* He eased out of his chair and removed his suit coat from behind the closet door, where he kept it unless he was in a meeting. It stayed crisp and unwrinkled that way. Donning the coat, he grabbed his briefcase and strode out the door. Mingling with the throngs of people, he soon entered the bowels of the New York subway system. It was dirty, old, and packed, but he loved the fact he could get anywhere in the city in minutes.

He got off at the stop near the quaint flower shop he visited once a week on his way home from work. The flowers there were exotic and unusual, but they also had his wife's favorite—roses. They were in pristine condition too, unlike the dented flowers the street vendors hawked. Since the day Laura had agreed to marry him, he'd bought her a single rose each week. He varied the color—his wife was a rainbow-of-colors sort of woman—and wrote on the card something he loved about her. Even after all their years of marriage, three kids, and a jet-set lifestyle, he'd never missed giving her a rose a week. Which day it was sometimes had to change, but not the thought and not the act.

As he stood in the cramped little shop, surveying the rose selection, he smiled. He loved the way Laura's hazel eyes lit up every time he gave her one. She'd clasp the rose, lift it to her nose, and inhale.

Watching her enjoy that rose never grew old. Making a stop once a week on the way home was a small way to say "thank you," "I love you," and "I'd marry you all over again."

Sean sat in a dark-paneled booth at a greasy spoon with worn, plastic-coated tablecloths. He had no idea how he'd arrived there or where exactly he was. All he knew was that the menu he held was smudged with ketchup. He swiveled a finger over the coffee cup, and the middle-aged waitress poured a muddy brew. He pointed blindly at an item on the menu, and she nodded.

"Don't talk much, do you, sugar?" When he didn't respond, she added, "Order'll be coming right up."

Was he still even in New York City? The last thing he remembered was striding out the door of his parents' building, and then the slate was blank.

Sean slumped against the back of the tall booth. It was in a corner, shielded from any onlookers.

It all made sense now—the restlessness, the instinct that

he was out of place among his family, that he didn't fit the Worthington mold. It was because he wasn't really a Worthington. He was half O'Hara from his mother and half Rich from his—

Father. He wasn't Bill Worthington's kid. He was Thomas Rich's kid.

Sean leaned forward, propping his elbows on the table, and held his head in his hands. *I've been living a lie, perpetrated by my own mother.*

Anger stirred. How could she have done this to him? Lied to him? For over three decades? Watched him struggle to find his place among the Worthingtons, knowing all the while why he didn't fit and never telling him?

Suddenly the betrayal by the person he trusted most in the world made him physically sick. Slapping a $100 bill on the table, he slid out of the booth.

"You all right, sugar?" The waitress was standing by the table, holding a tray with his order. "You look a little peaked—"

But he was already running for the door. He had to get out of there.

28

Will walked into a firestorm the instant he opened his front door.

For the first time ever, Laura ignored the rose he extended toward her. "Will, you have to go to your mom's right now."

His joy in being home deflated. "But I just—"

"Sean knows."

"Knows what?" One glimpse of Laura's face put the pieces together for him. "How did he find out?"

"Ava told him."

He tilted his head. "She *told* him? Did she tell you she was going to?" Past experience had taught him that Ava often discussed matters of the heart with Laura first.

Laura shook her head. "I had no warning. She invited him over for breakfast this morning and told him. Only said she'd decided it was time, and she needed to do it while Bill was away in Arizona golfing."

Will sagged. "How did it go?"

Laura touched his shoulder. "Not well. He stormed out of there without saying good-bye."

"So you want me to—"

"Go over there and get the details from your mother. Then call your brother. He's not answering your mom's calls."

He exhaled. "I'm not surprised."

It would be a far different evening than he'd planned.

Sean walked the dusky streets blindly, not caring where he was going. Why didn't he ever guess? Was he that stupid?

Does my father know?

The thought struck him like a lightning bolt, and he stopped under the awning of a storefront. He hadn't asked his mother that before he took off . . . hadn't stuck around long enough to have the wits to ask. He just had to get away from the pain, the betrayal, before it crushed him.

Father. The irony was so overwhelming, he laughed out loud. The reference to *father* was now ludicrous. Bill Worthington had never been his true father.

Is that why he's treated me differently? Been harder on me? Ignored me and focused on Will?

Sean's hands started to shake from the intensity of the shock, and he stuffed them in the pockets of his zipped sweatshirt. His stomach roiled.

What about Will? Sarah? Do they know?

They had to know, he reasoned. Or at least Will did, since he was older. If so, then they too had withheld the information from him. Why? Thinking naïvely they could protect him? Protect the Worthington name?

Realization dawned. *That's why Mom didn't want me to run for governor. Didn't want Will to run for senator. Because this skeleton in the closet might come to light and ruin the pristine Worthington reputation.*

That was what she had meant by her enigmatic comment,

"Things that are hidden will be revealed." After a lifetime of secrecy, she had felt compelled to tell him the truth, before it was ferreted out and plastered all over the tabloids.

He shivered as the outside temperature dropped. Suddenly everything and everyone Sean thought he could count on eroded from him.

Then, right as the heavens opened and the drizzle began, he heard his mother's words: *"Sometimes desperate, lonely people do desperate things. And even good people can get desperate. I wish . . ."*

Sean knew what she wished for—that she had never had an affair. That she'd never become pregnant with him. That he didn't exist. After all, his very existence jeopardized everything she held dear.

As the rain sluiced downward in earnest, Sean made a decision. He stepped out from under the protective awning and stood in the onslaught, letting the water flow unheeded around his body.

He had nothing left to lose.

29

"You need to tell Dad the truth," Will insisted. He couldn't back down simply because of his mother's tears. "You can't afford not to."

Ava swiped at her overflowing eyes. "If I do, it may change everything for our family." She adjusted her position on the velvet couch in their living room.

"Mom, it already has. It did when Sean was born. He's the proof of that change. Don't you see?" His frustration mounted. "It's not *if* you should tell Dad, it's *when* you should. Do you really want him to find out from someone else?"

She wept. "I wish I had the courage."

"But Mom, you do," he said gently. "You've always had it. You've only lost track of it for the moment. I know you. You'll find it again."

Sean was waterlogged from head to toe, and his favorite Nikes were ruined, but it no longer mattered. The shoes squished as he headed toward what looked like a busier street.

Once there, he flagged down a cab.

"Bad night," the cabbie proclaimed as Sean opened the door and slid into the backseat.

You have no idea, Sean thought. Aloud he said, "Yup."

"Where to?" the effusive driver asked.

"Just start driving, and I'll tell you." He waved the cabbie onward.

Now he knew exactly where he was, where he must go, and what he had to do.

Sarah awoke with a start at 1:30 a.m., as if someone had poked her with a sharp object. She was sweating.

Must have been a bad dream, she mused. But she couldn't remember one.

Or perhaps the spicy Indian curry she'd had for a late dinner was making her pay. It was all Sean's fault. He'd introduced her to that restaurant four years ago and insisted she try that dish. One bite and she was hooked. Every once in a while she had to have some.

"Okay, Sean," she announced aloud when she still couldn't go back to sleep 20 minutes later, "it's payback. This time you're the one who's going to get a wake-up call." She grinned as she hit his speed-dial number.

30

It had been five days since any of the Worthingtons had heard from Sean.

The entire family was worried. Ava was distraught. She had fled to their home in Chautauqua Institution to stay secluded from the media. With Sean's globe-trotting life, they were used to him coming and going and sometimes not contacting them for days or weeks.

This time, though, was different. The media had been hot on Sean's heels since the rumors had flown about his potential bid for governor of New York. Suddenly he'd disappeared. The tabloids were concocting various stories. The one with the highest readership was tantalizing voyeurism:

> Sean Worthington, wealthy playboy extraordinaire, MIA? No one's talking, but reportedly no one has seen him for days. The middle Worthington sibling is known for his extravagant lifestyle and worldwide jet-setting, but is he a victim of foul play? Or have the Worthingtons decided enough is enough and taken steps to rein in his wildness? Especially since he's close to making a run at becoming governor of New York? The family has declined any interviews.

Will scowled and threw the tabloid in the trash. Another reason for him to hate the gossip-mongers. A pinch of truth and a heap of conjecture, and a seed of question was masterfully planted in the mind of the reader, who would keep coming back for more. The industry made billions of dollars each year based on that simple principle.

The family had worked hard to keep under wraps that they couldn't reach him, despite all their efforts. But his social circle was too large, too active, and had missed his presence. They'd spread the word, and the media was swift to pick up on it. The networking king had gone silent. No tweeting, no Facebooking, no texting, no emailing. Even Drew calling in a favor with a high-tech specialist to track Sean's cell phone had produced no leads.

Sean, where are you? Will tapped his fingers on his desk. He couldn't concentrate on his work.

When he finally reached his little brother, Will would hug him first. Then he'd yell at him for putting their family—especially his mother—through such angst.

Langley, Virginia

The man's knuckles turned white as he gripped the hard copy of last week's *Buffalo News* and read the story headline: "Unknown Man Dives off Peace Bridge."

> Thursday evening an unidentified man dove off the middle of the Peace Bridge. The man, described as wearing a sweatshirt, jeans, and athletic shoes, got out of the backseat of a cab heading north on the bridge when lane closures due to roadwork led to gridlocked traffic. He walked to the middle of the bridge, climbed up one of the steel supports, and the next instant was gone. "Just did a swan dive into the Niagara," one witness claimed.

> The Peace Bridge, the second busiest border crossing between the US and Canada, connecting Buffalo with Fort Erie, Ontario, is a little over 12 miles upriver of Niagara Falls. The body has not yet been found.

The man's source had been able to gather some additional information that hadn't been printed in the *Buffalo News*. Other onlookers described the jumper as around six feet tall and having dark or maybe reddish hair. One man said his shoes looked expensive.

Could this be Sean? The descriptions were vague, but they could be a match. But what would happen to make someone of Sean's background and character suddenly commit suicide?

Only one thought came to mind. *Maybe Sean found out about the photos with the Polar Bear Bomber and was afraid they would ruin the Worthington family. After all, the Worthingtons are intensely loyal. Or maybe . . .*

The man left his thoughts there. He could guess all he wanted, but the proof lay in the facts. His job was to uncover them.

He focused on his new task—using every contact at his disposal to find out who the jumper was and to speed along locating the body. If the jumper was Sean Worthington, he'd ferret out the reason and the person behind the reason. Then he'd make that person pay.

31

New York City

Drew looked unusually stoic as he entered Will's office. "There's something you need to know."

Will glanced up from his laptop. "Okay, shoot it to me."

"There's a report about a man jumping off the Peace Bridge last Thursday."

Frowning, Will focused back on the reports he had been reading. "And that has what to do with us?"

"The descriptions are general but could match Sean."

Will's hand froze. Slowly he raised his eyes to meet Drew's.

His mentor's gaze was troubled. "As you know, I've been using every source I can to track Sean's whereabouts. I came across the report in last Friday's *Buffalo News*. The basic description of the jumper matched what Ava said Sean was wearing when they had breakfast. So I called in a favor at the Buffalo PD headquarters."

As soon as Will opened his mouth in protest, Drew added, "Don't worry. I didn't mention anything about Sean. But the additional details they gave me said he was approximately five eleven to six feet tall, dark or maybe reddish hair, and wearing expensive athletic shoes."

Will frowned. "That could describe a lot of guys in New York."

"Yes, but the cab driver says the man flipped him a $100 bill and thanked him for the ride before exiting the cab. You know how much Sean hated the bother of making change."

So did Will, and he'd often done the same thing.

"Have they found a body?" Will asked.

"Not yet. With the location just upriver of Niagara Falls, that makes the search much more complicated. But suicide would be completely out of Sean's character." Drew cocked his head toward Will. "Then again, doing things that are out of character seems to be running in the Worthington family lately. You . . . Ava . . ." His keen eyes searched Will's, as if he were trying to put together the final piece to a puzzle.

Will squirmed.

"Something tells me there's more going on than just that photo," Drew stated in a quiet tone, "or the string of photos Carson likely has that could reveal how it was staged. Sean doesn't know about the photo, does he?"

Will's pulse skyrocketed. "No, I don't think so. At least not from me." *But what if he did find out somehow? What if he's not communicating because he's after whoever set him up?*

"And Ava doesn't know, does she?"

"Absolutely not," Will declared. "No one knows except you, me, and Laura."

Drew gave a single nod, as if his deductive line of questioning had proved a point. "Is there anything else you want to tell me?"

Will's mind was at war. He needed to tell Drew about the connection between Sean and Thomas Rich. He wanted Drew's advice about next steps. But how could he break his mother's confidence without asking her first? "There are events at work here that you might not know about yet."

"I see. Well, I may know more, or have guessed more, than you think. Desperate people do desperate things." Drew propped both hands on Will's desk and leaned in. "But I certainly know one thing. Your family needs you now, perhaps your mother most of all. That's far more important than any business deal going on here at Worthington Shares."

How much does he really know about Sean? Will couldn't help but wonder. But he also got Drew's gentle point. It was time for Will to leave the office. He was needed more right now at Chautauqua. News about the jumper and the possible connection to Sean wasn't something he could share with his mother over the phone.

He'd call Laura. She'd pack a bag for him and hand it to him at the doorway to speed him on his way. He could be in Chautauqua by nightfall.

"You're where?" Sarah asked Will. "In the middle of a workday?"

"On my way to Chautauqua. I need to give Mom some news. But I also need to talk with you."

It had to be serious if Will left work. Sarah waved off a colleague who held paperwork and shut her office door. "I'm alone now. What's up?"

"I'm going to say it straight."

Sarah rolled her eyes even though Will couldn't see it. How else could Will, Mr. Straightforward, say anything?

"A guy jumped off the Peace Bridge last Thursday night. The details sound like a close match for Sean."

Sarah lowered herself into her desk chair. Thursday night. The night she'd had the weird dream or indigestion, couldn't go back to sleep, and tried to call Sean but didn't reach him. Had he been jumping off a bridge?

If it hadn't been Will telling her, she would have laughed at the ludicrous nature of the information. But this was Will, who never failed to check his facts before moving on anything.

She shook her head, trying to clear the haze. "I can't believe it. I don't believe it. I mean, he's been on the edge, but that? No way. Can't be Sean. Not the brother I know who rolls with the punches."

"We're checking into every angle we can. I'll let you know if we find anything. But I didn't want you to be blindsided if the news leaked from somewhere else."

"Got it, and that's much appreciated. Let me know after you've talked with Mom. Then I'll call and talk her down off the ceiling."

"You always could do that, sis. Thanks."

"And Will?"

"Yeah."

"That's not Sean. I just know it's not."

But then why had she felt like her heart had been stabbed the night that guy jumped off the bridge? The coincidence was eerie.

32

CHAUTAUQUA INSTITUTION, WESTERN NEW YORK

Will focused like a laser on what he had to do the entire drive to their family's summer home in Chautauqua. By the time he'd reached the wood-framed, old stone mansion, the sky was streaked with gold and red. He inhaled deeply of the lake air as he stepped out of his Land Rover and stretched his tight back muscles.

He loved this place, had loved it since he was a boy. Gazing toward the house, he scanned the expansive front porch. This was the time of day his father would sit in his favorite rocker, book in hand, enjoying the view. Since Bill Worthington wasn't on the porch, he was likely out of town.

That meant Ava was down by the lake watching the sunset. "Maybe it's my heritage showing through, but I feel most at peace when I'm close to the water," she'd told Will once. Her family still owned a picturesque castle and grounds and several estates in Wicklow overlooking the Irish Sea. Will and Laura had honeymooned at the castle.

Perhaps the fact his mother was by the water would somehow make the news easier.

Will headed for her favorite spot. The year that he had left for his freshman year at Harvard, Bill had hired artisans to craft a winding cobblestone path strewn with Ava's favorite flower bushes and grasses. Then he'd added a selection of vintage rockers that could withstand the weather changes year-round. Bill had scoured the best antique shops nationwide to secure the rockers and surprise her. He'd told Will it would help Ava deal with the transition of her first baby heading off to university. Will remembered it distinctly because it was one of the rare times his father revealed his tender love for Ava. He was usually so pragmatic and business-oriented.

Will was right. His mother was sitting in one of the rockers beside the path. The lowering sun glinted gold on her auburn hair that peeked above the top of the chair. She held a wine glass in one hand.

"Mom," he said softly, so as not to startle her.

She turned and peered around the side of the chair. "Will? My goodness! What are you doing here? I didn't expect you." Setting her wine glass on the table nestled next to the chair, she got up to hug him.

Within a minute, though, she stepped back from the hug. "You're stiff. That means you have news to tell me. And it's not good." Her eyes met his. "Out with it. I can take it. Whatever it is."

She always could read him like a book. But he wasn't sure she could take this news.

"Why don't you sit down, Mom?"

A visible shiver coursed through her. "It's about Sean, isn't it? And no, I will not."

He stayed close, in case he needed to catch her if she swayed. "Yes, it is about Sean." He gave the news the only way he could—honestly. "Last week a man jumped off the Peace Bridge in Buffalo. His description has similarities to Sean."

"What day?" she asked.

"Thursday."

"When?"

"Very late Thursday evening."

She was quiet. He could tell she was calculating the hours. "He left our flat . . ."

It was a little over six hours' drive from New York City to Buffalo, Will knew—and so did his mother.

"Oh my." Ava swayed, and Will reached out to catch her. She batted his hand away. "So it's possible. But Will? It can't be. It just can't be. He couldn't have—"

"Drew is checking out every lead he can right now. No body has been found, and no one is certain of anything. But we know the possibility exists."

Ava's body trembled. "It can't end like this. Sean can't end like this. He always was fascinated with Niagara Falls."

Will remembered. Sean had been eight when the family visited there. He'd been enthralled with the racing white water and the story of Annie Edson Taylor, who went over the falls in a barrel in 1901. "Someday I'm going to do that too," he'd claimed. Will's careful research—of others who had tried and died—at last curbed Sean's desire to try it.

But the trip whet Sean's appetite for adrenaline-rush adventures. After he hit adulthood and was away from his mama bear's clutches, he'd trained with the best white-water rafting experts and had since traversed the gorge downstream from the falls many times. He'd never told his mother about those and other daredevil stunts. But Will knew, since he'd been called to rescue Sean from many of those stunts, especially when Sean was in his early twenties.

Now Will felt a kick in his gut. Would Sean choose to end his life there, near the falls? He shook his head to refocus. "You had to know, and Dad has to know of the potential connection. No matter what happens, I couldn't withhold this news from you until we knew one way or the other. I couldn't tell you on the phone. Laura agreed I should come in person."

"Thank you for telling me, son. But your father is in DC. He's not coming home for a few days," she whispered.

"I'll talk to him. He'll be on the next flight home, I can guarantee that."

Ava grabbed his arm. "I have to tell your father the whole story."

"Yes, Mom, you do. It's the right thing to do. For Sean, for yourself, for Dad, for all of us."

She dropped her head for a minute. When she looked at Will again, the haze of weepy emotion that had plagued her for weeks had disappeared. Her face was stoic, but fiery determination glimmered in her eyes.

"Yes, Will, you are right. Absolutely right." She lifted her chin. "I am afraid of what this might mean, especially for me, for your father. But I have lived with that fear ever since that night at Camp David. Now I need to face it. I can't hide from it anymore."

The Ava Worthington who took on challenges regally and defeated them was back.

Langley, Virginia

"The new witness you uncovered said what?" the man behind the mahogany desk demanded.

"That he swears he saw the guy pause before doing a nosedive into the Niagara. Oncoming headlights blinded the witness for an instant. The next thing he saw was the jumper had disappeared. But a guy was running down the Peace Bridge toward the Canadian side."

"Is the witness sure?"

"As sure as a dotty old man of 87 can be," his contact said. "But his granddaughter, who was with him at the time, swears he's fully all there in the head and has excellent vision. I checked the background on the witness. He was a sharp attorney in Maryland before his retirement. Seems quite credible."

So the options were getting more complicated.

The supposed jumper might be Sean, or it might not be.

The jumper might have jumped, or he might not have.

If he did jump, his body might be found, or not.

If he didn't jump, he might have exited the Peace Bridge in Canada and be hanging out there for a while, hoping to be incognito.

The last option was the one the man was most interested in right now, because the others were dead ends in finding Sean Worthington alive.

"You know what to do," he told his contact. "Pull strings with immigration in Canada. If he crossed, they should have a record. Check with the border officials on both sides."

"Already in motion. I was pretty sure you'd say that."

"Good. Call me with any leads."

"Always."

The man ended the call. His plan was set in motion. He knew his source would apply the right amount of pressure to get the job done. After all, his contact had never taken no for an answer in his career before, and he certainly wouldn't now. It was why the man had kept him on his payroll all these years.

33

Jamestown, New York

True to Will's prediction, Bill had not only been on the first flight home but had chartered a plane to get him there as early as possible. Since a storm had loomed the previous night, they hadn't been able to leave DC as swiftly as Bill wanted. However, Will picked him up at 10:00 the next morning at a private airfield outside Jamestown.

Bill was quiet, his expression bland, almost numb. He didn't hug Will or even greet him. He merely stashed his luggage in the backseat of Will's Land Rover and got in the passenger seat. They'd both agreed the 15-mile drive to their Chautauqua home would give them the opportunity to talk man-to-man before Bill saw Ava.

The instant they were on the road, he swiveled toward Will. "Do you think it's Sean?"

"I honestly don't know, Dad. The details seem to match, but . . ."

Bill nodded. "So you doubt it's him too. So do I. Sean's done a lot of wild things over the years—more than I want to know about. He's been hot under the collar sometimes, but I can't imagine him doing anything like that. Especially now, when he's considering running for governor. It doesn't make any sense. Sean wouldn't, couldn't, crack like that. Not without justifiable cause."

But there is, Dad, there is, Will couldn't help but think. *What Sean believed to be true all these years has been ripped away from him.*

His father plunged on, his speech almost a stream of consciousness. "It would have to be something big that completely crushed him to weigh him down so much. I have a theory."

"What's that?" Will asked, tightening his grip on the wheel as he drove. How much did his father know? Had he guessed?

"Sean has seemed more restless than usual lately. Maybe he needed some time away before he took the next step of the governor's race." Bill scratched his grizzly chin, which looked like it hadn't seen a razor yet that morning. That small detail told Will how upset his father really was. "Or perhaps he wanted to think it through for himself, make sure it was what he should do."

"Maybe," was all Will could say.

"I know I've been hard on the boy over the years. I simply want what's best for him, and sometimes that has meant exerting a little extra pressure. You never needed it. You were hard enough on yourself. But Sean, and later Sarah . . ." His father turned his head toward the window. "They needed more direction. I worried far more about them than I ever did about you in your teen years and early twenties." He added more softly, "Maybe that's why he couldn't come to me. He had to run away for a short while instead."

"He didn't come to me either," Will countered.

Bill's head whipped back toward him. "That's because you

and me, we're the same. Driving toward the goal. We forget to smell the flowers along the way. So Ava reminds me. That's why I need her in my life, and you need Laura."

"So true, Dad, so true," Will said.

They were silent the rest of the journey home. They'd said what they could, for now.

New York City

Sarah's mind wasn't on her DOJ meeting. It was on her mother, who still hadn't returned her call. Ava was an early-to-bed type, so Sarah wasn't surprised she hadn't reached her last night. The shock of the news received from Will had probably kept her mother up far later than her norm. Maybe she was sleeping in this morning.

Sarah checked her texts. There was one from Will at 9:30.

> Mom home and okay. Picking up Dad. Landing at Jamestown at 10. More when can.

She shook her head. *Leave it to Will to manage the details, even in crisis.* He'd not only contacted their dad but had remembered to text her, knowing she had to be worried about their mother.

Will was so much like their father, except he had another dimension—a much more tender side. Bill loved his kids. Sarah had no doubt of that. But he'd been reared in such a stiff, formal environment that showing outward affection wasn't natural for him. She couldn't count the times he'd told her, "So you fell down. Don't sit there. Get up, brush yourself off, think about what you learned through failure, and move on." There was no coddling with Bill, just straight talk. Will had similar proclivities, but Ava and Sarah had worked on him. Then Laura took over when she and Will got married and had done an admirable job.

In the boardroom, Will was a force to be reckoned with. But at home? Laura was the one who kept the henhouse and the rooster in order.

The analogy made Sarah grin.

34

Chautauqua Institution

Will had done many hard things in his life—even more so lately. But a glimpse of the resignation and pain on his mother's face when she greeted Bill almost broke Will. He and Laura were the only ones who knew the true depth of her pain and why her heart was doubly breaking.

Ava sat in the porch rocker, awaiting their arrival. Will lingered at the driver's side of the vehicle as his father moved toward her and up the stairs. Then, uncharacteristically, Bill didn't say anything. He simply gathered Ava into his arms and held her as she started sobbing.

Will left his father's luggage in his Land Rover and headed down the cobblestone path toward the lake. He sank onto a nearby rocker, his gaze flicking from the house to the lake. He felt torn in two. This day would change everything for their family. Will had no idea which direction it would go.

In the midst of his pain, the still small voice spoke. *It is when you are weak that true strength comes.*

Yes, he felt weak. It was a quality he would never have assigned to himself in the past. But the recent events had revealed how weak he was when his family was threatened.

Will needed that true strength. For the first time in his life, he realized he couldn't make himself strong. Perhaps his Bible-banging sister was right. Maybe he did need help from above, from the God who had seemed elusive, out of reach, and unnecessary to his life.

He gazed at the horizon. It was a gray day—both sky and water—with a hint of moisture in the air. A day as morbid and heavy as his thoughts.

Will closed his eyes. "God," he breathed, "if you are there . . ."

He sighed—the kind of long, drawn-out sigh that released years of weariness. Calm settled over him like a lightweight but warm blanket. He rested in its enfolding embrace.

Will had no idea how long he sat there in the rocker on the cobblestone path. But when he opened his eyes at last and looked skyward, a shaft of gold-white light pierced the cloud over him.

Langley, Virginia

The man paced the length of his large study, thinking. His source had checked with Canada immigration. No one named Sean Worthington or matching his description had passed over the Peace Bridge and through the entry point on the Canadian side. It was highly unlikely he'd been able to slip through unnoticed, since every visitor had to show ID once they'd passed over the bridge in order to get into Canada. Then again, Sean was a Worthington. Anything was possible with his type of high connections.

Perhaps he bribed someone to let him through, the man

thought. Still, that didn't fit Sean's profile. Then again, neither did a suicide attempt.

He'd had his source circle around again to interview the cab driver. No new information there.

No one could confirm Sean's whereabouts one way or the other if he wasn't dead. It was unnerving and exasperating.

The man evaluated the information his contact had gathered.

If Sean had jumped over the Peace Bridge, his body would have floated down the river toward Niagara Falls and gone over the falls. The body might be trapped under the 3,000-plus tons of water flowing down the falls every second. That meant it could never be discovered or retrieved.

The other option was that it could float downriver from the falls. The swift river currents averaged 7.5 to 12 miles per hour. Four of the five Great Lakes drained into the Niagara River before emptying into Lake Ontario. That meant if the body had gone over the falls, floated downriver, and somehow managed to make its way into Lake Ontario, weeks could pass before it was discovered—even if it was located. By then the body would be in such rough shape it couldn't be identified, except for dental records.

Not knowing what had happened was disconcerting. The man had to know.

His plan couldn't be ending this soon, and certainly not like this.

35

CHAUTAUQUA INSTITUTION

When Will finally walked up the cobblestone path to the house, his Land Rover was gone. So was his father.

His mother was perched on the edge of the living room couch. She looked up when Will entered the room.

"Mom?"

"It is done," she said stoically.

Silence hung between them. He wanted to ask, needed to ask how his father had responded. But he waited instead.

"No one said doing the right thing would be easy," his mother whispered at last. Pushing herself off the couch, she headed unsteadily down the hallway.

"Do you need h—"

She paused but didn't turn. "No," she murmured, "I need to do this by myself. Alone." She reached for one of the brass handles of her bedroom suite and opened the door, then shut it firmly behind her.

He moved back to the living room. That was when he noticed the item that had been next to his mother's seat. One of his parents' wedding pictures, in his mother's favorite frame, was upside down on the couch.

There was nothing more Will could do. The inertia nearly overwhelmed him.

Instead, he did the only thing he could.

He prayed.

LANGLEY, VIRGINIA

The man peered at the door of his study to ensure it was locked. Satisfied, he reached under his desk to unlatch the hidden drawer with the false front that he'd used over the years. He removed a small, lumpy package, laid it carefully on his desk, and stared at it.

The contents were more dangerous than a ticking bomb. They always had been.

But they were safer here, with him, than in anyone else's hands.

36

Chautauqua Institution

"Do what you need to do, Will. We're fine here. Your mother needs you there," Laura told him.

It was Sunday morning, and Will was still in Chautauqua. Neither he nor his mother had heard anything from Bill. Will's Land Rover was still missing. Ava had wandered like a shadow from room to room since Thursday. Will had barely convinced her to take a bite of food. Even her favorite tea had lost its flavor, she said.

There was no way he'd leave her in this condition.

Now she stepped into the kitchen. "You know I love him, don't you, Will? That I learned to love him?" she asked.

So there it was—at last in the open after all these years. It was why his mother had never used the word *love* when she told Will about dating and marrying Bill. She had said, "I admired him."

He wished Laura were there. She'd know what to say. "Yes, Mom, I know you learned to love him. And that you do love him now."

"Perhaps it's only over the past few days I've realized how much I do." Her eyes teared. "When I may have lost him."

"You don't know that," Will said. "But I do know he has to process. You need to give him that time."

She straightened. "You're right. So then, would you like some breakfast?"

Much like the old Ava, she busied herself making a breakfast Will didn't want to eat but did anyway to please her. Cooking made his mother happy.

When she retired to nap in the sunroom, he knew she would be all right, no matter what happened. It was her favorite room of the Chautauqua house, filled with tall, leafy palms and ferns and a 15-foot-long, rock-lined koi pond with a waterfall. She called it her "green room" and had spent hours there feeding and admiring the fish and adding various flowers until it was a garden extraordinaire. She'd avoided it since Thursday and had kept the blinds drawn in her bedroom, blocking out the sun and the beautiful lake view.

He kept an eye on her until he saw her breathing relax. Then he tackled the latest text from his sister.

Want me to come?

He'd stalled her by sending little texts since Thursday, such as:

Mom's still in shock. Needs some time.

Dad and Mom have a lot to discuss and work out.

I'm sure Mom will contact you when she's able.

I'll be here at least through the weekend.

He shot her another text now.

No need. Laura says I need a vacation. Think I'll stick around a bit.

That tactic would work for maybe another two or three days, if he was lucky and Sarah was buried in her work. Then Sarah would insist on talking to their mother, or she'd be in the car, headed to Chautauqua.

Will also left a message for Drew that he would be staying a few more days. Drew would give Will that time, but then he'd press for answers.

Will wasn't sure what he could or should say. He was caught even more in the midst of a dilemma. Only he and Laura knew the whole story—Sean's potential connection to the bomber, who his birth father was, and that Sean was missing. Now Bill was temporarily out of communication. Will had no doubt his father would come back. The question was simply when.

NEW YORK CITY

"So the president handed Carson over to the FBI, and they've finished questioning him?" Sarah asked Darcy over the phone on Monday.

"Not exactly," Darcy said. "The current attorney general actually referred it over to the FBI. By the time Carson showed up for his confession, he was surrounded by an army of attorneys. Everything had already been set."

"So President Rich handed Carson over to us and washed his hands? What exactly did Carson confess to? A campaign cash violation? And the deal was already in place by the time he showed up?"

"Yeah, it was all preordained. No one's talking, but it almost certainly contains some sort of an inappropriate campaign violation. Cash for a regulatory favor for American Frontier, ordered by the CEO. Not murder or mayhem, and not something that will put him or anyone else away. Fines, probation, and a black eye—but no jail time."

Darcy's voice became more bitter as she went on. "His lead attorney, Rick Wilson, did all the talking for him. Carson never said much. They rolled Eric Sandstrom under the bus. Carson will walk, and none of this will ever get anywhere close to the White House. Carson won't get any jail time for this. He'll have to resign, but it's not like he killed anyone. He just helped his company on a deal that went very badly."

Sarah sat up in her chair. "So it all lands on Sandstrom?"

"Sure looks that way from where I sit," Darcy said.

Sarah did some quick mental calculations. She knew she couldn't warn her older brother about any of this. That would be a clear ethical breach. It seemed strange that she was forced to sit on her hands while the prize that Will had pursued was about to come back into view. But there was nothing she could do.

Wilson was as powerful and connected as attorneys came in New York. He was a named partner on one of the top three law firms in the city that handled nearly every big civil case against the world's largest multinational corporations—many of which had their global headquarters in the city. Wilson led the firm's criminal division and had orchestrated so many white-collar plea deals over the years that this case was likely child's play for him.

What seemed curious was that American Frontier was represented by his firm in other civil matters. They'd almost certainly built a Chinese wall that allowed Wilson to represent Carson personally on the criminal side. But there were boxes inside boxes on this one. Who did Wilson truly represent here?

Carson? Or someone else? It made no sense that Wilson would sacrifice the CEO of American Frontier while protecting his consigliere—unless there were other much more powerful interests at play that needed protecting.

"It was all handled at the highest levels," Darcy declared, "and I just found out about it. Only the top echelons at DHS knew, and they're not telling anyone yet exactly what the deal was. I know a couple of the FBI agents who were brought in, and they'll eventually fill me in. But they're not talking right now."

Because Sarah was a Worthington and had at least a working knowledge of what a corporation like AF paid its top officials who worked directly for the CEO, she knew that Jason Carson would be set for life once he'd gotten clear of the noose. He almost certainly had tens of millions stashed somewhere outside the United States, in the Cayman Islands or elsewhere. He also likely had a second nest egg in another location, tax free, from the extra favors he'd done throughout his career. But she wondered who was really paying his legal bills on this.

"So Carson does get that get-out-of-jail-free card," Sarah murmured.

"He'll walk," Darcy said. "His basic story is that Sandstrom approached him to do a little campaign violation job under the table. Carson didn't feel comfortable with the request, since Sandstrom said it had to be just between them and not on the books, so he refused. He claims Sandstrom didn't tell him any more than that, and he didn't want to know."

"Right, and that he'd never done anything like this before. Like Carson is squeaky clean."

"He said Sandstrom let it slip later that the job was taken care of," Darcy continued. "Once they got their exclusive permit to drill in the Arctic, Carson said he put the pieces together. Cash for a permit. His testimony keeps it contained to a regulatory agency and away from the White House."

"Convenient."

"Yeah, it is."

"What can Sandstrom say to counter that? It's his word against Carson's, and Carson stepped forward first. If he says Carson was actually behind it, he indicates he had pre-knowledge of the campaign violation and also implicates himself as the mastermind. No judge would fall for Carson dreaming it up on his own out of misplaced loyalty to his boss. Carson was just an underling. But you can't tell me he wasn't the one who set up the quid pro quo. That kind of thing is right up his alley."

"Still, he claims he had no knowledge of anything."

"Let me guess. For that benign info, Carson also probably stays in the FBI's protective custody?"

"Yup, until the trial's over. AF has even been ordered to continue to pay his salary until this settles out and he can be free to look for a new position," Darcy said. "And you? You're now all tied up in knots with this. You can't tell anyone about any of it, especially your family."

"You got that right." Sarah exhaled in frustration. "I can't go after Carson in the DOJ's criminal negligence suit. And I can't go after him as the newly appointed AG either because of the previously existing deal."

"Isn't that grand timing?" Darcy's tone dripped with more than her usual sarcasm.

"Makes you wonder what else got pulled behind the scenes, doesn't it? This takes the wind out of all kinds of sails, including mine."

"This is lousy all the way around," Darcy announced. "There's one bright spot, though. We still have Sandstrom . . . maybe."

When Sarah hung up the phone, she wasn't so sure. Neither

was Darcy, Sarah knew. Deals got cut all the time, and they'd both been on the receiving and giving ends of them. Every time the deals concluded, though, Sarah battled with her innate sense of justice. Justice was not always done. That tension between the real and the ideal wore her down sometimes.

In that moment, a reminder of Bill Worthington's mantra, "Do the right thing and the truth will win out," flashed into her head. It had dogged every step she'd taken in her career. Yes, she would do her work with integrity, even if others didn't. She would stay on the path and relentlessly pursue her chance to make at least her corner of the world a better place . . . even if she drove her soon-to-be-former boss a little crazy in the meanwhile.

37

Chautauqua Institution

Tuesday morning Will was outside watching the sun come up when he heard a familiar engine noise. Minutes later his Land Rover rolled into view and made its way up the drive. His father was at the wheel.

Will edged to his feet and waited.

Bill exited the driver's side and closed the door. He gazed at the house for a minute, as if poised on the brink of a decision.

Will walked out partway to meet him. His father surprised him, covering the ground between them swiftly and nearly crushing him in a bear hug. When they drew apart, both men's eyes were damp.

"You're a good father, Will. Don't make the same mistakes I did. If I could change anything, I would have been there for your mother. For you. Your sister." His voice broke. "For Sean too."

"But Dad, you were—"

"Not enough, son. Not enough."

Will hesitated, then asked, "Did you know? Did you guess?"

"I wondered," he murmured. "We struggled to have you. It

took so long to conceive a second child. It didn't happen despite our efforts and the best doctors. Then, suddenly, Ava was pregnant again. I'd been gone almost a month to India after I left Camp David. After I returned, we—"

Will held up his hand. "I get it, Dad."

"I thought we had turned a new leaf in our marriage. Now I know she was pregnant and so desperate for me not to know the truth that she covered it up."

His red-rimmed eyes met Will's with intensity. "Sean was born eight months later. I was in London. I hadn't expected the birth for another month. In those days husbands didn't go to doctor appointments with their wives. At least I didn't. I just listened to her talk about her follow-up reports after she'd been there. Then, a month before the baby's due date, she called me on the way to the hospital to tell me she was going into labor. I took the next flight home from London."

Will didn't interrupt. He knew his dad had to tell the story.

"I arrived a few hours after she gave birth. Sean was over seven pounds and looked very healthy, not like a preemie. I never met the doctor. He had already come and gone. I was so happy to be holding my second son that I didn't question it then. I only remember being surprised that he looked so different from you." He shrugged. "I guess I expected a carbon copy. Crazy, huh?"

"Not so crazy. We expected the same thing when Patricia was born—that she'd resemble Andrew, only with girl parts."

"Will," his father whispered, "why did it have to be Thomas?"

Will had no answer. But he also knew his dad wasn't really asking him the question.

"I still don't know all the details. Maybe I don't want to know. Did it just happen? Was it a planned rendezvous? Did she want a baby that badly she was willing to go to any length? I don't have those answers. I fled because I couldn't hear any more. I couldn't take it. My best friend and my wife. I needed to be away to wrestle with the betrayal, to come to terms with it. To decide what I must do now."

Will had to ask. "Have you decided?"

"Yes."

Will shivered as if a sharp wind had accosted him. "And?"

His father sighed. "I can't change the past, and I have struggled with that. No, *struggled* isn't a strong enough word. There is no word strong enough to describe the pain." He inhaled deeply. "I can, however, be present in the now. I can shape the future to the best of my ability." Swiveling toward the door of the family home, he declared, "Now I need to talk with my wife."

As he strode with determination toward the front porch, Ava opened the door. She stood in her white robe and grasped the door frame. Her body trembled.

Bill rushed up the steps and swept her into his arms. As he held her, the blood-red and gold colors of the Chautauqua rising sun lightened and brightened.

Will sagged in relief.

Bill Worthington was home to stay. His parents would weather this ultimate storm together, no longer hampered by the lie that had lurked under the surface for nearly four decades.

For now, even with Sean missing, that was enough.

New York City

Sarah sat in her office, gripping her Visconti The Forbidden City fountain pen as she hovered over a stack of papers. The pen was her favorite. Sean had bid on it at a Sotheby's auction and presented it to her on her birthday two years ago.

Now looking at it was a painful reminder that something was

terribly wrong with Sean. No one in her family was talking, and the lack of communication was driving her crazy. She'd left several messages for her dad over the weekend, and he hadn't responded. Ditto for her mother. From her dad, she expected it—sometimes he, like Sean and Will, got caught up in business and didn't reply for days. But her mother? That was downright weird.

Will had kept her in the loop, but the more she thought about it, the more suspicious she became. Leave it to Will to sound like he was saying something when he was being enigmatic.

He's stalling, she realized. *But why?* Her attorney instincts kicked in. She scrolled through Will's texts. She stopped on the one that seemed the most mysterious.

Dad and Mom have a lot to discuss and work out.

What's to work out? Sean's missing. Nothing changes those facts.

She frowned. Lately a lot of things didn't make sense—Will turning down the Senate bid, her mother's weepiness, her brother disappearing. Then there was Carson lurking in the shadows at Will's Senate launch, making a deal with the president, then jumping into the fray with the media. The pieces jumbled together in Sarah's brain. The answer was there somewhere, if she could only sort it out.

Sarah tapped her pen on her desk as she phoned Drew to see if he had any new information about Sean.

He didn't. His advice was sage and cryptic, as always. "Some things will be revealed if you wait."

If there was one thing Sarah Worthington wasn't good at, it was delayed gratification. "Yeah, yeah, I know." She blew out an exasperated breath. "It doesn't make the waiting any easier."

Drew chuckled. "No, but it makes you stronger."

38

CHAUTAUQUA INSTITUTION

Midafternoon Ava took a nap in her green room. Will and his father had coffee in the kitchen.

"So, what next?" Will asked.

"I thought I was the one who asked that question." His father took a sip of the dark brew.

Will lifted his coffee mug in salute. "I learned from the best, you know."

"We pick up and go on from here," Bill stated. "And we find out what's happened to Sean. As for myself, I'm thinking of a trip to Buffalo. See what answers I can find."

"You know Drew's on it."

His father's eyes turned steely. "Yes, but Sean's my son."

My son. Not *the boy*. Things indeed had changed.

Will got up to refill his mug with hot brew, and his incoming text message dinged. Sarah again. "You know we have to tell Sarah everything."

"No," Bill said fiercely. "Promise me you won't tell her."

"But—"

"If Sean is dead, there's no reason to tell her. What good would it do? It would only wound her. We need to protect her."

"Sarah isn't a baby anymore. She deserves to know," Will countered.

"No, she doesn't. Promise me you won't," he begged. "If Sean is dead, I don't want the news to change her view of her brother in any way. The knowledge might drive her away from us, from her mother. Ava couldn't handle any more right now."

Will at last agreed, but he didn't like it.

New York City

Sarah was elated. The subpoenas of American Frontier's interoffice memos, emails, and phone calls had done their job well. DOJ assistants had been neck-deep in paperwork, following the convoluted trails in myriad directions.

Painstaking research of the decision made to drill in the Arctic clearly revealed that many of the scientists and engineers were apprehensive about such a venture in pristine, uncharted waters. Detailed risk percentages—unpredictable and often violent weather, the temperature of the water, freeze and thaw cycles, the ability to get emergency equipment and teams in and out quickly and efficiently, the strength of the steel and other space-age materials used in the platform against potential hurricane wind speeds, calculations about how swiftly a leak could be fixed, etc.—painted a dire picture of the consequences if even the slightest thing went awry.

Sandstrom's numerous memos to the various scientists and project heads acknowledged that he was aware of the dangers but that to make gains, one had to take risks, and he was willing to do so to benefit Americans. He noted concerns but directed them to proceed on the project. That implicated him directly and personally in the criminal negligence suit, which was one of the goals Sarah had been aiming for. Problem was, the memos also shaved a bit of the edge off the lawsuit, since Sandstrom's intentions appeared to have always been for others' benefit—namely the host of Americans who wanted their homes warm in the winter and gas in their cars—not for his own or the company's financial gain.

It was a masterful PR ploy, Sarah and Darcy had agreed, as if Sandstrom himself or his legal counsel had dictated that wording be in every single correspondence signed by him or coming from his office. That sticking point had made pursuing the full potential of the lawsuit much more difficult. Still, nothing would give Sarah greater pleasure than seeing the smug CEO in prison orange.

He wouldn't get any kind of maximum sentence, though, since no deaths—human, at least—could be attributed to him. There had been and would be a lot of bad press, which wouldn't help the stock price or make the board or investors happy. Pictures of dead whales floating in the Arctic waters and other oil-coated sea creatures washing up on shores far from the Arctic Ocean were enough to make Green Justice and any other ecological biodiversity organization angry for a lifetime. But for the public in general, Sarah knew the injured animals would make the worldwide news and rouse only temporary sympathy, until hotter news trumped them or people grew tired of the coverage and turned back to their own problems.

For now, however, Sarah had amassed enough evidence to put Sandstrom away for at least a few years, if the case went their way. Her best estimate was that it would. Judge Anderson wouldn't go lightly on Sandstrom, per his judgments on prior cases that had similar evidence. For years to come, Sandstrom would be penalized personally, and American Frontier corporately, in order to shell out money to the communities who now had oil coating their shores.

But Sarah knew from Will and her own common sense that Sandstrom didn't act alone. Frank Stapleton, a key member on the American Frontier board and the longtime CEO of City Capital, the largest financial power center in the Western world, not only had assisted Sandstrom in swaying the board to drill in the Arctic—despite Will's arguments to the contrary—but had pulled strings behind the scenes in the highest of circles. So had James Loughlin, the senior senator from New York. All it took was a little finagling on both their parts—as well as the promise of a healthy dose of funding from Eric Sandstrom for Loughlin's next political campaign—to get the tides turned to allow AF to be the first oil company to drill in the Arctic.

Problem was, with both men, Sarah hadn't been able to uncover anything illegal that they had done in the process. They'd simply called in some favors and completed and filed all the appropriate paperwork. Everything appeared on the up-and-up. With Sandstrom being the largest financial backer for President Rich's election campaign, the deal had moved through swiftly—far too swiftly for the standard time lapses of checks and balances that American Frontier should have proceeded through before building the platform and commencing the drilling. However, proving the full extent of the negligence was still a problem.

Meanwhile, the president had been smarting from his support of American Frontier. His poll percentages had dipped considerably. But the American public was fickle. When Mark Chalmers announced a press conference and President Rich appeared, saying he had information that he'd just become aware of, the average American was swayed in empathy. After all, the president looked transparent, seemed repentant for blindly supporting what had appeared to be a groundbreaking venture to help drive down oil prices for Americans, and promised full investigations into American Frontier's efforts in the Arctic.

Sarah rolled her eyes. Full investigations of the oil crisis and the Polar Bear bombing had been going on since the events occurred. Both had kept Sarah and Darcy taking catnaps and eating only fast food when they had the chance to grab it. And drinking coffee—way too much black coffee.

Announcing the news from the presidential podium made President Rich look good, though, and thus increased his ratings. To Americans, it sent two important messages. One, the president himself was actively involved and pushing to bring the perpetrators of the Arctic Circle fiasco to justice. Two, he had initiated the massive search to find the Polar Bear Bomber so that the truth would be revealed. President Rich stated that with the bomber choosing to end his own life and leaving a note as to his reasons and intentions, he had nailed the case against himself and executed justice all in one maneuver.

It was the all-in-one maneuver that bothered Sarah. She and Darcy still hadn't located any evidence of foul play in the death of the Polar Bear Bomber. As far as the world knew, the crazy eco-terrorist had committed suicide by jumping off a tall building in Times Square. But before he did, he'd written a letter explaining his actions and connections in detail, linking him in a loose way with Green Justice. He'd also ranted about how evil large oil companies were. It was clear as day even to a kindergartener who could connect dots with a crayon.

"Too neat and tidy," Darcy had declared with a raised brow.

Sarah agreed.

What made it worse for Sarah was that Green Justice had specifically been named in the bomber's note. Though the DOJ and DHS searches had concurred that the Polar Bear Bomber was not on the Green Justice rosters anywhere, there was still the possibility he'd been there under an assumed name.

Sean had always contributed to Green Justice causes, thus potentially linking the Worthington family to the scandal. He had even been aboard a ship in the Arctic with his Green Justice buddy Kirk Baldwin. With Will openly opposing American Frontier's Arctic operations and Sean's GJ connections, as well as his well-documented support of ecological causes, some of her more cynical colleagues were raising questions. It was only their respect for Sarah—her hard work and reputation—that kept the guesses and queries under wraps. Sarah had chosen to shrug them off for now, but they loomed in the back of her mind as an irritant. She was confident neither of her brothers would have anything to do with bombing a building, and they wouldn't even navigate the circles a homeless eco-terrorist would, but it would be natural for others to draw erroneous conclusions.

Sarah sat up suddenly in her chair. Was Sean the victim of foul play? Was that why he was missing? After all, her brother was a well-known face and befriended everyone he met. He would have been an easy target.

Her heart pounded, and she took deep breaths to calm herself.

No, she told herself, *don't go there. Focus on what you need to do.*

That meant a second good look at the recently deceased Polar Bear Bomber. His suicide note had been found in a Brooklyn flat, and his clothes and numerous fingerprints that matched his DNA showed that he had been staying there. Whether legally or illegally, nobody knew. Residents of the Brooklyn building said they hadn't seen the usual renter coming and going for some time. Those facts technically drew the Polar Bear Bomber case to a close at DHS. Knowing an eco-crazy admitted to bombing the building out of hate for a big oil company had been enough proof to end the official search. There was no one to prosecute.

It was time to give Jon a call to see if he'd uncovered anything recently. The man was relentless in his search for truth, and she was certain he hadn't given up either.

Langley, Virginia

"They found a body," his source said.

"Identifiable?" the man demanded.

"Hair and clothing. Matches the description bystanders gave of the man who jumped off the Peace Bridge. Gray sweatshirt, jeans, athletic shoes," the contact reported. "Well, shoe. One shoe is missing."

"Where?"

"Lake Ontario."

"ID search in place?"

"Yes, but the body's in bad shape. If they can ID, we should have an answer in less than 24 hours. If it's Sean, I'll be the only one notified, for now." There was a pause, then, "How long do you need this to be on the QT if it is him?"

"A minimum of 72 hours."

"Hmm. I might be able to buy you 48, but it'll be expensive."

"Not a problem."

"Then it's done. I'll check in when I know."

39

Chautauqua Institution

Wednesday morning Will rose with the sun while his father and mother slept. He had heard the murmur of their voices from their bedroom even in the wee hours of the morning. Now that his father had returned, Will would leave sometime today to drive back to New York City. He couldn't linger until Sean was found . . . if he was found.

It's time, Will decided, *to let go of some of the weight I've been carrying.* He could trust Drew.

Drew picked up on the first ring. "I had a feeling today might be the day you'd call."

He already knew why Will had stepped away from the Senate race. Now Will filled Drew in on Ava's revelation.

"I see," was Drew's only response when Will was done.

"Did you know about Sean? About Thomas?"

"I had my guesses. Some of your mother's responses led me to believe that my guesses were right. Later they were confirmed." How much later, when, or how they had been confirmed, he didn't say.

Will didn't press the issue. He'd learned long ago that Drew only revealed what he needed to, when he needed to. But he had no doubt as to Drew's loyalty to the Worthingtons or that he would keep this latest revelation to himself.

"But Will," Drew went on, "what if this blows sky-high? You want Sarah to find out by seeing it on the news?"

"Dad made me promise not to tell her. For now, I have to keep that promise."

"I don't agree, but I understand. Things that are hidden will be revealed sometime. And that sometime can hurt more than telling her in the first place."

With those sage words, Will realized he'd traded one dilemma for a new one.

NEW YORK CITY

It hadn't even taken a bribe of P. F. Chang's takeout to convince Darcy and Jon to join Sarah at her penthouse right after work the previous evening. Her friends had been more than happy to retrace what they knew of the Polar Bear Bomber's story and reexamine the evidence. They had done what they could to find the holes in a thorough search, which had spilled over into the early hours of the morning. Then Jon and Darcy had crashed at Sarah's place for a few hours of precious sleep.

Now all three sat in comfortable sweats and T-shirts in her dining room, hair still wet from their showers. None were worse for their scant hours of sleep. In their jobs, they were used to it. The table was cluttered with notes and empty Chinese paper cartons from the previous night. They'd just ordered out for bagels and a gourmet coffee delivery.

It was a little after 7:00, and they were again on a roll. They had two hours to go before Darcy and Sarah had to be at work for meetings, and they planned on making the best use of that time. Jon wasn't on assignment until the early afternoon.

A large whiteboard, propped up on Sarah's dining room hutch, sketched out a timeline of the Polar Bear Bomber. They had kept several additional colleagues in the loop, working through the night with them via phone and data links. The data was scattered, but there was a slight trail they'd been able to follow.

PB Bomber = Justin Eliot

26 years old

*Attended public school until age 10. Considered odd by classmates. Teased and bullied. History of mental instability, even as a child. On antidepressants. After manic episode, diagnosed as bipolar. Put on lithium and taken off antidepressants. Unable to focus or concentrate. After second manic episode, terrifying his teacher and other students, school asked for his removal midyear.

*Mother: Rebecca Eliot. Marital status: single. No other living relatives.

*No records or photos of ages 10–11.

*Age 11. Mother enrolled him in a special school for children emotionally and mentally challenged at nearby church, St. Mark's. Still on lithium. Added medication of Zyprexa (olanzapine). Out of school first three months often for blurred vision and/or nausea. Seemingly liked by other kids at the school from behavior section on report card.

"There." Jon pointed. "'Liked by other kids at the school.' So maybe he made a friend . . ."

Sarah nodded. ". . . who could tell us more about him if we could track him." She made a note on a nearby whiteboard of follow-ups.

"And how did a single mother pay for tuition at a special school?" Darcy mused aloud.

"Good question." Sarah added that to the list. She looked at the first whiteboard again.

*Ages 12–13. Background actor in two school plays.

"The guy wanted to be an actor and tried his hand at it," Darcy declared.

"That CNN field producer you talked to was likely right," Jon said. "He was treating the job like he was a street actor. Maybe because that's what he'd wanted to be since he was 12."

"And maybe somebody gave him the acting job of his life," Darcy concluded.

"Or death, however you want to look at it," Sarah countered.

*Age 14. One of four leads in school play.

*Age 15. Lead in school play. Missed classes multiple times for theater workshops and professional auditions. Record for work permit for a local talent agency.

Sarah stared at the photos taped to the whiteboard. "Look at his yearbook photos for those two years. A good-looking kid. Appeared normal, happy, confident. Not like the tormented, unhappy child from his previous school. Clearly he'd found acceptance."

"And also an agent to represent him since he had a work permit on file," Jon added.

Sarah made another note to follow up on his agent.

*Ages 16–17. Out of school often for photo shoots and other work with talent agency. Did a stint as understudy in local theater.

*Age 18. Missed most of school year due to talent agency work. When there, "hazy and unfocused."

"So he pursued his dream, got an agent, and worked in the field for three years in high school," Jon noted.

"That was high school. What happened from then to the bombing?" Darcy asked. "How did a troubled-in-childhood kid go from there to a few successful acting gigs, and then to bombing a building?"

"I found clippings in the paper's archives of a few of his appearances that year and the next," Jon replied. "Including at some high-end parties with crowds who tended to like their stimulants. You know what I mean."

"Yeah." Darcy nodded. "Recreational drugs, with cocaine at the top of the list."

Sarah tilted her head to study the board. "A guy longs to fit in. He gets a break in acting, starts circulating with some high-end rollers. He's already on a mood stabilizer and at least one drug for his bipolar diagnosis. Maybe he starts mixing in a recreational drug or two—alcohol, cocaine, whatever."

"Which would lead to the 'hazy and unfocused' note in the school files," Jon said.

They turned their attention back to the notes on the large whiteboard.

*Age 20. Mother passed away.

*Ages 20–22. Declining trend in his high-end agented work.

*Age 23. Mother's house went into foreclosure. Bills weren't paid for over a year. Bank couldn't locate Justin and assumed control of the house.

"No record anywhere of a father," Darcy said.

Jon raised a finger. "I checked on that. MIA since the birth. Not even listed on the hospital birth record. No way of tracking. No other relatives listed anywhere. Rebecca Eliot was an only child, with both parents dying when she was 16. She also had Justin before she turned 17."

Darcy frowned. "So she was pregnant maybe even when her parents died? Check the dates."

Jon flipped through more papers. "Yep, had to be. The baby was born seven months after her parents died."

Sarah started to pace. "So where did a teenager stay in between her parents' death and when she became a home owner? In a foster home? A resident facility for pregnant, unwed teenagers? With friends of her parents'?"

"Nowhere we can find. Records show that her parents didn't own a home. They rented a two-bedroom apartment. Both were blue-collar workers," Jon reported. "The apartment was leased a month after their death, and it wasn't to Rebecca."

By now Sarah's attorney instincts were in high gear. "So where does a teenage girl get enough money to pay for a place to stay, insurance, and her hospital bills, and then to buy a home in her name by the time she turns 21? Did her parents have some hefty life insurance?"

Jon shook his head. "Nothing that I can find."

"That means someone helped her," Darcy mused. "Housed her. Kept her off the grid. But why?"

Langley, Virginia

His private phone rang shortly after 8:00 a.m. instead of the usual 11:30 p.m.

"No go on the body ID," his source reported. "It was too badly damaged. They're moving to a dental record search."

"Make sure a certain dental record rises to the surface," the man prompted.

"Already done. We should have an answer within 24 hours."

40

New York City

"Maybe it was the unnamed birth father who wanted to keep Rebecca Eliot off the grid," Darcy suggested. "He or his parents wanted it to remain a secretive affair. The girl refused to have abortion be an option, so they bribed her with paying her doctor and the hospital expenses for the birth, gave her cash to buy a house, and provided enough cash to pay the taxes and essentials for a certain amount of years until her child was old enough to be in school, so she could get a job. Was there any record of Rebecca having a job?"

"Nope," Jon said. "She disappeared from the grid for almost four years, until she bought the house. No record of a job between that and her death either."

"How else would a 17-year-old single mother with no resources save enough for a house by the time she turns 21? And have enough so she wouldn't have to work for the rest of her life?" Sarah asked the questions as she moved toward the door. The intercom had just announced the bagel and coffee delivery. "Hold that thought."

After paying the delivery boy, Sarah began removing the breakfast items from their bags and cup holders. Jon and Darcy reached to help.

"Justin's mother was the one who supported him," Sarah said. "Nobody else in the picture. She dies, and he can't handle it. Between the recreational drugs and his meds, he goes haywire. Doesn't pay the taxes, the bills, etc. The behind-the-scenes cash flow disappears with her death. Maybe he wasn't even aware of it, or if he was, he didn't know who was specifically behind it."

"Like a magical Wizard of Oz behind the curtain," Darcy threw in.

"He comes home one day, and his mother's house is foreclosed. He must have hit the streets then or found somewhere else to live."

"The IRS says he didn't pay taxes himself either before or after his mother died," Jon reported. "No 1099s either. House was solely in the mother's name. She paid the taxes."

"So either he wasn't paid over $600 by anyone reputable, or he was paid in cash for any gigs." Sarah lifted a brow. "No reputable agent would do a cash deal. There would always be a record for the agency."

"No record of a bank account either," Darcy pointed out. "Which means he relied on his mother for funding, except for the odd jobs he did. Everything he counted on went out the door with her death."

"Which could swing a mentally unstable man off-kilter," Jon reasoned.

Sarah gestured to the last entry on the whiteboard.

*Age 26. Made sure he was noticed outside AF. Dropped off backpack with just enough C4 to blow a chunk off storehouse. Stuffed polar bear suit in garbage bin behind ecological office complex. Wrote suicide note. Jumped off 30-story building.

There the trail ended, except for the fact that startled bystanders had seen the body plummeting from the top of the 30-story building and landing amid the traffic below. It didn't take long for NYPD to identify the body as that of Justin Eliot. There was no driver's license, only a state-issued ID. There was only one other item in his wallet—a hand-laminated card that was a miniature of an outdated agency comp card. On it, scribbled in black permanent marker, was a note: *I believe in you, Justin. Love, Mama.*

"It doesn't add up," Sarah declared. "What happened to those lost years between 23 and 26?"

Jon shrugged. "A few odd jobs here or there cropped up on the grid. Nothing enough to support carrying a lease on an apartment, though."

"Or his drug habits," Darcy added. "So what else was he doing?"

"The only thing that's reasonable," Jon said. "The kind of work you do for cash, when you're down and out and desperate. Basically anything, whether it's legal or illegal. You hit up friends to stay at their places, even a few days at a time."

"All we know is that the suicide note was discovered at a little Brooklyn flat that wasn't his."

Jon checked his notes. "Belongs to a Michael Vara."

"So how did Michael and Justin know each other?" Darcy asked. "Is Michael's name on the Green Justice activist list? Could Justin have been doing a favor for an extremist ecological friend in exchange for staying at his apartment?"

"Or did Justin, since he was homeless, just crash at someone's apartment who was out of town?" Jon took a bite of his bagel.

"I could ask Kirk Baldwin if Michael Vara is on the Green Justice activist list," Sarah said. "He's always been a straight shooter. He'd check and keep things hush-hush."

"Where would a guy like Justin get the money to buy C4? Did he and his mom have cash stashed in a mattress somewhere? And how would he have the knowledge to put a bomb together—C4, a plastic binder, detonator?" Darcy shook her head. "Doesn't seem the type. Nothing in the records shows that he was a techie. The bit of bomb-making residue and leftover parts in that Brooklyn flat means nada. Could have been planted. No, I think somebody gave him that bomb."

"Nothing in his background explains a growing hatred toward big oil companies either. No record of him even being eco-friendly. So the guy suddenly became an ecological extremist overnight? Not likely," Sarah reasoned.

"Don't forget where that polar bear suit was stashed. You'd have to be an ecological activist to even know where those buildings are. They aren't on the normal grid for people to find," Darcy added.

"Unless the same person or persons who gave him the backpack with the bomb also gave him instructions where to plant the evidence to frame ecological extremists for the crime," Jon said. "And then arranged to kill him—forced him to jump off that building—to destroy the only person who could identify who had hired him and thus lead to the mastermind behind the whole thing."

"Whoa!" Darcy exclaimed. "That's a pretty big string of connections."

He nodded. "Yes, but also very logical."

Sometimes Sarah thought Jon was Spock from *Star Trek*, he was so maddeningly calm and reasonable. But, she had to admit, he was usually right. His thinking had proven clear and on target in everything they'd discovered thus far. "It's a theory. A very solid one. Someone had to have seen him entering that building or climbing the stairs."

"NYPD checked the traffic cams, including the helicopter ones of the Times Square area. None showed a man of his description entering the building or exiting onto the roof," Darcy reported.

New York was a big place, but someone had to know what happened. Had he been "helped" to his death to hide what he'd done for Sandstrom?

Sarah flipped through notes from the coroner. "No marks on the body to show he was subdued or resisting anyone."

That fact, coupled with his note, had led investigators to declare his death as a suicide. It didn't hurt that the president himself was screaming for closure of the case.

"But why would the man commit suicide?" she asked. "A sudden bout of conscience over his actions?"

"Doubtful," Darcy replied. "For dinging the corner of the building of an oil company he supposedly hated? He didn't harm any person, only property."

"If you were an eco-crazy and you'd just succeeded in getting your actions in the worldwide press, what's the next thing you'd do?" Sarah asked.

"Capitalize on that press by planning something else to make a follow-up point," Jon said. "I wouldn't celebrate my success by writing a detailed suicide note and killing myself."

"Exactly. Eco-activists are about making statements to turn others to their point of view. Instead, this guy goes to the top floor of a 30-story building and does a dive off the roof mid-afternoon. For what purpose?"

"Unless that was his ultimate purpose—do a dive in the middle of the day to attract as much attention as possible," Darcy argued.

"But then why not make a big statement and get the press watching?" Sarah asked. "If it's going to be your final hurrah, wouldn't you make it a big one? Not just leave behind a suicide note for the NYPD to find? You'd want to see news helicopters circling, be able to proclaim your final message against the horrible big oil companies who are out to ruin the entire planet, then use the jump to the cement far below as shock value for your viewers."

"So maybe Jon's right. He was helped off the roof." Darcy chewed on a fingernail. "Don't you think it's rather convenient that the building's roof cameras malfunctioned during those hours? Has to make you wonder . . ."

". . . how big this mess is?" Sarah finished.

All three exchanged a dubious glance.

"Okay," Darcy said, "so what's next?"

"I'll call Kirk and ask if Michael Vara is connected with Green Justice," Sarah replied. "And see if I can track down his phone."

"St. Mark's is on the way to work. I'll leave now and stop by to see if I can track down the director of the program," Darcy offered. "See if the school still exists and, if so, whether somebody there remembers anything helpful from the years Justin was there, including any friends he might have made." She grabbed a bagel to go in a napkin and headed out the door.

"Let me see Justin's agency card," Jon said to Sarah. "I'll track the agent down and ask about the last time he talked to Justin." He smiled. "Between the three of us, we won't give up until we figure it out."

"You got that right!" Sarah laughed.

As he moved toward the door, she sobered. "Jon, have you heard from Sean?"

He swiveled toward her. "No, I haven't."

"I just hoped—"

"I know." His blue eyes steadily met hers. He took a few steps back toward her. "I know," he repeated.

A second later, he enfolded her in his arms as she started to cry.

It was the nicest thing anyone had done for her in a long time.

41

En Route from Chautauqua Institution to New York City

Will was driving and nearly halfway back to New York City when Drew phoned.

"I'm afraid I have some news. A body matching Sean's description was found."

"Where?"

"Lake Ontario."

Will felt like the breath had been knocked out of him. He pulled the Land Rover over onto the shoulder.

"Are they sure?"

"There's no positive ID. But the clothing and hair color match. Even found a Nike shoe. Do you want me to call Sarah and give her the news? Or your dad?"

"No. That's something I need to do."

New York City

It wasn't even Sarah's lunchtime yet, and already Jon had been able to track down Justin's former agent.

No wonder Jon and Sean had hit it off, Sarah thought wryly. They both had the most extensive networks she had ever seen—well, except for Drew.

"Caustic," Jon told her on the phone. "Too busy and angry to give me the time of day, especially about someone like Justin Eliot, he said. Told me the kid could have been somebody but blew it on drugs. Got flaky. Didn't show up for gigs or showed up late. Too many complaints from key clients, so the agent dropped him. He hasn't contacted Justin in over two years, doesn't care, and good riddance. I didn't tell him Justin was dead, or that he'd become the Polar Bear Bomber. I'm glad the FBI and NYPD didn't release his name since they haven't been able to find a next of kin yet."

Sarah agreed. "Guys like that agent would sensationalize the news of being the former agent of the Polar Bear Bomber—and make a boatload off it somehow."

"Yes, they would. Didn't want to give him the satisfaction. He could've helped a kid in need not go down the wrong trail. Instead, that agent took advantage of him."

There it was again—the sweet, caring side of a veteran reporter who had seen a lot of awfulness in his career. Yet Jon stood immovable in the middle of any maelstrom. She'd seen it multiple times now, had admired it. Such a contrast to the men Sarah usually met, including the self-focused TV producer she'd been stupid enough to date for a year. Why it had taken a full year for her to see the light, she had no idea.

"Sarah?" Jon asked. "You okay?"

Jon was proof there were still some quality men left.

"Yes, I'm okay. Just had a weak moment there."

"Hey," he said softly, "it's not weak to love your brother."

Tightness clogged her throat, and she couldn't respond. She knew Jon would understand.

Ten minutes later, her cell rang again. She was expecting Kirk Baldwin's call, so she answered without checking caller ID. "Hey, Kirk."

"Sarah," a male voice said.

"Will! Are you on your way home or . . . ?" She wobbled and lowered herself into her chair.

"I just got a call from Drew."

She gripped the edge of her desk. "And?"

"They found a body in Lake Ontario. The clothing and hair color is a match to Sean. The man was still wearing one athletic shoe."

She gasped. *It can't be. It just can't be.* "But was it Sean?"

There was a long pause, then a pained, "Don't know. The body's in rough shape."

How could they confirm or deny it? Waiting for a positive ID through DNA testing and dental records would be agony.

Then an idea hit. "What color was the shoe?" she demanded. "And what specific kind?"

"All I know is that it was an athletic shoe. I don't know the color. Didn't think to ask."

"Find out what kind and color it was," she insisted. "Then call me back. I have an errand to run."

Minutes later she was hurrying out the door of the DOJ building. She caught a cab to Sean's flat.

En Route from Chautauqua Institution to New York City

Will, still roadside on the way back to the Big Apple, was stupefied. Of all the reactions he'd expected from his sister, "I have an errand to run" wasn't one of them.

He phoned his father next. Bill took the news stoically. "So we get closer to the answer, perhaps," he said. "I think I'll wait for a bit more information before I share that with your mother."

Will would have done the same thing—check out every potential angle first.

Next he phoned Drew about the athletic shoe. Will heard the rustling of papers, as if notes were being flipped.

"Nike Air Force 1 Low Lux Masterpiece Crocodile Edition," Drew stated. "Brown with a metallic gold, 18-carat."

Will felt sick. He'd teased Sean about purchasing a pair of those shoes, calling them "downright ugly." He got out of the Land Rover and stood, sucking air.

"Will . . . Will, you okay?" Drew's voice sounded hazy, distant.

Will's ears buzzed. And then the contents of his lunch spilled onto the road.

42

///

NEW YORK CITY

Sarah entered Sean's apartment and hurried toward his bedroom. "What kind?" she asked Will as soon as he called her back.

"Nike Air Force 1 Low Lux Masterpiece Crocodile Edition. Brown with a metallic gold. But what—"

"Thanks. Call you back." And she hung up.

Throwing open the closet doors, she scanned the jumble of shoes. It was the one place he'd told his housekeeper was off-limits. He'd jokingly told Sarah, "If I have to keep the rest of my house organized, I need at least one closet that reminds me I'm a human being."

It was the kind of mess that would have driven Will nuts. Maybe that was why, growing up, Sean had been the least organized of all of them. He'd worked hard to keep his closet a mess and the exact opposite of Will's soldier lineup. Now the rest of his place was organized and pristine—thanks to his housekeeper and decorator—but his bedroom closet was still a mess.

Sarah dug through the heap. She only needed to find one

pair—his Nike Air Force 1s. If she did, she would know that body wasn't Sean's. But as she continued to search, her anxiety grew.

Where are those shoes? Please, God, let me find them here.

Sarah attacked the last heap to the right of the door . . . and found them.

Grabbing the shoes, she hugged them to her chest. Sean could complain later about the salt stains on his crocodile leather. She didn't care. She'd buy him a hundred more pairs . . . after she wrung his neck.

En Route from Chautauqua Institution to New York City

Will's dread grew when he didn't hear back right away from his sister and she didn't answer his texts. He jumped back into his Land Rover and drove as swiftly as he could to New York City.

His cell rang right when he entered the city limits. He pulled over in a 7-Eleven parking lot. "Why didn't you—"

"It's not Sean," Sarah announced. She was sniffling, like she'd been crying.

"How do you know?"

"Because I found his shoes—his Nike Air Force 1s. They're here, in his closet."

A tidal wave of relief threatened to swamp Will. He sagged against the driver's door.

"But his favorite athletic shoes are missing. You know, the Nike Dunk 'Paris' ones. Mom says he wore them when he had breakfast with her the last day she saw him."

The tidal wave broke over Will's head, incapacitating him.

Langley, Virginia

The man had been pacing his office for nearly 20 minutes with his eye on the desk phone. He hated that phone—the cumbersome nature of it—but his wife had insisted on it. She'd said it "made" his office, whatever that meant. He didn't care about décor. Function was what mattered to him.

His contact was late. He was never late. When his phone finally rang, he snatched the receiver out of its cradle.

With no preamble, his source reported, "The dental record is back. It's not Sean Worthington."

So Sean was likely alive . . . somewhere. Unless he'd run into foul play and the body hadn't been discovered yet. Anything was possible.

"I have a tip," his source added.

The information relayed next made sense. The Worthingtons were resourceful. If one of them wanted to disappear for a while or for years, they had the wealth and connections to do so.

He, of all people, knew that loyalty could be bought. For how long, though, was the question. He simply had to locate the person or persons who could be turned.

43

New York City

Sarah had sat in a stupor right outside Sean's closet so long that she couldn't even see her hand in front of her. The sky was dark outside the large bedroom window. Her fingers were numb from gripping her brother's Nike Air Force 1s.

Her cell had rung and rung. Text messages had vibrated. She hadn't made a move to answer them.

That body isn't Sean, but where is he? The words reverberated over and over in her brain.

She couldn't handle being in limbo between life and death for much longer.

At that moment she heard the creak of the front door opening. *Sean!*

She dropped the Nikes and then tripped over them in her rush for the door. Before she found the light switch in his bedroom, a man's frame filled the doorway.

"Sarah?"

It was Will. She took two more steps and collapsed in his arms.

There had been five times in Will's life when he had felt helpless. He could remember each of them distinctly.

The first was when he'd seen his mother, a bastion of strength, sitting alone in their backyard garden at Chautauqua. She was crying. Will couldn't recall exactly how old he was, but he was young. He hadn't known how to comfort her, so he'd done the only thing he could. He'd climbed up into her lap and hugged her. To this day, he could remember the tears that dripped onto his cheek, the sadness, the heaviness, of knowing something had gone terribly wrong.

Now he realized that was likely the moment his mother had found out she was pregnant with Sean, before his father's return from India. That experience of seeing his mother's weakness had formed in Will, from an early age, a fierce protectiveness toward those he loved. That included the tiny packages of his brother and sister at their births.

The second time he'd felt helpless was also at Chautauqua. Will had hoped for one night's dose of peace and quiet and a sunset view before his campaign launched. Instead his mother had joined him and told him how Sean came to be a part of their family. The revelation had shaken his world and much of what he had thought to be true about his childhood and his parents' relationship.

The third and fourth times were both today. The third, when Drew had identified the type of shoe found on the body, and Will recognized that Sean had a pair just like them. The fourth, when Sarah had told him which other shoes were missing—the very ones Sean had worn to breakfast with Ava. Somehow, for

Will, those shoes became the icon of their brother, who had simply vanished into thin air. Where was he? They were no closer today to finding him than they'd been a week ago.

The fifth time was now, as he held his baby sister and bore the weight of her grief as well as his own.

44

Sarah awoke from her spot on top of Sean's bed. In the night, Will had thrown a large fleece blanket over her. She cuddled deeper into it, trying to forget why she was there.

The siblings had stayed the night at Sean's. The agreement wasn't voiced aloud, but both needed to be there, together, surrounded by as much of Sean as they could.

Sarah inched herself up and yawned. There, on the floor next to the bed, was Will. Her protective big brother was sound asleep, his right arm thrown over his forehead, his lanky form and feet sticking out of the too-short afghan. Sarah chuckled. He still slept in the same position he had as a kid.

She bet if she bounced him awake by jumping on him like she used to when they were growing up, he'd look just as annoyed. The touch of home brought a smile.

Peering at the time on her cell, she realized with a start it was after 9:00. Time only for a quick shower and to throw back on the clothes she'd worn to Sean's. That would have to do for the day. Hopefully nobody would notice how rumpled they were since she'd slept in them and mistake her overnight for something else. Gossip was abundant at the DOJ. At least 90 percent of it was false, but that didn't stop the rumor-mongering.

She tiptoed around Will, out the bedroom door, and down the hall to the bathroom. She didn't want to wake him by using the bathroom attached to the bedroom.

After her shower, she twisted up her damp curls into a chic bob and scribbled a note: *I love you to the moon and back.*

Tiptoeing back into the bedroom, she placed it by Will's side. He'd understand the phrase from their childhood.

The first person Will called when he woke was Drew. He'd left the man hanging after he'd asked about the shoe specifics. When he filled Drew in, his mentor was quiet.

"Drew?" Will finally said.

"If Sean was dead, we'd know. We'd sense it. I don't believe he's dead. I think he just needed some time and space away. He deals with things differently than you would. If you're overwhelmed, you plunge headlong into work. If he's overwhelmed, he retreats."

In all the years Will had known Drew, the man had never been wrong.

Tucking Sarah's note into his pants pocket, he headed out Sean's door to a nearby coffeehouse. Today he'd need two stiff cups, back-to-back, instead of his usual one.

In the cab on the way to work, Sarah checked her texts from yesterday. Kirk Baldwin's was short.

Not on roster. No GJer knows a Michael Vara.

So that was a dead end. Usually Sarah hated dead ends. This time she was relieved. Green Justice tried to go about saving the planet and its creatures in a reasonable way, even if the fact the organization existed and pointed out problems incensed a lot of big industry titans. Kirk too was solid, trustworthy. He'd been Sean's friend for 15 years. Though the burly, bald-headed guy stated his points with no apology, his speech and actions were laden with personal integrity. Sarah was glad she didn't have to burden him with any more digging.

She looked at her next text.

Darcy

St. Mark's school closed. Former headmistress at church tomorrow a.m. Volunteers there. Stopping by again around 9:45 or 10. Join me if you want.

Sarah eyed the time on her cell. She could make it if the cab driver hustled.

45

CORVO, AZORES ISLANDS

The view was impressive, crafted by a once-active volcano. The most northern island of the archipelago of the Azores, it was perfectly remote. No traffic jams, no high-rises, no shopping plazas, no fast-food drive-throughs. Not even a hotel. Best of all, litle chance of cell phone reception or internet.

To stay off the grid, Sean had gotten one of the best pilots for hire on the market to fly him to São Miguel, landing at Nordela Airport in Ponta Delgada. After a day's stay in a hotel that didn't check ID, his pilot had flown him to Flores. The man was sworn to secrecy, paid well for an extended "vacation," and provided amenities.

Sean had spent five days on the beautiful island of Flores—a lush paradise of birds and flowers. With only about 4,000 residents, it was quiet, a place he could hear his own thoughts.

The first three days he'd rested in a whitewashed one-room house he'd rented as the island was lashed by rain.

The last two days he'd taken in the sights—the bluest crater lakes surrounded by high mountains and the sloping hillsides and valleys of fertile farmland. When business potential for the area nudged into his mind, though, he knew it was time to leave.

So he'd rousted his pilot from snoring under his Tommy Bahama hat to fly him to Corvo. This time, for the remainder of the three weeks he'd decided to take, Sean told the pilot to return to Flores. He wanted the island all to himself, with the exception of the native villagers.

They landed at the tiniest airport and shortest landing strip he'd ever seen.

"Wait in Flores. Pick me up from the airfield in two weeks." Sean grinned. "Anything you want, put it on my tab. I'll take care of it when I return." With as much cash as he'd spent in Flores and the hotel over the last five days, the hotel hadn't minded keeping a running tab for him for the couple of weeks he was away. Nor had the pilot, with the promise of comfortable circumstances while he waited and pay for his additional services.

He'd given his pilot that instruction over a week ago. By now Sean had met most of the 400 friendly islanders on Corvo. With no hotel, they'd happily taken him in, welcomed him like family.

Corvo was simple and beautiful. The electricity was iffy. He'd visited the rocky coastline and peered over the steep cliffs, not surprised that merchants in the old days had had a tough time landing on the island. But it was also one of the natural wonders that had helped the island maintain its quaint charm.

He'd gazed to the south, where cattle and wild horses grazed—a larger population than the people. He'd enjoyed a diet of fresh vegetables and fruit, including maize and delicious melons. As he hiked the island each day, if he grew hungry he only had to knock on a door. Whatever they were having for lunch or dinner became his lunch or dinner. The villagers liked the American dollars and the outside company that was rare on their island.

Sean relished the new flavors of the cuisine, basked in the attention from the locals, and found their dialect—a unique language spiced with Old Portuguese words—intriguing.

He could get used to this lifestyle, he thought. Living more simply, making his way among people who were close to the land, and finding ways to assist their communities. He also loved feeling like family.

On Corvo, there were no locked doors. There was nothing to steal. Besides, everyone knew what everyone else had, so the perpetrator would have been found quickly. That meant there was no crime, no suspicion. Everyone helped everyone.

It was a bit of heaven right on earth.

Togetherness. That's what I've been missing. Longing for.

Her beautiful, passionate eyes flashed into his mind again. Strange how, even with the distance between them, she was the one person he missed the most.

New York City

"Justin Eliot? Oh yes, I remember him." Marie Chesterton, the gray-haired former headmistress of the special school at St. Mark's, lowered herself onto a pew in the church's sanctuary. "Such a troubled young man. No support except for his dear mama." She clucked in sympathy. "No father anywhere. No grandparents to come see him in his plays. I guessed that she'd had the baby very young, though she never said so. She was much younger than most of our parents."

"You said he was troubled? In what way?" Sarah asked.

"Emotionally, I mean, dear. The first year or so at our school he had episodes where he would become frantic—so frenetic that he'd run circles around the classroom and needed to be calmed. Other times he would retreat, say he was no good, worthless. He often couldn't concentrate on his studies, but we did the best we could. He was on medication, but that didn't always work." Her expression was sad, tender. "I sat with him many times and held him until his mama could come. She always had a calming effect on him."

"You mentioned the first year or so," Darcy noted. "Did those episodes lessen after that?"

"Yes, he seemed to settle in. Even made a good friend." The older woman smiled. "They were in plays together."

Sarah eyed Darcy and knew they were thinking the same thing. Could that childhood friend have grown into an off-kilter adult with an ax to grind against oil companies, and talked Justin into doing one last act for old times' sake? Such as dressing up as a polar bear and leaving a backpack by a building? Could it be as simple as that? "What was that friend's name?"

Marie's gaze flicked back from her memories to rest on Sarah. "Michael. Michael Vara. Both boys had no father."

Sarah and Darcy exchanged glances. The apartment where the suicide note was found had been rented to a Michael Vara. It would have been easy for Michael to fake Justin's handwriting and signature, especially since it wasn't on file anywhere officially, like at the DMV. The building manager said Michael paid the rent on time via checks from an account in New York, but the envelopes were sent from different locations, many of them overseas. Other apartment dwellers in the building said they hadn't seen Michael in a long time, perhaps six months or so.

"Do you know what Michael did after he left your school?" Sarah asked.

Marie nodded. "Indeed I do. We talk often."

Darcy perked up. "So he's local still?"

"Oh, no, dear. Well, he has a flat here in the city that he

keeps for the short times when he returns—says it's cheaper than staying at a hotel." She chuckled. "Always was economical. He's mostly been in England and Ireland the last four or five years." Her face lit up. "A success story for sure. He works with emotionally troubled young people, helping them work out their fears and find companionship in theater pursuits through acting camps. That kind of thing."

Darcy leaned forward. "Was he ever emotionally troubled himself?"

Marie lifted her chin and gave an icy schoolmarm glare. Now Sarah could see why she made a good headmistress. A kind, grandmotherly type on the surface but steel underneath. She wouldn't put up with any nonsense. "That boy went through a rough time in life," Marie declared. "Saw his father beat his mother nearly senseless, then kill himself right in their own living room. Michael was 11. Guess anybody would struggle after that."

Sarah nodded. "Indeed they would. I'm so sorry." In her pro bono work at Harvard Law, she'd seen too many of those sad cases. They hadn't been simply cases to her, as they were to some of the other budding attorneys who only wanted to use the experiences as stepping-stones for their career. She often couldn't sleep at night, seeing the real faces behind the trauma. At what stage might someone have intervened to help the family before the crisis reached the tipping point? It was a question she'd pondered often.

"But Michael is strong willed. He decided he wanted to turn the tough things that happened to him into something good to help others. Pursued that as soon as he graduated from high school. He studied drama at NYC, on a scholarship," she announced proudly.

That certainly doesn't sound like a guy who would have anything to do with a bombing, Sarah thought.

"Do you know if Michael and Justin were ever in contact after they left the school?" Darcy asked.

"Indeed they are," Marie answered. "Michael's worried about Justin. Says he isn't the same since his mama passed. Told Justin he could stay at his flat anytime he needed a place to stay. Gave him a key."

That certainly explained how Justin came to stay at the apartment, with no signs of breaking and entering.

"Were Michael and Justin interested at all in ecological causes while they were at school? You know, 'save the earth' and 'protect the whales' kind of stuff?" Darcy asked.

Marie appeared to be thinking hard. "Not to my knowledge. Michael wanted to help other kids. But that could be. Those boys had gentle souls inside all the hurt. Rescued a spider that had strayed into the classroom and carried it outside to live a full life before one of the other kids could kill it."

So both did care about animals. Had it become more than that? Perhaps an obsession enough to bomb a building for? If so, who had planted the seed for violence and then funded it?

Langley, Virginia

Once he'd known the body wasn't Sean, the man had ordered a track on private planes and limos for hire through his expansive network. That was when they'd located a man who'd been heard mouthing off at a bar in Chinatown in New York City. He'd boasted about his friend, a pilot for hire, getting a sudden job late one night a couple of weeks ago. Nick Delray was willing to talk for a price and some additional drinks.

"It was a cush job, out of the country somewhere," the contact reported after flying in to New York City and showing up at

Nick's apartment. "Clearly Nick had already had a few drinks, but he said it was a string of islands. Nice weather. Tropical. He hasn't seen or heard from his friend since." He chuckled. "He was working hard to prove to me they were good friends. He insisted the pilot wasn't back yet because, as he said, 'If he was back, he'd call me.'"

"So he didn't know any other specifics?" the man asked. "Including the name of his pilot friend's fare?"

"Nope, as much as he tried to make me think otherwise, to milk me for more money."

Still, the information was the first breakthrough for the man and well worth the price.

It hadn't taken long to identify and trace the pilot's flight path to São Miguel in the Azores.

46

Corvo

Sean stood outside his small island home, enjoying the early morning air before starting his hike up the Morro dos Homens, the highest point on the southern rim of the Caldeirão. He loved the spongy earth of the peat bogs of the caldera. They were some of his favorite places on the island. The bogs had been a good, natural reminder that the earth didn't have to be solid or predictable under his feet in order for him to move ahead and enjoy the view.

On Corvo, Sean had found solace when the underpinnings of his life were ripped out.

His mother, whom he'd respected and loved for more than three decades, wasn't who he thought.

His father wasn't who he thought.

The way he'd arrived on this earth wasn't how he thought.

He wasn't who he thought.

Now it made sense why his middle name was Thomas. Why he didn't have a generational Worthington first name or middle name like his brother and sister. Why his profile in the mirror wasn't one of a Worthington. O'Hara, certainly, from his mother's side, but not the Worthington nose his brother and sister had—the feature that seemed to mark every Worthington for generations. The Irish heritage side had definitely won out in his looks. Both his mother and Thomas had Irish blood running through their veins.

He shivered, thinking again of her betrayal. He'd asked her once, when he was in elementary school, why she'd named him *Sean Thomas*.

"Thomas is a good, solid name I've always loved," she'd said. She hadn't said, "Thomas is the name of my friend and your dad's best friend who I slept with when your dad had to go out of town. He's your real father."

He winced. That sounded crass, but wasn't it the truth?

His first name, meaning "God has favored," was ironic. How could God favor him, a mistake? The product of a one-night love—lust—affair? Why would his mother name him that? Each time he thought deeply about the meaning of his name, he got angry all over again.

Does anyone else in the family know? Does Will? Sarah? Dad?

The questions had played like litanies through his mind for nearly two weeks until they were well worn and ragged around the edges. The only way to find out, he knew, was by returning to the States and asking his mom face-to-face. She'd lied to him once, which made her capable of lying again. That was why he had to look her in the eyes to know the truth. It was the only way he could be sure.

But he wasn't ready for that yet. The heat of the betrayal was still too hot for him to handle facing her. He didn't want to say anything he might regret later.

New York City

"One last question." Sarah smiled at Marie. "I know we've taken a lot of your time."

"Not at all, dearie. Those are my boys. I care about them with a mother's heart. But I'm concerned. Is Justin all right?"

Darcy studied the headmistress. "You asked just about Justin. Any reason?"

Marie patted Darcy's hand. "I know Michael is all right. Justin I've been concerned about for a long time."

Little does she know, Sarah thought, but she wasn't going to tell the older woman how Justin's story had ended. At least not yet.

"Do you have a way to get in touch with Michael, other than mail at his apartment?" Sarah asked.

"Of course. Right now he's in London, but we talk by phone, and I have his number. He also gave me the address you type into the computer, but I've never used it. I'm not into such newfangled things," Marie whispered.

After riffling through her large purse, she extracted a dog-eared address book and jotted Michael's phone and email address on a piece of paper. "Here." She extended the paper to Sarah, then took it back again briefly to jot another note. "When he works in theater, he uses another name—Michael M. Madsen. That's his mother's maiden name. He never wanted to publicize his last name, Vara, because of what his father did. It was a terrible time in his life. Most folks know him now simply as Michael or Michael M. Madsen."

Darcy and Sarah got up from their spots on the pew.

"Oh," Marie said, looking flustered for a minute, "let me give you one more thing." She extracted another sheet of note-paper from her purse and wrote a message on it. "When you find Justin, give this to him, would you?"

Sarah took the paper. How would this dear old woman take finding out the truth? "Is it all right if I make a copy of your contact information for myself?" she asked. Once the name was going to be released, Sarah would circle back and let Marie know what had happened to Justin before the press hit. The headmistress who truly cared for her former students deserved to know.

As they exited the massive stone church, Darcy and Sarah paused outside the door.

"So we find Michael Vara-Madsen, and we might find some answers," Darcy said.

"Agreed. But how can we go about it so we don't tip him off, if he did have something to do with the bombing?" Sarah asked.

"Jon," both women said simultaneously.

"Bet he wouldn't mind writing a piece about special-needs theater camps, if Michael is on the up-and-up," Sarah said. "He told me once he has to have 'evergreen' pieces ready to go—human-interest stories that can be easily updated and slipped in if a hot news piece falls out at the last minute."

"There you go," Darcy declared.

Sarah would give him a call. She hailed a taxi and got in the back. Realizing she was still holding two pieces of paper in her hands, she opened Marie's note.

Justin, my dear, I have missed you. Remember you have a home at St. Mark's and in my heart. Call me anytime, day or night.

Fondly, Mrs. Chesterton

Sarah's eyes misted. Her mother often said that people who worked with children and adults who had special needs were the salt of the earth. Marie Chesterton had proved that truth once again.

LANGLEY, VIRGINIA

The man was brisk and businesslike as he mounted the stairs of the private jet that would take him to the Azores.

"Welcome aboard, sir." The middle-aged pilot, experienced and confidential, greeted him at the doorway.

The man carried only a small overnight bag and his briefcase. He wouldn't need more than a couple changes of clothes and the packet in his briefcase. A quick phone call to someone high up in the Portuguese government had ensured that his plane would be able to land without delay and that he wouldn't need to go through the usual customs check.

No one but himself and the pilot was on board. The pilot already had his instructions. No further conversation was needed. The man liked it that way—quiet, simple, streamlined.

His contact had already caught a flight from New York to Boston, and then to São Miguel. They'd meet at the hotel on the island.

If Sean was in São Miguel, the man would do what he needed to do.

47

Corvo

Midway up the Morro dos Homens, the question that had cropped up the most on Sean's hikes assaulted him again. Did Thomas know?

How could he get my mother pregnant and not know? Sean's pragmatic side argued. *Or at least consider the possibility she might become pregnant from their tryst?*

Sean's anger kicked in. Or had Thomas callously done the deed and then let her leave Camp David, never following through to make sure she was okay? Had Thomas waited for the right moment to seduce Ava? To take advantage of her? Especially with the convenience of his wife returning to the White House? Did Thomas bribe the Secret Service detail to keep a few hours of the president's dalliances private from the rest of the world?

If so, Sean's disregard and distaste for the Rich family grew even more.

Then reality struck. Sean himself was part of the family he lambasted from time to time. *No wonder Mom chided me when I did that. I was attacking my own father and half brother.*

Had Thomas wanted to know he conceived a son out of wedlock when he was president of the United States? Did he ever see Sean in the society pages and wonder at any resemblance? *Especially with my middle name being Thomas?*

And what role exactly did Ava play? Was naming him *Thomas* her backhanded slap at the man who had used her? Or an attempt to give Sean a bit of the father he would never know?

A new possibility startled him, and he sank onto a large volcanic rock nearby. Was her interlude with Thomas her way to get the second baby she'd wanted? She had told Sean how long she'd waited to have him. Did her longing and desperation for that baby drive her into another man's arms?

He clasped his head in both hands. Was he judging Thomas wrongly? Had Thomas agreed somehow to be a surrogate lover in order to produce the child his university friend longed for?

If so, did Bill know about the arrangements? Had he even been part of the planning? Was that why Bill had to leave Camp David? Because he couldn't handle seeing his wife in the arms of another man, even if it was to produce a Worthington baby? And why he had been the hardest on Sean, of the three children? Because he knew Sean wasn't really his child?

Overwhelmed, Sean gasped for air. He struggled to sort through logically what he knew was fact and what was guesswork.

The two families had stopped seeing each other after that summer at Camp David. Was it simply because both men got too busy with their high-profile careers? Bill with growing Worthington Shares, and Thomas with being president of the United States for two back-to-back terms and then the host of philanthropic ventures that followed? That was the explanation Sean had accepted over the years, at least the one time he'd cared to ask. To him, the Riches were merely faces on a society page, figures who held high government positions. They didn't have anything to do with him, so he didn't track them.

Now he tried to recall anything Ava, Bill, or Will had said about the Riches.

Ava hadn't said much, other than giving Sean that stern mom look when he vocalized his view of Spencer Rich as president. But Sean had seen her flipping through her Harvard yearbook from time to time and had come across multiple pictures in a university scrapbook she'd made of herself, Bill, and Thomas, arms around each other's shoulders.

Before Camp David, the families had made a point of attending each other's key events. Sean remembered seeing a picture of Ava and Bill, married not even a year, with Thomas at his wedding. Victoria was not in the photo—only the three Harvard schoolmates. When Sean had joked once about the missing bride, his mother had simply said, "Victoria is . . . different. From the best of circles and very beautiful. But I think Thomas married too quickly."

Had Thomas done that because his heart had been broken by Ava marrying Bill?

Bill, come to think of it, had never mentioned Thomas by name in front of Sean. Odd, since they had been inseparable for three years at Harvard. The only reference Sean could remember was when the media reported on President Spencer Rich throwing a tantrum in the Oval Office. An intern had seen the display and let it slip to the outside world—and she'd since been dismissed. Bill had commented, "Like father, like son," in disgust.

Ava had frowned and said, "Bill . . ." in that warning voice she had.

Would Bill have said that about his best friend at Harvard unless something or someone had come between them? Had

Thomas also been in love with Ava, but Bill had won the prize? Or did Bill know about what happened at Camp David?

Will had once told Sean his memories of that time were fuzzy. He only recalled being glad when Spencer Rich left with his mother, since Spencer was a bully. Will preferred to explore Camp David solo.

No matter how much Sean raked his memory, he couldn't come up with any further discussion about the Rich family.

Why did the families stop seeing each other? Was it because Ava knew she was pregnant? Or because Thomas and Ava wanted to hide their affair? Perhaps they feared that communication between the two families would allow hints of the truth to slip. Or that Bill would note the subtle exchanges between Thomas and Ava, and he might start to do the math on Sean's birth.

The questions grated, rubbing his heart raw, because he had no answers. He might never have answers. He had to decide how to live with that, or if it was possible to live with that.

Sean scanned the mountain that still rose at least 1,000 feet above him. Then he stared at the over 1,000-foot drop to the bottom of the caldera.

New York City

"Sure, I can go after a potential human-interest story on special-needs kids and theater," Jon said. "That's a unique spin my boss would like for a fill-in piece anyway."

Sarah gave Jon the contact info. She knew once the project was in Jon's hands, they'd get the answers they were looking for.

Jon had an understated but persistent way of extracting information that relaxed people. By the time the interview ended, that person had been added to his social network and was already in the category of loyal advocate. That was just Jon. It was one of the many admirable qualities that had made him one of the best reporters in New York City.

Ponta Delgada, Portugal

The man disembarked from the private jet at Nordela Airport in Ponta Delgada. He was waved through Portuguese security and escorted immediately to the hotel where a red-haired American and a pilot had supposedly stayed for a day nearly two weeks ago. His contact had done well, pulling the appropriate strings to prepare for his arrival.

There a meal awaited him—red mashed peppers served with fresh cheese, mackerel with a flavorful sauce, tea pudding feito, and fresh pineapple. It was the best local fare that São Miguel Island had to offer. In spite of the task ahead of him, the man enjoyed every bite while his source ferreted out additional information. One chatty busboy said the red-haired American had asked a lot of questions about Flores—the temperature, the weather, sites not to miss—in his short stay at the hotel in Ponta Delgada.

The next move wasn't even a decision. It was common sense. After a night's sleep, the man, his contact, and the pilot would be off to Flores.

The man lingered over a locally manufactured cigar, then retired to the same room where the red-haired American had stayed. He nodded in satisfaction. His contact was indeed thorough in his arrangements.

They were closing in on their target.

48

Corvo

It was midafternoon, and Sean was nearing the end of his goal—to reach the top of the Morro dos Homens. For the past hour, the peak had been shrouded in a murky mist, much like his cluttered thoughts.

They circled back to perhaps the biggest question of all—why? Why had his regal, do-no-wrong, reared-with-the-highest-morals mother fallen into an affair or chosen to have an affair? The fact she had done one or the other was irrefutable. Sean was living proof.

Heaviness descended, and dark thoughts taunted him. *She was weak. Willing and ready to fall into his arms. All they needed was a time and a place. If not for that mistake, you wouldn't be alive. You are a mistake. That's why you've felt at odds with life, like you never fit.*

The heaviness crushed him to his knees and shortened his breath. He closed his eyes in agony.

End the mistake, the dark voice insinuated. *Step off the top of the mountain. Simple as that.*

Sean grabbed his head with both hands. “No,” he whispered. “I will not.”

A quietness settled. *Yes, she was weak*, a gentle voice said. *Fragile because she was lonely. Fragmented. Craving love.*

In a flood Sean’s own loneliness in the past couple of months swept over him. *I’m lonely. Feeling fragmented. Craving love.* A memory of the night he met the exotic woman in the bar surfaced. She’d offered herself to him.

Would it really matter if I give in? he’d wondered. He was in a far-flung location. No one would know. He relived the two of them in the hallway. Her touch in just the right place. His craving that touch and more. Intense desire had weakened his resolve.

So what had stopped him?

The same gentle voice that spoke to him now. The voice that told him to stay on the right path.

The mist began to clear from his head.

He had been so close to doing the same thing his mother had. Only one step and a hotel room door away. Who was he to judge her? He’d almost made the same mistake . . . with a stranger.

“I’m so sorry, Mom,” he rasped, his throat clogged with emotion. “So sorry.”

Loneliness and the pain of the revelation intensified into an agonizing knot in his stomach, forcing gut-wrenching sobs. He didn’t know how long he lay on the damp ground or if he fell asleep.

When he at last had the strength, he struggled to his knees, then rose slowly. He opened his eyes and stared in wonder. He was at the top of the Morro dos Homens, surrounded by brilliant blue sky, with a panorama of green valley, rocky cliffs, and shimmering azure waters far below.

His clothing was damp, as if a light rain had misted him.

A Wilson’s storm petrel circled nearby. He’d seen them on

the island in groups, but this one was solo. Small in size and seemingly a weak flyer, it was yet a bird that weathered the roughest of seas around the world but always came home to the far southern oceans to nest.

"I understand," Sean said. He was like that bird, weathering the roughest of seas solo. It would be his choice, his determination that would take him home.

To those who are given much, much is required, the gentle voice said.

Sean nodded. His perspective was now unfettered. He knew the path ahead.

New York City

It wasn't even his usual lunchtime yet, but Will had been antsy and uneasy all morning. Stepping out of the Worthington office building, he headed for Central Park. He needed a brisk walk to take the edge off the foreboding. He hadn't been able to concentrate.

Is there something I should have done differently? He couldn't let the question go. It tormented him.

Was Sean missing or dead because he'd gotten mixed up in the bombing somehow? Fell in with environmentalists more radical than he thought and he couldn't extract himself? Or did he overhear something he shouldn't have, and someone got nervous and decided it was time for Sean to disappear?

Should Will have told Sean right away about the photo of him with the Polar Bear Bomber? Should he have pulled Sean aside before mounting the platform? Given him time to explain? To figure out what happened? To extricate himself, if need be? As much as Will couldn't stand Carson, could that photo be real and not a setup as he hoped? Perhaps Will's reticence to anger his brother had led him into deeper trouble.

Then his mind flipped to Thomas Rich. Should Will have told his mother not to say anything to Sean about his birth father until Will could be there? So he could be by Sean's side . . . follow him to make sure he was okay? Yes, she'd done it spontaneously, but might Will have prevented that revelation or at least controlled the damage of it by forcing a meeting once he knew the truth? Then again, would it have helped or hurt Sean that Ava had told Will first? He was well aware of the rivalry Sean felt toward him.

Business decisions were easy—black-and-white. It was the emotional ones Will struggled with because they never seemed to be reasonable. So he did what he always did in these situations. He phoned Laura as he strolled the pathways of Central Park.

"Can't settle, huh?" she said as soon as she picked up the call.

"You noticed."

"Of course. You tossed and turned until 4:00 this morning, when you finally got out of bed and went to your office."

He winced. "Sorry I kept you up."

"You second-guessing yourself?"

Laura knew.

"Yeah."

"Hmm."

That "hmm" meant one thing. A lecture was coming. His wife was a softie when it came to those she loved, but she didn't have a lot of patience with people who beat themselves up over what they couldn't control or change.

"Will, you can't go back," she said. "But you can act now. Do what you can with Drew to figure out what happened to Sean. We may find out. We may never know. But either way, your father, mother, and sister need you. Your sister most of all, since she doesn't know about the photo or Thomas Rich."

"You're right," he murmured.

"I always am," she fired back. Then, in a softer voice, she added, "Will, you know that photo will come to light sometime. The Jason Carsons of the world like to have and use such leverage. If Sean isn't here to speak for himself, you'll be that steadying force for your family as they try to make sense of it. But in the meanwhile . . ."

He knew the one-two punch was coming, and he braced himself for it.

"Life is much easier if you ride along for some of it, instead of trying to control every aspect of it."

///

"No way could Michael have had any role in the bombing," Jon reported to Sarah. "He's the real deal. Came out of a tough background sunny-side up because of good people in his court. He's actually become deeply religious. He's driven to help other kids like him. I caught up with him right before he boarded a flight from Heathrow to Dublin. Said Mrs. Chesterton had told a friend of mine about him and what he did." Jon chuckled. "That's all I had to say, and he was off running, excited to talk about the theater program and how it had impacted the lives of students."

"So how did you work your way around to asking about Justin Eliot?" she prompted.

"Oh, ye of little faith! Doubting my abilities," he teased. "I simply asked what the inspiration for the program was. He told me about going to St. Mark's school at a rough time in his life. Said acting helped him process what had happened. I asked if any friend was there for him, and he named Justin. Then he paused."

"What kind of pause?" she asked. "A pause like, 'Oh no, you caught me at something,' or like, 'We went separate ways,' or like—"

"Whoa there, missy." He laughed. "All he said with a sad tone was, 'Change is much easier for some people than others.' I asked what he meant. 'Justin's always been troubled,' he told me. 'Here I am, helping lots of people on a different continent, but I can't figure out how to help my best friend. I've tried for years. After his mom died, he felt like God and everybody else was against him. The meds he was on didn't help the paranoia either.' After that, Michael's flight was announced, and he had to go. He said he'd be happy to answer any follow-up questions, though."

"So he said Justin was paranoid," Sarah mused. "Did you ask when he got to see him last?"

"Yes. Said he hadn't seen him in person for a couple of years, but they usually talk on the phone at least once a month. But now it's been a long time since they talked. He admitted he's worried." Jon's voice grew quieter. "I asked him when they'd talked the last time. The date he gave was two days before the bombing."

"He remembered the exact date they talked last?" Sarah asked. "Isn't that a little too—"

"It was Justin's birthday. That's why Michael remembered." He chuckled. "And yes, I verified it against the paperwork we have even before I called you."

"Oh." Sarah deflated. Still, it irked her a bit that Jon could read her mind.

"Hey, it's okay," he said smoothly. "But that's why he could be so specific. Justin had called, excited, saying he got a gig. 'Maybe things will turn around for me,' he told Michael."

"And Michael hasn't heard from him since?"

"No. He says he hopes things did turn around for Justin and that he's been too busy to call. He just wants his friend to be happy."

"Wow. So sad. He has no idea. You didn't tell him, did you?"

"No. I called him for a story. And since the name hasn't been released, I couldn't tell him," Jon said.

"Well, sounds like we just found the closest thing to a next of kin. You'll let Darcy know?" Sarah asked.

"I will."

49

Corvo

The path ahead for Sean Worthington was as clear as the view from the top of Morro dos Homens. Perching on a rock, he dug his cell phone out of his backpack. He hoped it was still charged and he would be able to get a signal from somewhere on the island. It had been two weeks since he'd used it. He shook his head. *I really have been in a fog, haven't I?*

Holding the phone up, he turned in circles at the top of the mountain. One bar only. He hoped it would be enough. He dialed Elizabeth's number.

She picked up immediately. "Listen," she said in a heated voice, "this better be Sean Worthington. If it's not, and you kidnapped him and have his cell phone, then you'd better—"

"Elizabeth, it's me," he said. "Sean."

There was an intake of breath. "Sean?" she whispered.

"I can guarantee it's me. Remember when you climbed aboard the USS *Cantor* in the Arctic? That's—"

"Sean Worthington!" The explosion was full force in his ear, and he winced. "People think you're dead," she railed at him. "Your *family* thinks you're dead. How could you let them think that?"

"What?" He tightened his grip on the phone.

He thought he heard a sob in response. "*I* thought you were dead."

"Why would you think that? Why would they think that?" He frowned. He'd been away from New York City and his family longer than two weeks before on trips, and nobody had thought he was dead. At times Sarah teased, "Hey, I know you'll contact me when you're ready." His family knew he was often out of pocket. So did Elizabeth.

"You disappeared. No texts, no phone messages, no emails, nothing. That's not like you, Sean. Even when I've been too involved in research to check texts and email for a while, I found at least one or more from you when I was done. This time, nothing. I contacted Jon. He hadn't heard either. We've been worried. Jon found out how upset your family was when Sarah asked him if he'd heard from you. Then she started crying."

His tough little sister, falling apart? He was stunned.

Elizabeth powered on. "Drew got a report that someone of your description jumped off the Peace Bridge. Your family thought it was you."

"But why would . . ." Light dawned. He'd stormed away from his parents' place and hadn't spoken to anyone in his family since. Frankly, at that point, he hadn't cared about anything but getting away before he fell apart. He'd been so focused on himself, angry at his mother, wrestling with the betrayal, that he hadn't stopped to wonder how worried she must be.

"I have no idea. All I know is what Jon told me about Sarah. That he has never seen her upset like that."

"I'm so sorry. I didn't think. I just needed to get away." His heart pinched at the pain he'd unwittingly caused.

"Don't you think we all need to get away sometimes? But it's not you to unplug, Sean. It's never been you." He heard her take a shaky breath. "So what happened?" she asked in a gentler tone.

It was so like Elizabeth. She could let him have it with both barrels blazing when he was stupid. Every time she had, he'd deserved it. But she didn't hold grudges. She didn't even mention that she'd hung up on him the last time they'd talked because he was being stupid then too.

She added, "Why did you feel you had to get away?"

He wanted to look into her expressive brown eyes. He wanted to see compassion, understanding. But he also wished to see a hint of . . . more. There, he'd admitted it to himself.

Yet, in that instant, another startling reality struck. He would never do to Jon what Thomas had done to Bill—move in on his territory. He couldn't hurt Jon or Elizabeth that way. A pang of loneliness twinged, and he steeled himself.

"Sean," Elizabeth murmured, "you know I care about you, right? Whether you tell me anything or not about what happened won't change that."

He needed her steady presence, her good listening skills, her ability to process information with clarity, her uncanny awareness of the state of his heart and thoughts. "I know," he finally replied.

Elizabeth, like Jon, had never been impressed with social connections or wealth. There were no strings attached to her acceptance. Of that, he had no doubt. Any pretentions and sidetracks he would have tried with others were stripped away.

"I found out I wasn't who I thought I was," he announced.

"Okay, I'm listening."

She did just that, with no interruption, as he poured out his story. At last he stopped, spent with the telling.

"You said you weren't who you thought you were," she said. "But what really has changed about you? Who you are at your core is the same—your values, your desire to impact the world for good. Sure, your birth father isn't who you thought he was. The way you came to be on this earth is different from what you thought. But haven't you ever done anything you regret?"

A flash of his loneliness and moral weakness that night in Geneva surfaced. "Yes, of course."

"Well then," she declared, "your mother? She has only proved that she's human, capable of making decisions that can alter her own and others' lives. We all are, in more ways than we may ever know. However, without her making that decision, you wouldn't be here. You wouldn't have grown up as a Worthington. You may or may not have had the opportunity or backing to fund others' dreams. Think of the people you've helped—given their dreams the ability to fly. Improved the health and financial picture of some of the poorest communities. I guarantee that your gift to GlobalHealth is saving lives right now in Nepal."

She was on a roll. He didn't try to interrupt. He knew better. Elizabeth would finish what she'd set out to say.

"You've relentlessly pursued making your mark on the world. You've done it differently from the way Will does it and the way Sarah does it. That's because you're you, not them. Not because you don't have official Worthington blood and they do. So get that out of your head right now. Bill, Ava, Will, and Sarah—they're your family. Will and Sarah are still your siblings. They'll love you, even when they know how you arrived on earth."

"Do you know if Sarah—" he began.

"Don't know, and you shouldn't guess," she chided. "Don't go there with Will or your father either. When you look each of them in the eyes, you'll know what they know."

"But what if my father—"

"He may know, or he may not know. You've told me multiple times that he treats you differently. You may finally have the answer as to why, if he does know. If so, you can establish a new and better relationship based on the truth, with nothing hidden between you. If he doesn't know, you and your mother will figure out the right time and the right way to tell him, and your sister, and your brother. That will be up to the two of you to decide."

He was quiet, ruminating.

"You've been thrown a big curveball," she added. "I know you need time to process. But you don't have to decide or do everything at once. Just do one thing."

"Oh yeah? What's that?"

"Get yourself down that mountain and back to New York City. Pronto, buster."

He chuckled. "Yes, ma'am."

"And Sean? Don't ever, ever do that to me again." She ended the call.

He grinned. It was vintage Elizabeth. He'd missed her.

New York City

"I reached Michael Vara right after his flight arrived in Dublin," Darcy told Sarah. "To say he was shocked is an understatement. He told me it couldn't possibly be Justin."

"Why did he think that?"

"He said Justin would never intentionally hurt anyone. His favorite gig was dressing up as an animal for kids' birthday parties."

"That's interesting. So dressing up as a polar bear would make sense," Sarah reasoned. "It wouldn't have been out of Justin's realm."

"But Michael said that Justin couldn't even squash a bug on the sidewalk. He'd step around them," Darcy argued.

"Maybe he didn't like people who hurt animals?" Sarah tried.

"We can talk to Michael in person after he does a positive ID of the body, or what's left of it after the fall."

"He's coming?" Sarah asked. "All the way from Dublin?"

"Yup. Had just flown from Heathrow into Dublin when we talked and said he'd get on the next flight to New York City that he could find. Said it was the least he could do for a good friend—ID him and then make sure he was buried properly."

Now that was a good friend. Sarah was impressed. If someone had to do that for her, who would it be? Her mind evaluated her large circle of friends and discounted most of them. Sure, they were fun to hang around with, but would they stick up for her in the same situation? She doubted it.

Only two were in that category—Darcy and now Jon.

Interesting how swiftly she zeroed in on the truth.

50

Corvo

Sean descended the mountain far more rapidly than he'd ascended it. His cell was now dead. It was a miracle that it had worked anyway to call Elizabeth in such a remote location. With no landlines he knew about on the island, he wouldn't be able to call his pilot in Flores and tell him to come earlier than planned. Otherwise he'd be stuck on Corvo for another five or six days until the pilot arrived. The beautiful paradise now resembled prison bars since he couldn't leave at his leisure.

It took him less than five minutes to pack his belongings. He closed the door on his temporary island home and strode toward the closest inlet and a grouping of several small fishing boats.

In his wide travels, he'd picked up smatterings of languages. Using hand gestures and the little Portuguese he knew, he managed to get his point across to one of the native fishermen. When Sean pantomimed leaving now, though, the fisherman shook his head. He pointed to the setting sun and poured out a volume of words. The ones Sean picked out were "rough seas," "not night," and "morning fish."

He got the picture. His ride would be going nowhere tonight, but he could plan on it in the morning. To make sure he wouldn't miss it, he'd be there waiting as soon as the first ray of sun hit. The people of the island didn't go by schedules.

He smiled widely, bowed his head to thank his soon-to-be-host, and headed back for the small house.

New York City

Sarah had just walked in her front door that evening when her cell dinged with a text.

Darcy

MV on red-eye from Dublin. Meet my office 11 a.m.?

Sarah

Be there.

Tomorrow they'd hopefully have long-awaited answers about the Polar Bear Bomber.

Corvo

Sean lay restless in what the islanders considered a large bed. To him, it resembled a slightly wider twin, and his feet poked out the end. He chafed at the delay of the overnight, mentally kicking himself for being so thoughtless.

A line from the *I Love Lucy* reruns his sister loved to watch ran through his head: "You got some 'splainin' to do!" Boy, did he. But what could he say? Especially if three of his family members didn't know why he'd run? "Uh, I decided spontaneously to take a vacation away from everything, without letting anyone know"?

He shook his head. He knew that wouldn't fly.

His mom would be guilt-ridden and try to spirit him away privately to apologize. She'd say it was her fault and she'd find a way to make it right. But there was no way to make it right. What was done was done. There was no undoing it. He was living proof of her affair. If Bill didn't know about it, the truth about Sean's birth might drive his parents apart.

He shook his head. *My parents.* How easily he still thought of them as that, even though he now knew Thomas Rich was his father.

Bill? He'd be livid. "Of all the stupid things you've done in your life, this one's at the top. What were you thinking, worrying your mother and sister like that?" In every stressful situation, Bill only mentioned worrying the women in their family, never the men. Guys weren't supposed to have feelings. They were scripted to be steady, even-keeled, passionate only about growing Worthington wealth—like Bill and Will.

As usual, any emotional damage the family had suffered in the interim would be Sean's fault. Even more, if Bill did know about Sean's birth father, how would he treat "the boy" now?

Will? He'd adopt that steely, disappointed, "Wow, you went over the edge this time, little brother" expression. He'd watch with that condemning look from the sidelines while the rest of the family rained verbal chaos down on Sean's head. Later Will would wrangle the why out of Sean through rapid-fire questions that unnerved even his toughest adversaries.

And Sarah? She'd race to him and hug him fiercely. Then, after telling everybody else to back off, she'd personally give him grief for scaring them.

He deserved anything they dished out. How had he gotten so far off track that he'd only thought about himself? One night of pursuing his desires could have ruined what he wanted to build with someone like Elizabeth. Two weeks had seemed a short time away to process such a big revelation. But if he'd lived through 14 days of thinking Will or Sarah were dead . . .

He had a choice to make. Either he could let the guilt incapacitate him—for his night of weakness, for terrifying his family—or he could buck up, hightail it back to New York, and take the heat and any consequences that followed. Doing so would take courage, yes, but Sean had only backed down once in his life and fled. He would not do so again.

The gentle voice spoke again. *To those who are given much, much is required.*

And there it was. His time on the mountain had clarified his focus.

The media spotlight had often been on him as a Worthington. He'd played that up at formal events and anywhere else the paparazzi caught up with him. He was the Worthington most photographed—the one the tabloids buzzed about—and with just cause. Will, who spent his time mainly in the boardroom and secreted away in his office building, warranted a *Time* magazine cover or two but wasn't interesting fodder for the tabloids. Sarah had been in the limelight as a teenager and at university for her antics, diverse causes, fund-raising, and social networking. A week didn't pass without her face and most recent event splashed across the gossip pages. But once she'd taken her job with the DOJ and become deeply religious, she'd seemed to settle.

That left Sean, the high-living bachelor, as the king of the party circuit. But Sean had grown tired of the stilted, banal conversation and of himself being the focus, with the causes he believed in garnering only a brief mention amid the gossip.

The arena of politics was not for him, he had decided. Especially since he wasn't really a Republican and wasn't really a Democrat. He believed both political parties had their pros and cons, and it had always troubled him that people in general bought so blindly into one or the other, mainly because family or friends were Republican or Democrat. It was difficult for anyone to step away from their tribe and risk potential dissension.

Sean knew well how to work the system after Will's run for Senate. But he didn't want to. That wasn't where his passions lay. He knew he owed Kiki Estrada a call. She wouldn't be happy, but he needed to catch her before she got the steam engines rolling.

So what was he good at? What did he really want to do—for himself? If he could choose to do anything, and he hadn't been thrust into the role he had with Worthington Shares, what would he do?

As the night deepened, he wrestled with those questions. At last, exhausted, he squinted in the dark toward his backpack. After fumbling to light a lamp, he withdrew the book his sister had given him. He'd never cracked it open, never felt the need. The Bible stories he'd heard in childhood had stayed there, relegated to his past instead of his adult life. Now the book drew him.

Opening the first page, he saw his sister's scribbles.

To Sean. Light for your path. Love you to the moon and back. Sarah.

It made him miss her all the more.

He flipped a chunk of pages and read the words his eyes landed on in the flickering lamplight. "Whatever you did for one of the least of these brothers and sisters of mine, you did for me."

There it was again—the clarity that cut through the muddle.

Every life is precious, Sean thought. *Every life matters.* Suddenly he realized the truth of the creation story in Genesis. *God has breathed life, his spirit, into human beings. We are made in his image. That means something. That breath of life is what gives every human being infinite value, something not defined by wealth or circumstances.*

At last the something "wholly other" he always felt in Nepal made sense.

Somewhere, most likely in a paradise now beneath the Persian Gulf, God had chosen to create man and woman in his image. There, in that paradise formed at the nexus of fertile land and abundant freshwater, he had literally breathed life into the human species that had evolved for hundreds of thousands of years and struggled to survive on the surface of the earth. And humankind moved forward to conquer the entire earth from there—a "wholly other" species endowed with the breath of life from God. Sean closed his eyes, remembering the infinite spirit he saw in the faces and lives of the Nepali people. The same kind of spirit he always felt among those who had little and often struggled for survival. Yet they were the most joyful people he had ever met.

In a flash, Sean knew the path ahead. What he loved most was meeting new people from financially challenged areas and seeing the light of joy in their eyes when he told them he could back their dream, improve life for them and others in their communities. He smiled as he thought of the summers he'd spent in Malawi with his mother, squatting in the dirt with the villagers as they figured out the best location to dig a well or build a medical clinic.

What would he do now? He laughed out loud as he placed the book on the floor by the bed. Exactly what he had been doing, but with a very different goal. He had pursued growing

Worthington Shares through start-ups—and had won overall in the financial bottom line for the company. Along the way he had assisted fledgling businesses in underdeveloped countries and helped improve scores of communities.

But what if, instead, he flipped his thinking? Started with the goal of finding the best ways to make a positive mark on communities for the long haul? What if he even moved to a particular place in the world, got to know the locale, and then brainstormed or identified ventures that Worthington Shares could put their financial muscle behind that could benefit people the most?

As Elizabeth had said, who he was at his core had not changed. He would combine what he was best at—networking, brainstorming, problem solving, traveling at a moment's notice, maneuvering multiple cultures and languages and feeling comfortable doing so—and use it strategically to benefit those with the deepest need. Instead of considering the company's financial growth model as the tipping point—that the ventures would contribute to the Worthington bottom-dollar spreadsheets—he'd make his goal first to improve the lives of the poor across the world, in whatever way he could. Sure, the Worthingtons gave to a lot of charities. Giving a check and putting boots on the ground were completely different ventures. A combination of the two? Just think what might be accomplished!

The ideas were a shot of adrenaline.

Elizabeth was right. Worthington money was a gift, even though at times he'd considered it a curse because of the social trappings and responsibilities that came with it. Now, however, no matter how he had become a Worthington, he was committed to using the resources that had been granted him to make a lasting mark on the planet for good.

Those decisions made, serenity cloaked him.

At last he slept.

51

NEW YORK CITY

Michael Vara settled shakily into the chair Darcy offered him in her office after he viewed the body. His hands were trembling. His olive-toned face was pale and sickly. "I know that's Justin, but I still don't believe it. There's no way he bombed that building."

"We have film of him carrying that backpack and leaving it next to the building," Sarah said gently.

"Then he couldn't have known what was in the backpack," Michael insisted, gripping the arms of the chair. A lock of his dark curly hair fell over one eye as he looked up at her. "A couple of days before the bombing I talked to him. He said he was just hired for a gig. He was so happy—it was the first one he'd had for a long time. Maybe he'd even make enough to get out of the city, to get a plane ticket to meet me in Dublin, he said."

Michael dropped his head into his hands. "He'd talked about needing a fresh start. I'd told him for a long time that he needed to get out of New York. He was doing things lately that he didn't want to do. I told him he could always stay at my place for free."

Sarah and Darcy exchanged glances.

"You said 'doing things he didn't want to do.' What kind of things do you mean?" Darcy asked.

Michael shuddered. "Dangerous underground shows. Metal bars on windows, bulletproof glass . . . those kinds of things. I told him to stay away."

"Ah."

"That's why he was so happy to get an easy two-hour gig that paid well. All he had to do was dress up in some kind of costume, carry a backpack, and wander around for a while, he said. Make sure he was noticed. Then he'd get a couple grand. I thought it was kinda weird." He looked up. "Then again, New Yorkers are weird."

Sarah nodded. "That matches what we saw in the video."

"He definitely didn't say anything about carrying a bomb. He was happy and not nervous. If he'd been about to do something illegal, I would have known. It would have come through in his voice, like when he told me about the underground shows."

"Okay, so let's follow that theory—that he didn't know what he was carrying in the backpack," Darcy said.

Michael frowned. "There's no way he knew."

"How do you think he would have reacted psychologically when he discovered that he'd delivered a bomb that took out part of a building and could have hurt a bunch of people?" Darcy asked.

"He would have been devastated."

"Enough to jump off a building?"

"No." The answer was sharp, definitive. Then he wavered. "Maybe." A long sigh. "I don't know. Justin went through a lot of ups and downs, but he never once told me he wanted to end his life."

"Michael," Sarah asked, "if we showed you the suicide note, could you identify it as Justin's handwriting or not?"

Darcy crooked her finger at one of the DHS staff outside the glass partition. He poked his head in, handed the note to her, and shut the door again.

"What do you think?" Darcy handed the note to him.

Michael was silent as he read. Then his eyes moved back to the top of the letter, and he traced it line by line with his index finger. At last he looked up. "Justin didn't write this note. If he was upset enough to decide to kill himself, he wouldn't be able to think clearly enough to be this organized. He'd be rattled. Writing sporadic words, phrases, in stream of consciousness, not full sentences explaining why he decided to bomb the building and kill himself. And Green Justice? He never mentioned Green Justice or hating oil companies."

He swept his hand over the paper. "And see the type of pen he used? I hate blue ballpoint pens, and so did he. It was one of those quirky things we had in common. I only have black fine Sharpies and calligraphy pens in my apartment. So if he wrote it there, where did he get the blue ballpoint pen? Did they find it in the apartment?"

Darcy looked startled. "Don't even know if anyone searched for that."

"If it isn't there, that would mean he, or whoever wrote the note, didn't write it at my apartment," Michael reasoned. "Unless Justin had the pen in his pocket . . ."

". . . and it flew out when he jumped off the building," Sarah finished.

"The handwriting is totally different," Michael added. "Before I started working overseas, he'd write me notes when he was doing fine and when he was doing badly and leave them at my flat sometimes. The handwriting styles were hardly recognizable as the same person. When he was doing fine, he used my calligraphy pens in a beautifully flowing script. When he was doing badly, he printed with the black Sharpies, and it was jerky. Short words, but sentences. Never in blue ink. This?" He shook his head. "It's not Justin."

"Did Justin have the technical ability to figure out how to put a bomb together?" Darcy asked.

Michael blinked. "Justin? He didn't know how to check the circuit breaker in their house when the electricity blew. I had to come over and do it for him and his mom. No way. Somebody had to have delivered that bomb to him ready to go."

"Perhaps it was set on a timer when he was given the backpack or had a remote detonation," Sarah said.

"Justin wouldn't have done it if he had known anyone could be harmed. Dressing up in a costume was second nature to him. We do it in the theater all the time. But planting a bomb? No. Not even at his worst. He only wanted his name in lights. Said his mother told him he'd make it big someday . . . be in the news." Michael slumped. "Never would have guessed it would be this way."

"One last question," Darcy said. "Did anyone other than you know that Justin sometimes stayed at your place?"

He frowned. "Only Mrs. Chesterton. I'm pretty sure I told her he sometimes stayed there. Neighbors in my building might have noticed him coming and going, but they wouldn't know he was staying there. They'd probably assume he was visiting someone. The tenants change a lot in that building."

Sarah and Darcy exchanged a glance. Neither Michael nor Mrs. Chesterton would have anything to do with Justin's death. Dead end there.

Michael winced. "She's such a dear lady. I hate to tell her the news . . . if it's okay for me to tell her?"

Darcy nodded. "Now that you've officially identified the body and there is no next of kin, the name will be released."

"How soon?" he asked. "I'd like to let Mrs. Chesterton know and make burial arrangements for Justin. I think it would be better to have that taken care of before his name is released."

"I understand," Darcy said. "If you can make arrangements right away, we can have the body moved and I'll make a request to stall the release of the name for 48 to 72 hours to allow you to make the final arrangements."

"Thank you." Michael lifted his chin. "Justin had problems, but he was my friend. I believe someday the truth will be revealed, and I want to be there when it is. If you need my help on anything, count me in." His dark eyes narrowed in determination. "My friend doesn't deserve a role in history as a terrorist."

After Michael left, Sarah eyed Darcy. "You thinking what I'm thinking?"

"Yep. Justin was helped off that building."

Sarah nodded. She got out of her chair and paced as she talked, ticking the points off on her fingers. "Not only did somebody make sure Catherine Englewood got him on camera, but they provided him with the backpack and bomb. They gave him instructions where to leave the evidence—incriminating the ecological activist contingent. Nobody would be that dumb to leave evidence behind their buildings. Evidence of his insanity and a signed confession were planted at Michael's apartment."

"Hey, wait right there. Who else other than Michael and Mrs. Chesterton knew that Justin stayed there sometimes?"

"That," Sarah declared, "is the million-dollar question. It means there's another player, or two, or more. And to ensure that Justin couldn't help us put together the pieces, he was lured to the roof of that building."

"Maybe even herded off it."

"Exactly. Now we have to prove it."

En Route from Corvo to Flores, Azores Islands

The sun was barely up. Sean inhaled the briny scent of the North Atlantic. Like his mother, he felt most at home on the water. She'd joked it was due to her generations of Irish roots. Now he knew why it was doubly so for him.

He'd crossed a lot of oceans on his start-up trips lately, but the last time he'd been on a boat was the USS *Cantor* in the Arctic Ocean. The ice floes there were a far cry from the tropical warmth that surrounded the fishing boat he was on now, even early in the morning. Yet he preferred that icy, untamed wilderness because Elizabeth had been there. Yes, he admitted, wherever he was with her felt like home. Upon hearing her voice yesterday, he'd been ready to say, "Remember when you climbed aboard the USS *Cantor* in the Arctic? That's when I knew I was in love with you."

But he'd halted midstream. With Jon revealing his interest, Sean could never betray those friendships. They were too important to him. Still, his heart twinged at the possibilities that would never be. Lifting his face, he welcomed the breezy mist from the ocean.

Soon he'd be back on Flores. He'd gather his pilot from the hotel courtyard where he likely lay soaking up the sun and the views of the beautiful native women. After a short jaunt to Ponta Delgada, where they'd fuel up and stay the night, they'd head to New York City.

He'd be there sometime the next day.

En Route from Ponta Delgada to Flores

The man was irritated with the delays at Nordela Airport that had kept his private jet grounded until midmorning. When they were at last in the air, he settled back in the white leather chair.

His contact approached hesitantly. "Sir?"

"What now?" the man barked.

"His cell number has popped up on the grid as being in use," the contact reported.

There were only three options. One, Sean was alive and had taken a mini vacation from technology. Two, he'd been taken against his will, and now the kidnappers were making demands. Or three, someone had found his cell and was using it.

"Where?" the man demanded.

His contact flinched at the tone. "We're tracking it as we speak. I should know soon."

"I want to know when that call was placed and to whom, and triangulate the origination."

His contact nodded and placed other calls rapid-fire. Within five minutes, he announced, "The call was placed midafternoon yesterday."

"Yesterday! So why are we just finding out about it now? And to whom?"

"An Elizabeth Shapiro. I'll have a bio and other details shortly."

But the man didn't need the bio and other details. He knew who Elizabeth Shapiro was. It was his business to know. His contact didn't know everything about him. He'd learned early in his career that the best way to keep matters private was to keep them to yourself. So he only nodded. "She is a secondary issue for now. Focus on the triangulation of the call."

"Got it, Boss."

52

FLORES, AZORES ISLANDS

As soon as Sean stepped off the fishing boat in Flores, he sprinted to the nearby hotel where he'd retained rooms for himself and his pilot while he was on Corvo.

He was right. The pilot was sunning himself and enjoying being waited on by the local women. A dark-haired beauty was holding a fruity drink out to him as Sean approached.

Sean waved her off with a finger. "Hey." He nudged the pilot. "Gotta go."

The pilot sat up, looking disoriented for a minute. Then he was all business. "Okay, sir. Where to?"

Sean liked that. The pilot didn't argue or ask why he was almost a week earlier than they'd planned. He simply asked for next instructions.

"To Ponta Delgada as soon as you get the plane ready and fueled. Then when we're in the air, I'll let you know where to next."

The pilot nodded once. "On it." A split second later he'd

grabbed his towel and was off the chaise lounge, striding toward the hotel building.

The pilot was a man of few words, didn't pry or need to know reasons, and moved quickly. He also didn't seem to be the gossipy type, and he'd been paid well not to reveal anything about his passenger.

Sean had learned a thing or two about secrecy as a Worthington. Whenever he didn't want to be splashed across the press, he used his middle name and no last name in any arrangements. He'd done that this time to hire the pilot and had paid for everything in cash. When that many Ben Franklins were handed over, the pilot seemed more than happy not to press for any other details.

Sean headed back to his room. While he waited for his cell to charge, he sat with his head in his hands. He knew the call he needed to make next—to Jon. He had to apologize for his actions and come clean about his jealousy. In the meanwhile, he took a shower to clear his head. The last time he'd had one was when the rain washed him on the mountaintop in Corvo.

New York City

Drew shut the door, then took a seat across from Will in his office. "You know what it means as well as I do."

Will nodded. "Sure. When Sandstrom is arrested—and that's a foregone conclusion from what Sarah has been able to tell me—they'll be looking for a new or at least an interim CEO."

There were rumors of the board being nervous and restless. Sandstrom continued to claim to the inside circle that any proof the DOJ had was circumstantial only—that the internal memos revealed his purpose to make oil economical to the American people. That was what would hold up in court, Sandstrom was confident. But several board members had been heard muttering that they should have listened more closely to Will, instead of being swayed by the silver-tongued Sandstrom.

"Nobody knows more about AF than you." Drew studied Will.

"Except Frank Stapleton. His business experience is broader than mine. After all, he's the guy who took me under his wing."

Drew lifted a brow. "Yes, but sometimes the student can learn to outperform the teacher."

Will laughed. "Your proverb for the day?"

Drew's eyes twinkled. "Maybe. But Stapleton isn't in the direct loop of all your research before AF drilled in the Arctic. He doesn't have the combination of scientific knowledge and business acumen that will be required to guide AF through the Arctic crisis." He paused. "Neither has he been following every move of AF's and Sandstrom's like you have, even since you left the board."

"Okay." Will shrugged. "You got me. You know I can't let it go."

Drew tilted his head. "Maybe that's because you aren't supposed to let it go."

"But we sold the Worthington shares," Will argued for the sake of arguing, even though the tactic rarely worked with Drew.

Drew lifted his hands. "So? Shares are bought and sold every day. You said so yourself. There are lots of places to invest in New York. That means nothing. But it does pave the way for you to be clearheaded about the decision, should you be asked."

"And you know this because . . ."

"The way I know everything. Now is the time to start thinking about how you might want to respond."

"Already have. You know I can't say no to that challenge. I've been groomed for it. I thought I wanted it, that it was mine to take on. Got sidetracked for a while. Never thought I'd need to take it on when it was in the worst crisis of its history, though."

Drew got up from his chair, smiling. "That's exactly what I thought you'd say." He strode to the door, then swiveled right before he grasped the handle. "Interesting about companies in crisis. That's when the greatest change for the good can occur."

He didn't have to say anything else. Will knew what he was implying. They'd talked about it before. There was no one better prepared or more able to tackle AF's needed move toward clean energy than Will Worthington. He already had a road map. Had planned the sign markers along the way for several years. The fossil fuel era was ending. The clean energy revolution was dawning. Great business leaders recognized these tectonic changes in the marketplace. Will did in a way that Eric Sandstrom never would. Now was the time to create a new blueprint for American Frontier that would be good for the bottom line—and even better for the planet.

As Drew exited the office, Will stared out the large glass window with the impressive overview of Madison Avenue. Yes, he could and would make that blueprint happen. Now all he needed was the opportunity, which he had no doubt would come his way.

En Route from Ponta Delgada to Flores

The contact's phone rang again. "Okay, got it." As soon as he ended the call, he announced, "Corvo."

The man's eyes widened. So Sean was alive. The other two options fell by the wayside. He twirled his finger in a single circle.

The contact hurried toward the cockpit.

Within a few minutes, the plane had changed course toward the small island of Corvo.

53

Ponta Delgada

Sean took a deep breath before he phoned Jon.

"So you definitely didn't jump off a bridge," Jon said in his usual unruffled manner. "I told Elizabeth there was no way. That wasn't you. She was frantic."

Elizabeth, frantic? About me?

"I'm not going to ask where you've been—or why," Jon added. "But you've had a lot of other people frantic too, including your sister."

Remorse flooded Sean again. "I, uh, needed a little time away."

"Nice line, but I'm not buying it. Tell me you're on your way home to face the music."

"Yes, as soon as I can get there. Looks like tomorrow."

"And you're not going to call them until then, are you? You're just going to show up?"

"I have things to tell them that I need to say in person," Sean explained. "But I called Elizabeth. I also need to say something to you."

The newsroom noise faded into the background as if Jon was moving to another room.

"I'm listening," Jon said.

"Remember the last time we talked? When you said you wanted to pursue Elizabeth, and I said that was fine with me?"

"Sure do, but—"

"Wait. Let me get this out. It isn't fine. When we were on board the *Cantor*, I realized something but didn't have the courage to act." He paused, knowing his next words might irrevocably alter his friendship with Jon. "I love Elizabeth and have for some time. But I will never act on that love, if you feel that way about her—"

"Sean—"

"Shut up, man." Sean paced the hotel room. "It's hard enough to get this out without you interrupting. I recently learned something about myself, and that's why it's so important I explain this to you now. I refuse to make the same mistake that someone else did. Betray the two friends most important to me in the world."

"Okay, now you shut up," Jon retorted. "Because you're not making sense. But there's something you don't know since you've taken your trip to . . . well, wherever you are. When Elizabeth thought you might be dead, she was a mess. She said her last words to you weren't kind. Evidently you two got in an argument."

"Yeah, I was stupid—"

"Hey, don't want to know why. That's between you and her. I could have told her at that point that I was interested in her. But I kept hearing this little voice in my head saying, 'It's not her. But you'll know when you find her.'"

"Wait—you mean you're not interested in Elizabeth?"

"Are you even listening to what I'm saying?" Jon said more

loudly. "Elizabeth is my friend. You're my friend. I thought I might be interested, but when she thought you might be dead, I knew why the voice had told me to wait. She loves you, not me."

Sean was stunned speechless.

Jon's voice broke through the fog in Sean's head. "Hello? You still on the planet?"

"You're sure?" he managed.

"Of course I'm sure. So when you get your miserable carcass back to New York and make things right with your family—good luck with that—you better get on the first flight to Elizabeth and make that declaration. Time's a-wastin'." Jon laughed.

"So you're okay with it?"

"Absolutely." The single word rang with Jon's usual tone and confidence.

Sean sighed. "I'm so glad."

"There's one thing I'm not okay with, though." Jon chuckled.

Sean frowned. "What's that?"

"Standing any longer in the bathroom to have this conversation. It's the only quiet place to talk around here."

Near Corvo

The man peered out the jet's window as the lush island of Corvo came into view. His phone rang.

He listened briefly, then hung up.

So, Sarah Worthington would be nominated as attorney general. The vetting would be a brutal process, with no certainty that she'd be confirmed by the Senate. The Worthington name carried both prestige and political baggage, even though no family member had ever cashed in their deep political and financial chips for a seat in the Oval Office. Senators on both sides of the aisle would praise and condemn her, for their own reasons.

The man stroked his lip. Suddenly the reason for the sudden promotion became clear.

It's Frank Stapleton, isn't it? He's the power broker. Stapleton had convinced Spencer he had to buy Sarah off. What did she know? Or was this solely an attempt to end her passionate search for connections on the AF bombing?

Word had reached the man that Darcy Wiggins, a DHS veteran not known for giving up, and *New York Times* reporter Jon Gillibrand had teamed up with Sarah to research the case about the Polar Bear Bomber. The man frowned. Anyone else in the know his contact had talked to seemed to think the case was dead, just like the bomber. End of story. Why then did Sarah and her colleagues continue to pursue it so relentlessly?

And why was Stapleton working so hard to distract her? What did Stapleton, AF, and Spencer have to lose besides a little potential embarrassment in the media? Sure, they were connected to the Arctic crisis and thus were smarting. But it wouldn't take long for the press to refocus all the heat on the CEO, Eric Sandstrom. He'd be the scapegoat, and AF and the board would simply look caught in the middle of a dirty-dealing CEO.

The man scowled. So why would they pull so many strings to get a hot young DOJ attorney from one of the most prominent families in America off the case?

Something more was brewing. And it had to be big. The man wouldn't rest until he ferreted out what it was.

But first things first. Soon they'd land on Corvo. With any luck, they'd be able to finish the mission that had taken them to an archipelago of tiny islands that many hadn't even heard of out in the Atlantic Ocean.

54

NEW YORK CITY

Sarah was glad for days like today, when work had been so busy she'd barely had time to think about anything else. It dulled the deep ache of her brother still being missing.

But when her world slowed down and she entered the door of her suite, loneliness descended. She tried to shake it off. Maybe it was because she'd waved off the requests of a couple of co-workers to join them for Friday night dinner and had headed home instead.

She slipped into yoga pants and a simple T-shirt. As she contemplated what to have for dinner, the doorbell sounded.

She frowned. People didn't show up unannounced in her building if the bellman was doing his job. He knew her family, though, and which frequent visitors were approved, and he had her permission to let them come on up. But her mother and father were at their home in Chautauqua, and Will would always call. So that left Darcy. She grinned widely as she opened the door. "Hey, Darc—"

But it wasn't Darcy. It was Jon, holding a large bag of aromatic Thai food.

"Called work and was going to stop by there," he explained, "but you'd already left. Thought you might like an easy dinner. Maybe some entertainment." He extended several movie rentals in his other hand.

"Wow, perfect. Who am I to turn down an offer like that?" She waved him in. Leave it to Jon to charm his way in through the friendly doorman. Then again, maybe the doorman had gotten used to seeing Jon when he, Sarah, and Darcy had been working on the Polar Bear Bomber case at her penthouse.

They unpacked the food on the kitchen countertop, pulled up stools, and dove in like neither of them had eaten in days.

"You have no idea how much I needed this." She gestured with her chopsticks. "Or the company. Thanks."

His gentle gaze rested on her. "Maybe I do."

Why did she have the feeling he knew more than he was telling her?

Corvo

The man peered out the bedroom window of a small white house. There were no hotels on the island, but a villager had told him he knew of a house recently vacated and had escorted him there. His contact would bunk on the miniscule sofa in the living room that was a breath away. The pilot was staying with a local family nearby.

The villagers were friendly but seemed wary. *They must not receive visitors often. Good*, he thought. It would be easier to track Sean. A stranger, especially a redheaded Easterner, would stand out.

But rain had descended, sending the villagers scurrying inside and turning the paths into mudslides. His contact had come back drenched and filthy and said it was hopeless finding anything out tonight. He'd try again in the morning.

The man sank onto the thin mattress. He tried to roll over and almost fell off the narrow bed. As his hand swept the floor, he touched the corner of something hard. He reached further under the bed and pulled out a book. A Bible.

Disgust swept over him. Even here, in the middle of the Atlantic, he couldn't get away from it. Lately he'd had the uncomfortable feeling that he was being pursued. All the mistakes he'd made in life had loomed even larger.

He flipped open the book to the first page. In the dying light he squinted at what was scribbled there.

To Sean. Light for your path. Love you to the moon and back. Sarah.

He sat up, then jumped up, nearly hitting his head on the low ceiling.

So Sean had been here, right here, not long ago.

But where was he now? Still on the island? Or had he already left?

It would be way too long until morning.

55

New York City

As soon as Sean's private plane touched down outside New York City, he hailed a cab and headed immediately for Will's place. One peek at his face reflected in the cabbie's rearview mirror and he winced. They'd left Portugal at dawn. He was grizzled and grubby, looking too much like a mountain man. He hoped he didn't smell like one. But he didn't want to stop at his apartment first. He had to set things right with his brother.

Sean admitted it. He needed Will's wisdom—his brother's clear thinking—even if it came with a boatload of sternness and the lecture Sean knew he deserved. Half of him hoped Will knew about Thomas Rich. The other half dreaded it if he did.

Sean knew that Will would be home. His brother was predictable, his weekly schedule like clockwork. At this time on a Saturday he'd be home. There was no time like the present for a reunion.

After smiling at and greeting the doorman, who did a double

take at Sean's appearance, Sean took the elevator to Will's place. He rang the doorbell and waited.

Footsteps neared the door, and then the door opened partway.

Will stood there, dressed casually. He looked tired. Upon seeing Sean, his eyes widened and he sagged against the door. "You're . . . here," he managed. "Alive!" Hurt, confusion, and happiness warred for a place on his face. He seemed unable to move.

"You're right," Sean said brokenly. "You've always been right. I don't think through my actions, how they'll come off to others. I am so sor—"

Will grabbed Sean in a fierce embrace. "I thought you were dead. All of us thought you were dead."

Then the distanced, upright, proper Will did something uncharacteristic. He began to cry like a baby. "Sean," Will whispered, "I . . . love . . . you."

It was the first time Sean could remember hearing those words from his brother. His own eyes brimmed and spilled over.

Shock, grief, and the release of pent-up emotions skittered down Will's spine as he embraced his brother. Sean was alive. Home.

All too soon, though, Will's thoughts raced. *Where has he been all this time?* He wanted the details, had to know the details, to make sense of the situation.

Not yet, the still small voice said. *The answers will come. Be patient.*

So instead he stood with his brother in the private space outside his front door. Never had Will been more grateful that only his family and Drew's family knew the code to get to their penthouse suite. Here they could talk unimpeded.

At last Sean broke free. "You know, don't you? About Thomas? Now I understand why you walked away from the Senate bid."

Will blinked. So Sean thought that was the sole reason. He didn't know the rest of the story.

Not yet, the voice said again. *For today this is enough*.

Someday Will would have to tell him, but now wasn't the time. As important as it was for him to be in control, he was learning to trust that voice. "Yes," Will replied. "A brother's love."

"All this time," Sean whispered, "I was angry at you. I had no idea."

"I promised Mom I would do all I could to protect you."

"So you gave up your dream for me." Sean stated it directly, but there was pain in the words.

"No, I gave up one dream."

"I should have trusted you."

Will looked him in the eye. "Yes."

"Does Dad know?"

Will nodded. "He does now."

"He didn't before?" Sean asked.

"Not for sure, though he had some guesses over the years."

"I see. And Sarah?"

"I don't think so. Mom didn't tell her. Dad doesn't want us to tell her, so I haven't. He wants to protect her."

He saw the acknowledgment in Sean's eyes. "I understand."

"So are you going to let Mom know you're alive? And Sarah? Right away?" Will pressed.

Sean laughed. "Now you're sounding like my brother."

56

Sean stopped by his place at One Madison to drop off his backpack, take a shower, shave, and grab fresh clothes before heading to Chautauqua. Both he and Will had agreed it would be best if their mother saw him in person.

He leafed through the stack of mail that his housekeeper had brought in while he was away. One envelope with no return address and handwriting he didn't recognize stood out. He opened it out of curiosity.

Think twice about running for governor. Secrets have a way of becoming public.

The text was written in blue ballpoint pen.

He turned the note over. Blank. *Weird.*

So who else knew that Worthington blood didn't run through his veins? That had to be it. It was the only secret he had. Thank goodness he'd already decided that politics wasn't for him. The note only confirmed it. He would never put his family—especially his mom—through the scrutiny the family would face now if he ran for public office.

Still, the note grated. He balled it up in his fist. Sean hated bullies. He wasn't about to let them get the upper hand. His brother was the only human he'd allow to play that ace-card role in his life. Sean acknowledged that now. He would have made a lot fewer mistakes if he'd listened to Will instead of trying to compete with him as they grew up.

His eyes flicked back to the note in his hand, now a mangled ball. Maybe he should keep it. He spread it out on the desk, smoothing out the wrinkles and tears, and slipped it inside a book. Who else knew about his birth father? Only Thomas himself, as far as Sean could figure it. Then a flash of recall hit. Just before his brother had announced he wouldn't run, Sean had seen Jason Carson standing by the stage. Had Carson somehow found out about Sean and threatened Will with releasing that knowledge? Was that the entire truth about why Will stepped out? Because not only had their mother told Will, but Carson had dangled the secret in front of Will like a hangman's noose?

The idea incensed Sean. The slime! What exactly did Carson have against the Worthingtons anyway? Or was he merely a puppet, with his master behind the scenes pulling the strings? Had Sandstrom been behind that too?

"Will," Laura cautioned, "let it go. You can't control things in this situation. You have to let Sean handle it—alone."

Will knew she was right, but he felt helpless. He hated that feeling. He wanted to control the situation, halt his mom's grief and Sarah's by letting them know immediately that Sean was alive.

Laura hugged him. "I know. You're a fixer. This goes against your grain. But Sean isn't little anymore. Big brother can't and shouldn't fix things in his life now."

So Will painfully relinquished control. He couldn't do anything but that, since Laura had taken his cell phone from his pocket. He knew she was right, though.

"Okay, okay, I promise I won't call."

Laura stepped back. "Good for you. And I'll help you keep that promise." She smiled, waggled his cell phone in her hand, and made her way into the kitchen.

He felt limp. Emotion had never been easy for him. Things that could be quantified—numbers, statistics—were much more comfortable.

He absentmindedly picked up the morning paper from the foyer table. He'd been about to start reading it after waking up late when Sean knocked on the door.

Jason Carson seemed unstoppable. The whistle-blower was still being painted as a good guy whose conscience had led him to reveal Sandstrom's dirty dealings. Will wondered what Carson's next revelation would be. Not only had he derailed Will from the Senate race by holding a photo of his brother with the Polar Bear Bomber over his head, but Carson still held that power. At any time he could choose to destroy Sean—and the Worthington family as a whole in the eyes of the world—by revealing that photo. And what better way to do it than in the eyes of a primed public? Especially with the speculation about Sean running for governor of New York?

Will it happen all over again—what happened to me? Except hold my brother hostage this time?

Other than his father and Laura, Will didn't care what people thought of him. But Sean's network was critically important to him. He thrived on what other people thought of him. That was why he'd been so upset and embarrassed when Will conceded the race. So what would it do to Sean to have his own neck in a noose?

Will's big-brother protectiveness rose to the forefront again. He couldn't let that happen to Sean. He knew exactly who to contact.

Corvo

At last the man had gotten answers. The contact had wangled the information out of a local fisherman that he'd transported a well-paying red-haired American to Flores.

Irritated, the man ordered his pilot to ready the plane for an immediate departure.

He took Sean's book with him.

57

NEW YORK CITY

Once Sean was in his Jeep, he paused before he put it into gear. *Might as well get it over with*, he chided himself. *Stop being a chicken.*

He phoned Sarah.

"Sean?" She sounded out of breath.

"Yup."

There was a deathly silence. Then he heard a door slam so hard that windows rattled. She came back on the line. "How could you! Let us think you were dead?"

Sean listened painfully as his sister let him have it with both barrels. When at last she was done, he said, "Okay, I deserved that."

"You bet you do, and a lot more too," she retorted. "Where on earth have you—"

"Hey, I'll explain as soon as I can. I promise. But I wanted you to know I'm okay. I'm home. But I need to talk to Mom first."

"She's in Chautauqua, mourning," she snapped. "Because she thinks you're dead. Dead, Sean."

"I know. I understood that the first time you said it. Will told me she's there. Listen—I have to get on the road now, but I'll call you back soon, when I'm not driving. Okay?"

"Make that double soon," she said. "You owe me. Big." And she hung up.

He shook his head. Sarah never had been big on patience, and she was a fireball to boot. He chuckled. Sounded like someone else—himself. Maybe he was more a Worthington than he knew.

One more down. Two to go.

And they would be the two hardest.

En Route from Corvo to Flores

Once his jet was in the air, the man smacked the table next to him in frustration.

His contact winced. The reason didn't need to be stated. They were once again behind on Sean Worthington's movements.

"Track that cell," the man ordered.

"On it already." As they neared Flores, he added, "Got it. Satellite GPS photo coming through now."

The grainy photo of a Jeep and a man in the driver's seat popped up on the jet's computer screen.

The man nodded. Sean Worthington. No doubt. He was alive.

The computer screen switched to a map and a blinking red dot. So Sean was back in New York City. But he was driving out of the city, heading for . . .

"Keep following him on the GPS," the man barked. The orders weren't necessary. He knew where Sean was going. "Set course for Western New York. Chautauqua Institution in particular."

58

New York City

Sarah had plunged into her least favorite task—cleaning out her bedroom closet—as a distraction after hearing from Sean. Doing anything else was hopeless. Clothing, shoes, purses, and scarves were strewn over her bedroom floor and bed. She ricocheted between joy that he was alive and an intense desire to kill him.

He'd made her promise two things—not to call their mom, and not to come to Chautauqua that weekend. He'd explain later, he said. As angry as she was, she still honored his requests.

Now she flopped back on the bed and stared at the ceiling.

Her cell rang a little after 6:00. Convinced it was Sean again, making sure she was keeping her promises while he drove to Chautauqua, she fired at him, "What now?"

"Wow," a male voice said. "That was some greeting."

"Jon! I'm so sorry. I was . . . annoyed at somebody. I didn't know it was you."

A good-natured chuckle resounded on the other end of the line. "That somebody couldn't be Sean, could it?"

She sat up. "You know? That Sean's alive? Did he call you?"

"Yes, yes, and yes."

"When?"

There was a slight pause, then, "Yesterday."

"You mean you knew he was alive yesterday, and you didn't tell me? How could you not tell me?" Now she was ticked.

"Let me in, and I'll explain," Jon said.

"What do you mean, 'Let me in'? Where are you?" she asked.

"At your door."

She eyed her mess of a room, then her own clothing—her oldest sweats and an old Yale sweatshirt. Oh well, it was just Jon. "Okay, but your explanation better be good."

He was in sweats himself and held out a bag in one hand as a peace offering. It was hard to stay mad at a guy like Jon for long.

"Come on in."

He placed the bag on her kitchen counter.

Her stomach growled, as if on cue. "What's in the bag?"

"Ethiopian cuisine." He winked at her. "Lamb, rice, veggies, and sourdough flatbread."

Yes, it was impossible to stay mad at him. He knew what she liked. "Jon, why didn't you tell me?"

"I couldn't. I promised Sean that I'd let him tell you and work the details out in his own way."

She crossed her arms and glared at him. "You tried to distract me so I wouldn't worry."

"Yup. I think it worked—at least for the night until he could call you today." His eyes twinkled.

She smacked him in the bicep.

"Whoa there, little missy," he said with a John Wayne swagger and voice.

She rolled her eyes. "You've been hanging around Sean way too long."

His gaze was kind, knowing. "I wanted to make sure you were okay last night and then today, once you knew."

"I just want to know why, and he couldn't tell me." Her voice wavered.

"He didn't tell me either, and I didn't ask. For now, it's enough that he's back."

She nodded. "Don't know what's wrong with me lately."

He studied her. "Sure you do. You've been on a roller coaster since Sean disappeared. Even rock-solid Worthingtons have feelings."

"Yes," she threw back, "but we're not allowed to show them in public. Dad taught us that."

He turned in a circle, gesturing widely around her apartment. "Is this public?"

"No, but—"

"Sarah, you can trust me. Always."

Chautauqua Institution

Sean hurriedly pulled his Jeep up to the front of the estate. He'd driven the 400 miles from the city in an hour's less time than usual. He didn't bother going into the house. This time of day, his mother would only be one place—sitting in a rocker among the grasses by the water.

He hurried down the path, looking for her. He'd wasted enough time. She didn't deserve what he'd dished out over the past two weeks. Now that he'd seen the weakness, the loneliness, in himself, he understood the desperation that had driven her into her university friend's arms. He could no longer judge her for that, because he'd almost been guilty of the same thing. If it hadn't been for the gentle voice telling him to stop . . .

Now he needed to find his mother—to tell her that he didn't hate her, that he understood.

At last he spotted her sitting in one of the rockers, her face turned wistfully toward Chautauqua Lake as the day edged toward evening.

When his jet landed in Jamestown, a luxury car waited on the tarmac to drive him the 15 miles to Chautauqua Institution. His contact had arranged for a sleek boat to take him out on the lake. The man would be his own pilot.

This time he was satisfied. He'd guessed right and had arrived early enough. He'd left his contact on shore, awaiting further instructions via cell phone. What he had to do next, he wanted no one but himself privy to.

The man watched the estate through high-powered binoculars as Sean arrived in his Jeep. Then he swept the binoculars to scan the interior of the home. No movement. Good. It matched the satellite intel he'd been provided.

He followed the stone path around the house, toward the water. At last his vision landed on a woman in a weathered rocker.

His focus wavered, and he sank onto the driver's seat of the boat. His hand fell on the bulky package he'd carried with him.

59

"Mom?" Sean called softly as soon as he was close enough for her to hear him.

Ava tilted her head upward, as if she'd only heard his voice in the wind or in her imagination.

"It's me, Sean," he said, now only yards from her.

She froze, then slowly turned his way. The minute her eyes lit with recognition, she leaped from her chair and embraced him. Together they rocked, standing up, as she cried.

Then she drew back and touched his wet cheek. "It really is you. I thought I was dreaming."

She didn't ask where he'd been all this time. He knew his presence was enough.

"I'm so sorry," he said. "I didn't think. Or I did, but only about myself, not about how you might feel."

She reached to shush him, but he caught her hand. "I need to say this. I understand now why you had the affair—the loneliness, the desperation, the craving for love. I've felt those myself."

Her eyes brimmed with sorrow.

"Maybe I understand for the first time how hard it is to be

a Worthington—the expectations, being in the limelight, continually needing to be strong. You did a desperate thing. I did a desperate thing. I ran away—from you, from everything. We all do what we need to do to survive."

"I was so lonely," she murmured. "Nothing like a family vacation without your husband. It was the first of many I would have after that, but somehow the first was the hardest. And when Thomas comforted me, I . . ." She sighed. "These many years I've held in the pain, wondering when the truth would be revealed, knowing it would change our family. That I might lose Bill."

Sean ached for his mother. Until a short while ago, she'd always been cheerful, holding the family together. Yet she'd lived for years with intense loneliness. "I know it hasn't been easy. Living with Dad—or any of us." Strange how easily he continued to think of and speak of Bill as his father.

"Your father . . . when I told him, he didn't show any emotion. Took the news like he would the announcement of any business deal. Then he walked out the door." A single tear traced down her cheek. "Took Will's Land Rover and was gone for a long time."

Sean closed his eyes. So the truth of his existence had separated his parents. He would have to live with that for a lifetime.

Her gentle hands cradled his face. "Oh, son, he came back. Told me how sorry he was for not being there for me when I needed him. Thanked me for telling him the truth."

"So he didn't know?" Sean had to ask.

"I never told him. But he said sometimes he wondered. Because you were supposedly born early but didn't look like a preemie. Because we'd tried so long to get pregnant with Will and then had failed in our attempts to have a second baby. Then suddenly, after Camp David, you were in our lives. Later, he saw flickers of his friend in the way you smiled, your mannerisms, the color of your hair. You were so different from your siblings in the way you approached life."

So Bill had guessed. Was it any wonder he'd called Sean "the boy" and never "son"? Little clues—his treating Sean differently, his dissatisfaction with anything Sean did, his focus on Will as his son—made sense now. Yet out of love and loyalty to Ava he had provided for Sean. It was no wonder he had cut off any contact with Thomas.

"I know you wish it had never happened, Mom. I remember you saying that when I left."

"No, son, I never said that. I said 'I wish . . .' and you didn't allow me to finish. Now I want you to listen to me." The steel was back in her voice. "I never have wished I didn't conceive you. What I wish is that I had told you sooner. I held information that you needed to make sense of who you are. Of why you and your father sometimes butt heads."

He was confused. She still used the phrase *your father* naturally. "Is Bill here?" he asked.

She stiffened. "*Your father*," she said, "is out taking a walk around the grounds. He'll be back soon."

"I understand. I'll be gone before he gets back."

"No, Sean," she begged. "He needs to see you, say things to you. Please—wait until he gets back. Until you two can talk."

He'd put her through so much pain, he could give her that much, he decided. "Mom, I've got all the time in the world. I'll wait."

He couldn't believe those words had emerged from his mouth. A first for someone who fled from even the suggestion of family get-togethers.

As the bell tower at the point rang out the early evening hour, the man focused his binoculars on the poignant embrace. His gaze lingered first on the young man, then on the woman, as their auburn hair mingled in shades of dark and light red. It was only when they stepped apart that he swung the binoculars to inspect the house again and the shore on either side of the estate. Still no movement.

Now is the time, he decided. He powered up the idling boat so he could make his way to shore. He reached for the bulky package and started to open it.

At that instant, though, unrest swept over him. He refocused the binoculars on the man and woman. She was weeping, holding his face in her hands.

He couldn't do what he'd come to do. Instead he withdrew only a creased photo from the packet. Dropping it over the side of the boat, he watched until the faces blurred, waterlogged, and the photo at last sank into the lake.

Perhaps it was time for some things to end.

60

NEW YORK CITY

Sarah and Jon were almost done with their meal when his cell rang. He frowned, got up from the kitchen bar stool, and moved into the living room to take the call.

"You sure?" Sarah heard him say. "Absolutely sure? . . . I see."

He looked troubled when he sat back down on the stool.

"Hey, you've been babysitting me enough lately." Sarah chuckled. "Not that I needed it or anything. Need a listening ear?"

He swiveled toward her. "I just got confirmation on a rumor I came across a couple of days ago. Turns out it's real. Or they're real."

"What's real?"

"Take a look for yourself." He handed her his cell phone. "Scroll through the images."

Frowning, she took the phone and scanned the photos. "Hey, that looks like the Polar Bear Bomber—Justin Eliot. Where did you get these? And that looks like . . ." She zoomed in on the images. "There's only profiles of the other guy, but Jon, I swear that's . . . Sean."

"It is," Jon murmured. "It's been confirmed as an undeniable match."

She now stared at him. "Sean knew Justin Eliot? But that's not poss—"

"The photos show that Sean and Justin had a conversation of some kind. Looks like it was at a bar. What exactly they said, we don't know. We haven't been able to trace any recording. This is the first time I've seen the photos," he added. "They were only a rumor before."

"You don't think—"

"No," Jon replied, "I don't think."

But Sean had disappeared, she knew. Had he gone off the deep end because he'd somehow gotten involved with an eco-crazy group that had hired Justin Eliot to playact and then plant a bomb? Had he been wrestling with his conscience and couldn't take it anymore, so he had to leave the country for a while? Or had he discovered his unwitting role the night he disappeared from New York City? Is that why he couldn't explain to her where he'd been?

Then the full extent of the legal, ethical quandary hit. In her relentless search for the accomplices behind the bombing, had she actually been searching for her brother?

Chautauqua Institution

The man's contact phoned while he was still on Chautauqua Lake. "Stapleton's at it again," he reported. "Convincing the president to buy Sarah Worthington off with the AG job isn't enough. Word is, she's still not backing off the AF case. She's not happy with only taking Sandstrom down."

The man nodded. So Sarah was still digging. She didn't yet know how dangerous the game could get.

"The president threw another tantrum in the Oval Office," his contact added. "Says he wants the Worthingtons controlled. So he and Stapleton are putting the heat on Sarah's boss. They aren't taking no for an answer. Let's just say John Barnhill isn't having a restful Saturday night. Can't say no to the president but is defending Sarah and her instincts too."

"And Sean's already in a headlock," the man mused. *Even if he doesn't know about the photos yet.*

Carson, Sandstrom, and Spencer had been in on that setup. They'd already used that card to keep Will in check and take him out of Senator Loughlin's way. They'd use it again, the man knew, if Sean even hinted that he might step into any political race.

"Yes," his contact agreed. "So Will is left. Getting him out of politics wasn't enough. Spencer is after all three of the Worthington kids. Makes you wonder why he's so vitriolic against them."

The man knew why, but he'd let his contact come to his own conclusions and not confirm or deny them. "So what's his next plan for Will?"

"Word is that he and Stapleton have agreed that Stapleton is going to offer Will the CEO position. He says Will's always wanted it, and he can use that to control Will and the Worthington family. Stapleton has a lot of confidence in himself."

And that's exactly what will take him down someday.

"With Sarah as AG, her hands will be tied on the AF case because of the deal in place. With Will as CEO, the White House and AF will control him. And Sean will stay meek, or

Will might force him to be so out of fear of what might happen if those photos become live."

"Maybe." The man frowned. "I guess that remains to be seen."

But somehow he knew it would take more than that to alter the destinities of the three Worthington siblings.

61

New York City

The room spun crazily around Sarah as she considered the possibilities.

"Wait," Jon said. "Look carefully at the photos again."

His quiet voice cut through the dizziness, and she blinked. "What about the photos?"

"Check every photo. Note the angle of the camera. Sean is always a profile. But the bomber? He changes positions for each photo, as if he's mugging for a camera . . ."

". . . so his face can be viewed from all angles, for positive ID," she finished.

"Exactly."

"You're thinking this is a setup," she said.

"You bet I am. Sean might be a wild card sometimes, but he'd never be involved in a bombing."

She shook her head. "This looks really bad." It was hard enough that Will was on the board of AF and Sean was with a Green Justice buddy in the Arctic when the oil fiasco happened, and now she was the one prosecuting the DOJ's criminal negligence suit against AF. Even though she'd given up any legal decision-making power to Worthington Shares when she'd taken her DOJ job—a decision her father would never understand—that wouldn't mean anything to the public. She was still a Worthington in their eyes. And if it was the least bit possible Sean had anything to do with the bombing and with trying to control the flow of information about the oil crisis by having a *New York Times* reporter on board with him . . . well, her thoughts couldn't even go there. The press would crucify the DOJ, the entire Worthington family, and Jon Gillibrand.

"I agree. The evidence looks pretty incriminating," Jon admitted. "Then again, any evidence can be manufactured. We both know that. My guess is that he was just being Sean. He met a guy at a bar when he was killing time waiting for somebody, and they talked. Sean had no idea he was being captured on camera."

"How long can you keep this info under wraps?" Sarah asked.

"I called in a favor with a lab tech friend to run Sean's facial recognition and body profiling software, to make sure my gut was right—that the profile was a match for him. My friend will keep his mouth shut until I tell him it's okay to open it. But there's no guarantee other people don't have or won't receive copies of these photos and won't come to other conclusions."

"There's only one person who can tell us the truth—Sean." She speed-dialed his number.

"Actually, two," Jon corrected. "Whoever set him up."

Chautauqua Institution

Sean was sitting on the porch, enjoying the peaceful view. His mother was moving happily around the kitchen, rustling up a simple dinner. Sean didn't want anything to eat, but his mother needed to prepare it. His stomach still churned at the confrontation soon to come.

Out of habit, he checked his cell for calls and messages. Sarah had phoned three times in the past 15 minutes and left a terse text.

Call. Now.

Like he needed more tension in his life at the moment. He wasn't ready to explain anything to his sister.

The phone rang again with her ringtone. Leave it to his attorney sister to be so persistent.

He took the call. He knew she wouldn't give up until he did. This time he couldn't claim he was in a meeting halfway around the world and too busy to take it—a tactic he knew she was wise to but he still tried.

He was right. Her lawyer side was in full swing, and she was in interrogation mode.

"You met some guy at a bar and talked to him. Who was it?"

"What?" Now he was confused. This wasn't about where he'd been the last two weeks? He hadn't been in any bars in Portugal or the Azores.

"A bar near 20th and Madison," she clarified.

He searched his memory, and guilt set in. That was the night he'd been trying to duck the family dinner that Drew had set up. The night Drew had given the three siblings the spiel about how the American Frontier crisis would change each of their destinies. He'd been late. "Yeah, I was there once, for a meeting with an executive, but that's been a while. And the guy never showed."

"So who did you talk with?"

"And this is important why?" he tried.

"Just answer the question!"

It was like dealing with a younger version of their father. He acquiesced to get it over with. "I had a long wait, so I chatted with some people." He thought back. "One guy in particular, who sat next to me at the bar. Seemed nice enough, but a bit odd, or maybe he'd already had too much to drink."

"But you didn't know him?"

"What? I'd never seen him before. Haven't seen him since. Don't know his name. So now are you going to tell me why you're grilling me?"

"I've just seen photos of you with that guy. And he happens to be the Polar Bear Bomber," she announced.

He dropped his phone. "You have what?" he said after he'd fumbled to pick it up from the porch steps.

"Wait, and I'll send one to you."

He raised a brow when he saw it. "Yes, that's me, and that's the guy who was a little off. We just chatted for a bit about nothing, I guess. Can't remember. Then I left to go to the dinner at Drew's. So why would somebody take a picture . . ." Reality set in. "Are there more?"

"Yes. Jon's got them on his phone."

"Jon? He's seen them? What does he know? Where did he get them?" He fired the questions at her.

"Jon's here. He showed them to me."

Jon was there? Sean didn't have more than an instant to ponder that.

His friend's voice came on the line. "You know what this means, right?"

He did. His heart was racing as he put together the pieces. "But you don't think . . ."

"Of course we don't think," Jon replied, "but you should probably—"

"—let Will know." He would as soon as he hung up with Jon.

"And Sean? Don't worry. I'll be here with your sister."

Leave it to Jon to be the knight in subtle armor.

62

New York City

Will was sitting with Davy in their biggest chair, reading *Mike Mulligan and His Steam Shovel*, when Laura handed him his cell. "It's Sean."

He raised a brow. She simply nodded.

"Hey, pardner," she told Davy, "I'll take over and finish, okay?"

Davy wrinkled his nose but got up from his dad's lap.

Will took the phone out into the foyer. This wasn't the best time to have an intense conversation—on a Saturday evening right before Davy was heading to bed.

"Okay," Will said into the phone, "I'm clear."

"I need to tell you something," Sean said.

Will's heart sped up. What had happened when Sean was gone? Where had he gone?

"There are some photos of me, taken with the Polar Bear Bomber in a bar," Sean declared.

Will felt sick. So Sean knew about them? And he knew the guy was the Polar Bear Bomber? So that meant . . . wait. Before he deduced anything, he needed to ask. "Is there anything you want to tell me about them? Or how you know about them?"

"You don't seem surprised."

"I knew," Will murmured.

"What?"

Chautauqua Institution

Sean gripped the phone and headed down the cobblestone path. "You know I'm not involved in the bombing, right? It was a setup."

"Just tell me what happened," his brother said. "We'll put the pieces together."

After Sean told him about the secretary who'd called last-minute about the meeting at the bar, Will commented only, "Hmm."

"The executive didn't show," Sean added.

"Hmm," Will said again.

Sean knew his brother's code. Will's mind was working at light speed to pull together myriad scattered information and form a precise picture. Sean's own thoughts flashed back to the day Will had passed on the Senate bid. Jason Carson had been lurking around the side of the stage during Will's announcement. Suddenly Sean knew the truth.

"Carson told you right before you were to announce your run, didn't he?"

"Yes."

"And you didn't know my role in it, so you took a pass?"

"As far as the public is concerned, your role in it doesn't really matter," Will said. "Point is, the pictures exist. For most people, that would be enough."

Sean stopped walking. He was stunned at the depth of his brother's love. "You put yourself on the chopping block. Not only for one reason but for two. Everything you'd dreamed of, you gave up . . . for me." How greatly he'd misjudged Will.

"No, not everything. Only one thing. And nothing is worth losing you or risking your reputation."

"So what do we do now?" Sean asked.

"We fight back. We leverage Carson's own setup—and all who are involved with him—against him."

"How?"

"Leave that up to me."

Sean heard the determination in his brother's voice. Will had a plan, but he wasn't willing to share it. Sean knew better than to push. It was enough that his big brother believed him and would fight for him.

"Caped Crusader, huh?" Sean joked.

"Always."

New York City

Will stepped outside his front door so he'd have absolute quiet to assemble the pieces of the puzzle.

Sarah's and Will's suspicions about American Frontier bombing their own building, which Darcy and Jon concurred with, had to be true, even if they couldn't fully prove them yet.

Will also was fairly certain the convenient confession and quick death of the bomber was orchestrated by AF somehow, particularly Sandstrom and Carson. Sarah was on the trail and wouldn't give up until she had answers.

The photos of Sean with the bomber were a hackneyed attempt to frame the easiest Worthington sibling to get to. Sean, by nature, was friendly and social. He didn't have Will's natural cynicism or Sarah's attorney instincts. Plus his ties with ecological causes made him a prime target—a good excuse for hating big oil companies.

Will narrowed his eyes. So they thought they could control his political run—saving Loughlin's ineffectual hide for another term in office—and force him away from American Frontier in order to continue their Viking drive forward into new ventures without a naysayer voice. They thought they could control how hard and deep Sarah dug for the criminal negligence suit. All by holding set-up pictures of Sean with the bomber as a noose around the Worthington family's necks.

Those moves infuriated Will. Might did not make right. His keen sense of justice and his determination to go after Carson—the key to felling the other chess pieces, he believed—hardened like cement. Sandstrom was already soon to fall. That left Frank Stapleton, his old mentor but secret enemy, in temporary leadership of AF. Stapleton didn't care about whales and polar bears or oil-coated shores. His interest was purely financial. And he had strong ties to the current president of the United States for extra backing.

Everyone, though, had their Achilles' heel. Will simply had to find it.

He thought back to the night of the setup—the same night Drew had called the three siblings together. What would have happened if Sean had said he couldn't make the meeting at the bar and been at Drew's house on time?

Will shook his head. He knew the answer. Carson would just have found another time and place to set up Sean with the bomber.

Drew had been right. The Arctic crisis indeed would alter the trajectories of all three Worthington kids' destinies. More deeply than any of them could have known, until now.

His next call would be to Sarah. Other people underestimated her, but Will never would. He knew what she was capable of. She didn't have to prove it to him.

As an advocate, she was die-hard loyal and would fight to the end. But do something dirty or fight against her? You'd lose every time.

63

CHAUTAUQUA INSTITUTION

The sun was slipping into the horizon when Bill Worthington, clothed in walking attire, approached the house.

Sean spotted him, stepped out the screen door, and waited with tensed muscles. On the drive to Chautauqua, he'd run every potential scenario of this meeting through his mind. Now his head ached. He and Will had already agreed that tonight was not the time to inform Bill about the photos with the Polar Bear Bomber.

Sean's heart ached at how old his father suddenly appeared. At that moment, Bill looked up. Seeing Sean standing only feet away, he halted.

Sean's heart sank. Was that it? The end? Would his father not even greet him? Would he turn away?

Bill tottered for a minute, as if uncertain. Then he stumbled forward, his face a torment of emotions. "Sean!" he called and reached out tentatively to hug him.

The two men stood in an awkward embrace as the tension drained from Sean's body.

All is not lost. Perhaps we can rebuild. Or maybe we can build for the first time. Sean could never remember his father hugging him. Showing any physical affection was rare.

"I understand now—what I hadn't understood as I was growing up," Sean began when his father stepped back. "I know who my birth father is, and that explains a lot. About me. About you. It must have been hard for you, wondering and not knowing until now."

"But—"

"You treated me differently. Well, I am different. I didn't know how much so until now. I didn't understand you or why you were so hard on me. But I'm beginning to."

"I'm so sorry, Sean. I have already apologized to your mother for that, but I want to apologize to—"

Sean plunged on. "But Thomas Rich is not my father. He's not the one who raised me. You are. We haven't often seen eye to eye. But Dad, I still love you and will always love you."

"My son!" It was a strangled cry of anguish and love. This time he wrapped his arms around his son with passion, as if he never wanted to let Sean go.

For the first time ever, Sean felt accepted by his father. He returned the embrace, standing on equal footing at last with the man he respected more than any other. The man who had been the solid backdrop of his life, prompting him to stay on the path. The man he'd butted heads with, even avoided at times, but whom he now understood.

What would it be like, for over three decades, to not know if one of your children was truly your biological child or your best friend's? And still to treat that child as one of your own? The depth of his father's sacrifice was unfathomable when Sean glimpsed it from that perspective.

The screen door creaked, and Ava stepped out. Bill gathered

her close until the trio formed a circle, standing in the embrace of a dazzling Chautauqua sunset.

The man watched the reunion from his boat on the lake. No matter what the end would be, he had to allow time for this scene to play out. Focusing the binoculars on the two men's faces, he saw the tension between them. He couldn't hear the words exchanged, and that grated on him. There hadn't been enough time or advance warning to tap into the Worthingtons' extensive security system to get a listening device planted.

He saw the flutter of the screen door opening, and then a woman stepped out. Ava. The man refocused the binoculars on her as she moved toward her husband and child. When Bill reached out to include her in the circle, the man decided he'd seen enough.

He powered up the boat to head for shore.

The three Worthingtons stood together, watching the last of the brilliant sunset before retiring inside.

"I have something to give you," Ava told Sean after Bill headed for the shower. She crooked a finger toward her green room.

Sean followed. It had always been his favorite place in their summer house—the palms, the koi pond, the waterfall. Perhaps someday he'd give up city life, work from the tropics. With the kind of work he did for Worthington Shares, his base could be anywhere. Strange how he'd never thought of that before. It was as if the time on the mountain had torn off the veil covering his mind. Now the possibilities seemed broader. Even the colors of the green room were more vibrant.

Ava moved toward the corner and her beloved sea chest, the

weathered antique that had belonged to her grandmother. Since she'd been a girl, Ava had adorned it with shells and other sea treasures from Ireland and other countries where she'd traveled. It was a work in progress, she said, and a good reminder that life was an odd assortment of experiences found along the way, not a perfect masterpiece whose pattern was distinguishable from the beginning.

She opened the chest, removed a small item, and handed it to Sean. It was a baby shoe that didn't even fill the palm of his hand.

"Turn it over," she murmured.

On the back of the shoe was handwriting he recognized as his mother's. The shoe was inscribed with "Sean," and then below it, "A Gift."

"When you outgrew this first pair of walking shoes," she said, "I turned them upside down and wrote on them 'Sean Thomas, A Gift of Love.' I wanted you to know, no matter what, that you are a gift of love and that you are very loved. I want you to have it now."

He nodded. "I understand."

Pain flickered over her regal face. "I no longer have the other shoe. I wish I did."

64

New York City

Sarah had been pacing her apartment, waiting for Will's call. "About time," she shot at him after answering her phone.

"It was a setup," Will reported with no preamble. "But then you knew that already."

"Still, it's good that's confirmed. Carson?"

"And how did you figure that?" he asked.

"Give me some credit, big brother. I'm not as airheaded as you think."

He chuckled. "I've never thought that. And yes, you're right. Jon still there?"

"No." She laughed. "He does have to work sometimes. He only rarely babysits. So tell me all you know, and then I'll tell you what I know."

After a short briefing—something the Worthingtons were masters of in their rapidly moving universe—both had the information they needed.

"We're agreed then," Will said.

"Yep. Sandstrom and Carson go down, whatever it takes—

and anybody else who decided to hitch their wagon to those two," she proclaimed. "It's time for a little justice, Old West style."

"So you did learn something from those Westerns you said you hated," he teased.

"I did. But you're sidetracking the point. When I said anybody else, I meant *anybody* else."

"Even the president of the United States?" His tone was sober.

"Yes, especially him."

"Then I have another phone call to make," Will said.

He didn't explain. Then again, that was Will. He simply took care of things.

Will paused only a minute before he connected to a phone number he'd been given but had never used. What he planned next could backfire terribly, but he had to act. Not acting would put his brother and sister directly in the line of sight of those who had no scruples. He'd thought through every angle for weeks.

Will was surprised when Thomas Spencer Rich II picked up on the first ring. He'd expected to at least go through one or more assistants who would tell him Thomas wasn't available, but that he could leave a message. Maybe Thomas only answered because it was late on a Saturday night. Will hadn't realized until that moment just how late it was.

"Will Worthington," Thomas said in a deep baritone. "What can I do for you?"

"Mr. Rich, as you know, we're old family friends. My mother doesn't know I'm calling you. Neither does my father. They might not approve of what I'm about to ask you. But because of our connection—your friendship especially with my mother—I am requesting your assistance and your confidence on a highly delicate matter."

"Oh? And what might that be?" Thomas's tone was curious but also a bit pensive.

Was Thomas aware that he was Sean's birth father? Will didn't know and had decided not to bring it up. If Thomas knew, it would make what Will had to relate much easier. If not, it still needed to be said. Will would have to trust the deep friendship his mother and father had forged with Thomas at Harvard to encourage him to do the right thing.

"It has to do with some photos that have come to my attention, and what they really mean."

65

Chautauqua Institution

Sean awoke late the next morning with the sun beaming into his bedroom. Stretching, he flung back the luxurious coverlet and caught a whiff of breakfast aromas. His mother was doing what she loved—cooking. It smelled like Swedish pancakes, one of his favorites. Nothing wheat-germ, too healthy, or cardboard-tasting today. He exhaled in relief.

He was admiring the view out the window when his mom knocked on his door, then stuck her head in. Only mothers could get away with that.

"Good morning, sleepyhead. I'm making Swedish pancakes. Come when you're ready."

So he was right. His stomach rumbled in acknowledgment. "Fabulous. I just want to give Will a quick call first. Then I'll be there."

"All right." But she lingered. "Welcome home, son," she whispered at last, then padded back down the hallway.

He smiled. For the first time, he truly did feel at home among his family.

New York City

"Did you just get up?" Will asked when he heard Sean's voice. "Come on. It's past 11. My kids had me up at 7:00."

"Hey," Sean said in a serious tone, "I only wanted to thank you—for having my back. I know this time it cost you a great deal, and I won't forget it."

"That's what big brothers do for annoying little brothers," Will teased. For once he was the one lightening the mood. It still felt unnatural, but maybe Laura's coaching over the years was paying off. "If you've got a minute, let's loop Sarah in and figure out a plan."

"Three of us against the world. We can't go wrong," Sean teased back.

"It's really good to have you home," Will admitted.

"Okay, enough of the mushy stuff. Let's get to business."

Will laughed. Their roles were still reversed.

It only took about 10 minutes for the three siblings to conference and figure out next steps.

"I'll brief Jon. He knows he's got the exclusive story on the full exposé of Sandstrom, once we're ready, and we'll be working with Darcy," Sarah said. "It'll happen fast. Jon's got most of the story pulled together. He's just been waiting for the final details and the go-ahead."

"So we're good. Then I have somewhere to go," Sean said.

"Oh, where's that?" Sarah asked.

"Hey, sis, if I wanted you to know, I would have told you."

"Well, if you think for one minute you're going to disappear again and not tell me . . ." Sarah started in on him.

Will shook his head and chuckled. His brother was back to

his enigmatic self. His sister was back in attorney mode. Both were back to bickering. Things were getting back to normal.

It felt good.

Chautauqua Institution

After Sean's stomach was full of Swedish pancakes and lingonberries, he had one more call to make.

Elizabeth picked up immediately. "You working things out with your family?"

Leave it to Elizabeth to go straight to the heart of any matter.

"Yes, I am."

"You okay?" Her warmth and concern poured over him like a balm.

"I am. And I was wondering if you might have a little time."

"Sure," she said, "I'm here. We can talk about anything you want. Take as much time as you need."

"I was thinking more a little visit out your way. I could catch a flight to Seattle in the morning. If you could carve out a few hours, that is."

"Wow! That would be fabulous!" Her voice was radiant, happy. "And it's perfect timing. I just finished a huge research project for the boss—you know, my dad—and I bet the old salt would give me a couple of days off."

"We could even do the Space Needle, anything you want."

"You? Tourist stuff?" She laughed. "Things have changed."

"Maybe more than you know."

She sobered. "Okay, just tell me when your flight will land, and I'll be there."

As soon as they ended the call, he booked the earliest Monday morning flight to Seattle that he could find.

Langley, Virginia

The late-night call was unexpected and startled the man.

"Looks like it's going to happen soon," his contact said. "Tuesday morning, latest."

"And the other?" the man asked.

"It'll be a done deal by tomorrow noon."

66

En Route to Seattle, Washington

Sean stored his carry-on and settled back in his first-class seat. He closed his eyes, putting the past behind him. Even though Sandstrom had messed with Sean's life behind the scenes, Sean didn't need to see the guy arrested. The photos couldn't yet be proven, but Sandstrom's criminal negligence now could. His sister had done her job well. Sean might never get any personal revenge for what Sandstrom had tried to do to him—and what Carson could still do to him—by revealing the photos, but Sandstrom would at least pay for some of what he'd done. He'd likely spend time behind bars, thinking about what he should have done differently. That was enough for Sean.

He focused now on what was in front of him—the new plan that had been working through his head since his time on the mountain in Corvo. That plan had everything to do with a certain quirky scientist named Elizabeth Shapiro at the University of Washington.

New York City

CEO Eric Sandstrom looked like he was in shock. Now in handcuffs, he was being led out of the American Frontier headquarters under police escort. He would be arraigned for criminal negligence—knowing there were problems with the oil platform, drilling, and other procedures, and ordering the process to not only continue but be pushed ahead—and also for numerous counts of environmental abuses that had devastated international waters and communities along those waters since then. But it was the campaign cash violation that had triggered the arrest. Carson had turned on him.

Will had joined the shareholder suit against AF, giving muscle and confidence to the other shareholders.

With only a few texts, Sean had engineered the agreement of multiple ecological NGOs across the world to also file suit against Sandstrom. Their signed agreements had been scanned or faxed to Sarah and already were sitting on her desk this morning.

At the very least, Sandstrom would face some jail time and stiff penalties that would strip him of any resources.

Sarah and Darcy watched as he was urged into the backseat of the squad car. Sarah wished they'd also been able to prove he'd set up the bombing of his own building and perhaps also engineered the death of the Polar Bear Bomber. But she, Darcy, and Jon hadn't been able to do that yet, nor could they touch Jason Carson, who was protected by the former attorney general's deal with the president.

As the squad car drove off, Darcy high-fived Sarah. "One down, more to go." She grinned.

"You got that right," Sarah declared.

It was her job to take the CEO down, but in this case she felt a personal satisfaction. The man who had tried to attack her family in multiple ways would now go through the due process of law. She'd closed the book on Sandstrom.

Jon's full exposé of Sandstrom's criminal negligence in the Arctic fiasco would run online at the *New York Times* within the hour and then in hard copy on the front page Tuesday morning. The rumors of the end had given Sandstrom just enough hours to be nervous, try to lawyer up, and then realize he'd need to get out of the country pronto. He'd been throwing a thumb drive of key documents in his briefcase and erasing a sector of his laptop when the squad cars arrived.

Sarah and Darcy exchanged a look of steely determination. Now that Sandstrom was wrapped up with a bow, Jason Carson was next in their sights.

Will couldn't help it. He didn't need to be there officially. He was no longer a board member of American Frontier. But his long history with the company and his sense of justice won out. He had to see Sandstrom taken down. So he stood now just outside the AF building—the scene of one of the most notorious domestic terror incidents in American history—and watched as Sandstrom ducked into the backseat of the patrol car.

What would happen to American Frontier next? Will had an idea, and it wouldn't be pretty. If it was to survive as a company, AF would need to find new leadership, redirect their efforts, invest heavily in research before jumping the gun on any project, deal honestly with the media nightmare that would surround them, and push forward on any and all efforts to repair whatever environmental damage could be fixed. In other words, the company faced an overwhelming mountain.

However, Will also knew that somehow the company would

survive and press forward. It just wouldn't be on his watch, as he'd thought. Things would have to greatly change in the mix of board members for Will to have the opportunity to assume the CEO position.

When the squad car drove away, Will turned to leave. He caught a flash of a familiar figure out of the corner of his eye, across the street from him. But it couldn't be . . .

The man watched the arrest of Eric Sandstrom. He nodded to himself, then walked away into the throng of people that crowded New York City.

So the White House thought they'd distract Sarah Worthington by throwing her into the pool of AG vetting, he thought. *And by falsely framing Sean, to take both Sean and Will down.*

He chuckled. *They don't know the Worthingtons at all.*

Bill Worthington had trained his kids well.

67

Will was almost amused. Almost.

"Will? Frank Stapleton. Wondering if you'd have a minute today for coffee," the GOP kingmaker said in a friendly tone.

Will wanted to reply, "It couldn't have anything to do with the fact that Sandstrom was arrested, would it?" but he didn't. He'd learned a long time ago from Drew and his father that it was smart to keep your enemies close, especially if they were old friends.

"Sure," he answered in an upbeat tone he didn't feel. *What are you up to, you wily old fox?*

They set up the time, in an hour, for a local diner.

Will called Drew.

"You know what this is about, don't you, Will?" his trusted mentor asked.

"Search and rescue."

En Route to Seattle, Washington

An hour into his flight to Seattle, Sean stopped wrestling with what he would say to Elizabeth. He had to trust in the plan. So he tackled his other concern. How would Sarah respond when she found out Sean was her half brother? Was Bill right in wanting to protect her from that knowledge, even when the rest of the family now knew?

Would that knowledge really change anything for Sarah? She and Will had still backed him even when faced with "proof" that he'd met with the Polar Bear Bomber.

Now is not the time, the gentle voice said.

On Corvo, he'd learned to trust that voice, even though he hated to wait.

For now, he would follow his heart in a different direction—toward a leggy, opinionated blonde.

New York City

"So what do you think, Will?" Frank Stapleton spread his arms wide, dwarfing the small diner booth where the two of them sat.

Stapleton, the acting chairman of the AF board, had just offered Will the CEO position on a silver platter.

"You're the obvious choice," Stapleton proclaimed. "No doubt about it." He was in his usual kingmaker mode, relaxed and confident that his offer wouldn't be turned down.

"I'll think about it," Will replied.

Stapleton stiffened. "What do you mean, you'll think about it?" He leaned forward. "Will, this is what you've been working toward, what you've wanted all these years—to be CEO of the most powerful company in the world. What's there to think about?"

"Still, I'll think about it and let you know." Will's voice was firm. When his eyes met Stapleton's, he saw a flash of concern before the man composed himself.

"Okay then. I'll hear from you . . ." Stapleton's brows raised in question.

"When I'm ready," Will announced.

The two shook hands. As soon as Will was around the corner of the building, he phoned Drew.

"Was it what we thought?" Drew asked.

"Indeed."

The timing of the offer wasn't a surprise. The CEO position had been suddenly vacated. Stapleton was correct—Will was the obvious choice. However, was this the moment he'd been created for? To lead a powerful company through its worst imaginable crisis and onto the right path? Or was it a distraction from another path that would be revealed?

"Your dad's flight will be at JFK in less than an hour," Drew said.

"You called him." It wasn't a question.

"I did. I was pretty sure how your conversation would run. I knew the two of you would want to discuss it in person."

Good old Drew, always a step ahead, Will thought.

So it's Frank Stapleton, the old snake charmer, the man thought. *He's the real force behind trying to take the Worthingtons down. But why, besides the obvious?*

He tugged his cap lower over his face when Will Worthington and Frank Stapleton exited the small diner. Seeing the pair together wasn't unusual. For years, Stapleton had been grooming Will to become the next GOP candidate for president of the United States.

The problem had come when Will had decided to run for Senate as a Democrat, thus threatening not only the Republican Party but also the long-standing New York senator James Loughlin, who was beholden to Stapleton and Spencer. With Worthington muscle and financial backing, Will was a shoo-in to win, especially as New York tired of Loughlin.

With Will as senator, it wouldn't be too far of a stretch for him to decide to run for president. That would put him in direct competition with Spencer's reelection campaign. That threat in itself would be enough to get Spencer to back anything Stapleton wanted to make happen. With rumors of tantrums in the Oval Office, plus his backing of AF, a company now buried in scandal and criminal negligence, the president's ratings had dipped.

Was Will Worthington aware of how much Stapleton was pulling the strings behind the curtain? If so, Will was even smarter than the man thought, to play it cool and keep his now-enemy guessing.

So Stapleton and Spencer had teamed up to promote Sarah, to distract her with the glitz of the AG job, to keep her from going after AF with guns blazing. The man shook his head. Clearly that hadn't worked.

That meant Stapleton also likely had something to do with the photos of Sean and the bomber—or at least had been looped in that Sean would be taken down. Sean had been the one single link that could break the Worthington resolve. The man knew from his history with Bill that the Worthingtons would protect their own.

Disgust spewed from his lips in a long exhale. *And Spencer was weak enough to allow himself to be manipulated into trying to destroy a blue-blood family, all over reelection money.*

Greed had made people and kingdoms fall throughout history. It was an old, well-trod story.

The story would replay again when Stapleton and Carson were taken down. The man wouldn't rest until that happened. Spencer? That would be more difficult.

But nothing was impossible.

68

Sarah finally had the chance to call Jon a little before noon. "Great story. Well done," she told him.

Jon's exclusive online interview was now being parroted by every television network and news agency around the country. The media was scrambling to present any angle they could. One network revealed a photo of Sandstrom's disgruntled wife, waving off the cameras to get in her Jag. Sarah had seen the pattern before. The woman would file for divorce, hoping to get her share of their nest egg but not realizing their funds had already been frozen.

"I especially loved the part where you hinted that the investigation about the Polar Bear Bomber was still under way since questions have been raised." She laughed. "That frosted Darcy's boss, but it also kick-started him to reopen the investigation an hour ago. That ought to bring Carson, Sandstrom, and the president some sleepless nights."

"We'll put the pieces together somehow," Jon said.

"I have no doubt."

American Frontier was being bombarded from all sides. Their

stock price had plummeted within minutes of the breaking news. Ecology-minded picketers already clustered outside the headquarters. Frank Stapleton was surrounded with microphones and news cameras, disavowing knowledge of Sandstrom's criminal activities and stating that American Frontier would assist the authorities in getting to the bottom of what had happened.

"There's one sad thing about all of this, though," Jon added. "The oil washing up on the shores can never fully be cleaned up."

"I know. And it didn't need to happen."

Mistakes were sometimes unavoidable. Oil leaks happened. Equipment failed. Nothing was 100 percent foolproof. But criminal negligence? That was something different.

En Route to Seattle, Washington

Mid-flight, Sean realized how much had changed in his life in less than a month. Learning about his past had freed him to step into the present with confidence. His relationship with his father had changed. Sean no longer had to please him, avoid him, or fear being a failure in his eyes. That meant the sky was the limit on the NGOs and start-ups, Sean's true passion. But his focus had changed—people first and money second. When the two went hand in hand, even better.

He thought back to the day when Drew had said, "Maybe it's time to stop trying to be your brother and just be yourself. The man I know you are. The man I know you can be."

Sean owed the sage Drew an apology. Their beloved mentor had been right, as always.

But even better, now Sean knew who he was, and he would passionately pursue that destiny.

He also knew he had to end the speculation in the media about him running for governor of New York. A political run was not for him, at least not right now. With the recent revelation about his birth father, this was not a good time for the Worthington family to face the digging and mudslinging that dogged every political campaign. They had already been hurt enough.

His father's dream of a Worthington running for the top office of the United States might come true someday, but not right now. Not through Sean. Maybe someday Will would choose to run again. If so, and if Will asked, Sean would be by his side again as campaign manager. After all, they were brothers and would watch each other's backs.

As soon as Sean's plane was on the tarmac, waiting to taxi to the arrival gate, he took advantage of the few minutes to make another call.

Jon picked up immediately. "You in Seattle?"

"Just landed," Sean answered. "But how did you know? Oh, of course. Elizabeth."

"Yup. She's pretty happy you're coming to see her. You are coming to see her, right?" Jon teased. "To say what you should have said a long time ago?"

"Hoping to," he admitted. "Guess I'll know soon. But that isn't why I called. I thought you might like another exclusive."

New York City

"What do you think, son?" Bill Worthington asked Will.

The two men were sitting on the couch in Bill and Ava's New York penthouse.

"About the opportunity?" Will asked. "I don't know. Drew

told me I should think about it awhile back, in case the possibility came up. I have been. But I can't seem to get past a big bump in the road. I keep asking myself, 'What could I have done differently to keep American Frontier from getting to this point?'" He shrugged. "If I can't figure that out, will I make a good leader for the company?"

His father nodded, understanding the quandary. "I have often asked myself the same question in different business ventures. In this case, though, you followed the path of integrity. You pushed for research, for more time before drilling in the Arctic. Sandstrom and the board didn't listen."

"What could I have done to make them listen?" Will asked.

His father shook his head. "You can't always change people's minds. They can be pigheaded sometimes. Look at me. Took me over three decades to come to terms with who Sean might be. I never asked Ava the question I should have—is he really my son? And you know why I didn't?" Bill didn't wait for an answer. "Because I was afraid. I was afraid of knowing the truth, of losing her." He looked fiercely at Will. "Fear can keep you from asking questions you should, from doing things you should. You, son, were far more of a father to Sean than I ever was. I sacrificed my family to build an empire."

"But Dad—"

"Let me finish. I thought I was doing the right thing for you kids—ensuring a solid future so our family would endure many more generations. But along the way I didn't learn the lessons I should have from my father. I remember often feeling lonely and fatherless as I grew up. My father wasn't one to give me time or affection. I followed the same path, leaving Ava and you kids alone far too much. When I think . . ." He choked up. "Will, you have what I never had."

Will frowned. "What's that?"

"Balance. I see the time you spend with Laura and the kids, the way you put them first, the decisions you make as a result. I think you learned the hard way about being lonely, because I was gone a lot of your growing-up years too." He held up a hand. "And don't deny it. Ava and I have talked about it. She's set me straight, as hard as it was to hear. But you? You've watched what I've done right and what I've done wrong, and you're a better man for it."

His father was right. Will couldn't deny he'd made some decisions about his own priorities because he'd wanted things to be different for him, for Laura, for his kids. "That's one of my concerns," he admitted. "Running Worthington Shares and also juggling CEO of AF. I'm not certain I can do both. And do both well."

"But you don't have to do both by yourself. You've already surrounded yourself with capable people—people you can trust, like Drew, like Sean. But do things differently than I did. Learn to let go. Will, you've seen the upside and the downside of me being off balance. And you have something else too—Laura on your side. She's a different generation than Ava, and a different temperament." He chuckled. "She won't let you get off balance."

Will laughed, thinking of this week, when she'd reined in his business schedule because it overlapped with an event of Andrew's. "You're right."

"Will, you're on the right path. And now I think Sean is too. He's run some ideas by me for fine-tuning his role at Worthington Shares that he wants to talk with you about. Making that side of the business his own, and even better." Pride glimmered in his father's eyes. "Both of you have chosen to do what's right, as hard as that is sometimes. There's no greater legacy I can leave my sons or my daughter. God knows I haven't been perfect. I've made some big mistakes along the way. There's a lot

I have to make up for—with Ava especially." Bill straightened, his stance once again that of a business titan. "I had to make a decision. To no longer be held back by the fear of what might happen. I need to live by my own creed. The only failure is in not trying, in not giving something your all."

"So, Dad, what would you do? Would you take on AF? Now?"

His father studied him. "You'll figure it out. You always do."

Will leaned back against the couch. This time there was no pushing. No "Will, you can save the world, and you're the only one who can do it" speech. Only a few words that showed his father believed in him and in what he could do.

69

Seattle-Tacoma International Airport

Sean exited the flight with only his carry-on. He loved traveling light, never waiting for baggage when he got to his destination. When he was almost at baggage claim, he phoned Elizabeth. It would only take him a couple of minutes after that to walk out the doors to where she could pick him up.

Her line rang and rang. She didn't pick up. Assuming she was stuck in traffic, he turned toward the outside doors.

There Elizabeth stood, only feet away. She was dressed simply in jeans, a khaki shirt, and boots. Very Elizabeth. Comfortable, never caring about any fashion trend.

"Surprise!" she called and dangled her car keys.

She'd never looked more beautiful.

He hurried toward her, dropped his bag, and hugged her. They stood unmoving, surrounded by the maze of people and baggage at Sea-Tac.

At last she drew back. Her brown eyes flashed warmth. "Come on. The Space Needle awaits."

"Huh?"

"Your suggestion. Remember?" she teased.

"Well, aren't you full of surprises?" he teased back.

"Every day." She grinned.

He paused. "For the rest of my life?" His gaze lingered on her.

She stilled. The car keys trembled in her hand. "If that's what you want," she whispered.

He reached for her. "It is."

Her smile was radiant.

LANGLEY, VIRGINIA

The man removed the bulky package from his desk and eased it open. Time had worn the brown paper of the packet thin and made it crackly, but he still kept it.

He drew out the first object—a white baby shoe, scuffed from a child's learning to walk—and ran his fingers over the toes. He turned the shoe over and traced the delicate lettering that said "Thomas," and beneath it, "Of Love." Someday, perhaps, he would return this shoe to its rightful owner.

The next item was even more familiar—a tiny white shirt, embroidered with the fuchsia flowers that grew wild along the roadsides in Ireland. He held it up to his nose and inhaled. It still had the slight scent of baby powder.

The third item, a photo of a happy red-haired baby revealing a first tooth, always made him smile before heartache descended.

This time, though, the heartache was swift and intense.

One photo was missing from the packet—a university photo of three best friends, heads together, laughing. He vividly remembered the night it was taken, over four decades ago now, when they shared their heartfelt dreams about changing the world with each other.

What had happened in between? Real life. One night of moral weakness had altered their friendship. That was why he'd let the photo go, let the waters of Chautauqua Lake blur the faces until they were unrecognizable.

He sighed. He'd missed so many years, years he might have had if he'd gained the courage to act, to do things differently. He had spent years of regret tracking the red-haired baby's progress. The baby had grown into a man to be respected, a true Worthington in character.

The man had lived continually with the fear and the secret hope that once Bill Worthington knew, he would reject the boy, reject Ava. That day in Chautauqua he'd almost made his move—driven the boat up to the Worthington summer home. Then Bill had arrived. The reunion scene the man had viewed from the lake had closed off any possibilities of his own dream. Once again, Bill Worthington had revealed his sterling character, the loyalty he was known for. But this time, the man had glimpsed something new in Bill's face—an understanding of what love really was, what it could cost.

That small glimpse had unnerved him, changed his plan.

He loved Ava, always would. But bygones were bygones. He couldn't change the past. Now he was left only with the shreds of his ever-active, condemning conscience.

With one last glimpse at the shoe, shirt, and photo, he tucked them back into the packet in the secret drawer. He locked the drawer and pocketed the key. His glance swept to the book that Sarah had given Sean, the one he'd left behind in Corvo. It now nestled among the hundreds of books in his voluminous library, but he'd never forget its spot. Perhaps someday he'd pull it out and see if Sarah had written anything else.

At last Thomas Rich, former president of the United States, closed the door of his study. He stepped out into the hallway of his lavish home and into the life that he'd built for himself.

Even if it wasn't the life he'd always longed for and wanted with all his heart.

Epilogue

New York City

Will scanned the room. The chagrined faces of board members who had formerly served with him gazed back at him—at least those who weren't too embarrassed to look. The others stared down at the conference table.

It was Will's first official meeting as CEO of American Frontier. Drew sat in at the back of the room, at Will's request.

Will stood and gestured around the room. "In this very boardroom, not long ago, we all heard a story. Former CEO Eric Sandstrom told it, in fact. It was a story about the Vikings—fearless, courageous explorers who took enormous risks so they could expand their realm. American Frontier has done that. Sometimes those risks paid off well. Other times they've led to unprecedented and very public failures."

He didn't need to note the Arctic crisis. Everyone in the room was well aware of it.

"We now have a choice. We can continue and fine-tune

American Frontier's mission—to innovate and search out new sources of energy—or we can die. As the world's largest and most powerful oil company, what we decide in this room today will have a significant impact on the planet.

"My father always taught me, 'To those who are given much, much is required.' Our former CEO used that same statement to convince the board to continue the Arctic exploration and drilling for oil, even though we all knew the risks. Each of us in this room shares that blame, myself included, for making that decision. But it is what happens next that will go down in history as our response to one of the largest oil crises the world has experienced."

The expressions of so many CEOs and titans of industry were now uplifted, hopeful. Will looked at Drew, who gave a subtle nod.

"So here is what I propose. American Frontier will accept the responsibility that is ours. We will work hard to recover and clean up what oil we can. We will pay reparations—yes, even though that will mean a vast cut in our profits and unhappy stockholders. We must do what is right.

"But that is only the beginning. We will continue our explorations for new oil, but also broaden our research budget. Especially in the area of clean energy. This is the time in our planet's history where oil companies and ecological concerns should be working together instead of fighting each other. Together we can save civilization. Our efforts can spark the beginning of a dialogue, a campaign to bring parties together, and increase the public's awareness . . ."

As Will continued sharing his extensive plan, board members began to nod. Frank Stapleton sat back and smiled, as if the ideas were his own and he agreed fully.

The vote was unanimous to go with Will's plan. Board members were enthused about the next steps. They all shook Will's hand as they left the room.

Frank Stapleton was last. "Well done, son. Well done." He too shook Will's hand. "I told you that you'd be a great CEO for AF. You've got those board members believing in you already."

"I truly believe 'To those who are given much, much is required,'" Will said. "To me, it's not simply a mantra. This is only the beginning. Before this is done, we will all be called to make difficult choices. Some will choose wisely." He studied Stapleton. "Some will not. Each of us will have to live with our decision."

Drew walked up to stand beside Will. "A wise person once said, 'Things that are hidden will be revealed.' I sincerely believe that."

Stapleton cleared his throat. "Yes, I suppose that is true. Mr. Simons, always a pleasure to be in your company." He swiveled back toward Will. "Until the next time, Will."

Will leveled a steely gaze on his former ally. "You can bet on that."

Sarah's attorney skills were in hyperdrive. She'd met several times with the legislative affairs staff at the White House to prepare for her Senate confirmation. They had not been gentle with her. The process would be ugly, hateful at times, even vengeful. She had to be prepared for challenges from unexpected quarters.

The White House staff had assumed that their counsel would scare Sarah. They were surprised. It caused the opposite reaction. Sarah had been very still while the staff walked her through the weaknesses that would be exposed. Even her faith would be challenged, they told her. At the end, she simply nodded, pulled out a binder to take notes, and looked them in the eye. "Let's get to work, then," she said. "I do not intend to lose this."

Now, in the quiet of her office, she was having second thoughts. Had she truly earned the chance to serve as the nation's attorney general? Why now? Did the sudden move have to do with American Frontier and the story Carson had leaked to the media? Who was trying to play her? Who exactly was protecting whom? And from what? Might there be some loophole in the agreement between the president and the former AG, in which she could go after Jason Carson?

If she was confirmed, she'd have considerable authority. But in relation to American Frontier, Jason Carson, and the Polar Bear Bomber, her hands would be tied. The White House staff had advised her that she would need to recuse herself from any cases involving the company that her older brother now ran.

Somehow, in some fashion, Sarah was determined to aggressively pursue the truth about the bombing. Darcy and Jon would continue to keep her in the loop on anything new they discovered.

The media was having a field day with her brother as the new CEO of American Frontier. Will was often on camera—his answers calm, to the point, and so logical that the naysayers were muted. It helped that thanks to Jon Gillibrand, Will had already emerged in the press as the voice of reason that had attempted to pull AF back from the brink of poor decision making. The world now knew that since Will had been unable to sway the vote, he had walked away from American Frontier. He'd even sold his family's shares in the company. His conscience was clear. But he had stated unequivocally that he felt called to the helm of AF now, to take the company through this dark time into a promising future with a new vision of pursuing clean energy that would benefit the planet.

Several of Sean's ecological NGOs were already backing Will with their comments, and the chatter of the online community was mostly favorable toward the new CEO. Will, Kirk Baldwin, and Sean had met with heads of a dozen of the largest environmental groups in a sort of makeshift summit. More such meetings were planned to establish common ground and a working plan that both sides could agree on.

Sarah, as the president's nominee for attorney general, and Will, as the CEO of American Frontier, had appeared together briefly for a media conference. It was a bit unorthodox. But Sarah had not yet been confirmed, so it was cleared by their respective media offices. Their appearance together served to send a clear message that both AF and the government wanted justice to be done and wrongs righted as much as humanly possible. Sarah and Will outlined an agreed-upon plan to move ahead with those goals in mind. The plan was very public, transparent, and straightforward.

That one press conference alone lowered tensions in several quarters. Once again, the Worthingtons were in the limelight, heralded by one national news magazine as "The Most Respected Family in America."

It was the only press article Ava had ever posted in their home. She'd had the cover framed for their Chautauqua kitchen. All the kids had rolled their eyes over it, but not so their mother could see.

Sarah knew she should be satisfied. Sandstrom was behind bars. But if she'd learned anything over her years at the DOJ's Criminal Division, and from her friend Darcy, it was that many things weren't as they appeared. People's motives were usually self-seeking. Eric Sandstrom had been led like a lamb to the slaughter. Why had it been relatively easy?

The answer was clear. Someone else—or multiple persons—

had something big to hide. And Sarah, Darcy, and Jon would keep digging until they found it.

On a Boat off Corvo, Azores Islands

"I see you made the paper," Dr. Leo Shapiro said to Sean in his gravelly voice. "No more run for governor, huh?"

"Dad!" Elizabeth chided. "Did you finally read that? It's weeks old."

He waved her off. "We've been busy. Vacationing for the first time in years . . . well, combined with a little scientific work." He turned his attention to Sean, who leaned over the boat to retrieve a water sample from the inlet. "Smart move, son, not to go into politics. You must have something else on your mind." Leo grinned and cocked a thumb toward his daughter.

Sean looked at Elizabeth, who was lying on her back on the small boat, her feet dangling in the azure water. He'd never seen her so happy, so relaxed.

He'd never been happier himself. In a month, Sean and Elizabeth would be back at Chautauqua for a family get-together. For once, he looked forward to it instead of dreading it. Elizabeth would fit right in. All the Worthingtons, and Drew and Jean too, would love her. Of that, he had no doubt.

Then Sean, Elizabeth, and her father would team up for a mission that combined marine research for the University of Washington and a couple of NGOs that Sean wanted to check out.

Perhaps someday he'd take Elizabeth to his mother's home in Ireland. Maybe someday he'd contact Thomas Rich. Close the loop on his remaining questions. For now, though, Sean was content.

Elizabeth sat up. The sun shimmered on her blonde hair as she draped it over one shoulder. She reached for the plastic travel vase Sean had purchased in Flores and inhaled the fragrance of the purple wildflowers he'd picked for her that morning off the shore of Corvo. Maybe he had learned a thing or two from his brother, who bought Laura a rose every week.

"Mmm, these smell so good," she said and flashed him "the look."

That look said everything.

He was home.

Bonus Feature

Birth Order Secrets

Have you ever felt compelled to act a certain way, as if you've been programmed?

The Worthington siblings—Will, Sean, and Sarah—grew up side by side in the same family, yet each sees life through a completely different lens. As a result, they respond to events differently.

Have you wondered why your sister or your brother is so polar opposite to you in lifestyle, behavior, and everything else? Why you're a neat freak and your sibling is a messy? Why you're a procrastinator and your sibling is a finisher? Why you pick the friends you do? Why you're driven to succeed? Why you're less comfortable around your peers and more at ease around people older than you? Why you're attracted to a certain type of person, or to a specific occupation? Why you struggle day to day with never being good enough? Why you're always the one mediating between warring family members or co-workers?

The answers to these questions have everything to do with birth order secrets. Your place in the family has a lot to say about why you do what you do. It gives you important clues about your personality, your relationships, the kind of job you seek, and how you handle problem solving.

This Birth Order Secrets bonus feature highlights key traits of firstborns, onlyborns, middleborns, and lastborns. You don't have to meet all the criteria in a certain list to be a specific birth order. In fact, if you don't, there are reasons for that too. (For more intrigue, read *The Birth Order Book*.)

Discovering and understanding the secrets of birth order can powerfully change your life and revolutionize your relationships at home and at work.

Millions of people have already seen the results. You can too.

I guarantee it.

Dr. Kevin Leman

Firstborn

First on the scene.
Held to a higher standard.
Star of the show.

If you're a firstborn:

- You are a natural-born leader. People look up to you.
- You have a strong sense of what is right and just.
- You love details and facts.
- You like to know what's expected of you and have high expectations for yourself and everyone else.
- You love rules . . . well, you call them "guidelines." In fact, you may have a few too many.
- You always feel under pressure to perform.
- You don't like surprises because you're a planner and organizer.
- Books are some of your best friends.

Onlyborn

Goal-oriented.
Self-motivated.
High-flying achiever.

If you're an onlyborn:

- You are a planner and an organizer and work well independently.
- You have high expectations for yourself and others. The word *failure* is not in your vocabulary.
- You were your parents' first and only guinea pig in child rearing.
- You were a little adult by age seven, comfortable with those older than you but not always at ease with your peers.
- You find yourself saying *always* and *never* a lot.
- Add *very* or *really* in front of any firstborn trait, and that describes you.
- You are extremely conscientious and reliable.
- Books are your best friends.

Middleborn

Navigator.
Negotiator.
Relational genius.

If you're a middleborn:

- You're determined to choose your own path.
- You're pretty good at avoiding conflict.
- You're even-keeled, the mediator, the peacekeeper. You see all sides of an argument.
- You sail through life with calm and a sense of balance.
- You thrive on relationships.
- Friends are your lifeline.
- No one in the family ever asked you, "What do you think we should do?"
- You navigate life's seas in your own subtle way—although you may be the only one who realizes you're the peanut butter and jelly of the family sandwich.

Lastborn

Winsome.
Natural entertainer.
Rule breaker.

If you're a lastborn:

- You're great at reading people.
- You've never met a stranger.
- You can be very persuasive.
- Admit it—you like to be the center of attention.
- You're good at getting other people to do what you want them to.
- You're a natural salesperson.
- Many people still call you by your pet name, even if you're an adult.
- You love surprises!
- Although you don't like to admit it, you were just a little bit spoiled.

Acknowledgments

Grateful thanks to:

- All who read our books, enjoy the journey, and find their own “aha moments.” You make writing worthwhile.
- Our family members, who each relentlessly pursue making a difference in the world in their own unique ways.
- The Revell team, especially Lonnie Hull DuPont and Jessica English, for their enthusiastic support of this publishing dream.
- Our longtime editor Ramona Cramer Tucker, who is the peanut butter and jelly of our sandwich.

About Dr. Kevin Leman

An internationally known psychologist, radio and television personality, speaker, educator, and humorist, **Dr. Kevin Leman** has taught and entertained audiences worldwide with his wit and commonsense psychology.

The *New York Times* bestselling and award-winning author of over 50 titles, including *The Birth Order Book*, *Have a New Kid by Friday*, and *Sheet Music*, has made thousands of house calls through radio and television programs, including *Fox & Friends*, *The Real Story*, *The View*, Fox's *The Morning Show*, *Today*, *Morning in America*, *The 700 Club*, CBS's *The Early Show*, *Janet Parshall*, CNN, and *Focus on the Family*. Dr. Leman has served as a contributing family psychologist to *Good Morning America* and frequently speaks to schools and businesses, including Fortune 500 companies such as YPO, Million Dollar Round Table, Top of the Table, and other CEO groups.

Dr. Leman's professional affiliations include the American Psychological Association, SAG-AFTRA, and the North American Society of Adlerian Psychology. He received the Distinguished Alumnus Award (1993) and an honorary Doctor of Humane Letters degree (2010) from North Park University, and bachelor's, master's, and doctorate degrees in psychology, as well as the Alumni Achievement Award (2003), from the University of Arizona.

The Leman Academy of Excellence, a classical charter school founded by Dr. Leman, launched in 2015.

Originally from Williamsville, New York, Dr. Leman and his wife, Sande, live in Tucson, Arizona, and have five children and two grandchildren.

For information regarding speaking availability, business consultations, seminars, webinars, or the annual "Wit and Wisdom" cruise, please contact:

Dr. Kevin Leman
P.O. Box 35370
Tucson, Arizona 85740
Phone: (520) 797-3830
Fax: (520) 797-3809
www.birthorderguy.com
www.drleman.com

Follow Dr. Kevin Leman on Facebook (facebook.com/DrKevinLeman) and on Twitter (@DrKevinLeman). Check out the free podcasts at birthorderguy.com/podcast.

About Jeff Nesbit

Formerly Vice President Dan Quayle's communications director at the White House, **Jeff Nesbit** was a national journalist with Knight-Ridder (now the McClatchy Company), ABC News' Satellite News Channels, and others, and the director of public affairs for two prominent federal science agencies: the National Science Foundation and the Food and Drug Administration.

For nearly 15 years, Jeff managed Shiloh Media Group, a successful strategic communications business whose projects represented more than 100 national clients, such as the Discovery Channel networks, Yale University, the American Heart Association, the Robert Wood Johnson Foundation, and the American Red Cross. Shiloh Media Group helped create and launch three unique television networks for Discovery Communications, Encyclopedia Britannica, and Lockheed Martin. They developed programming and a new cable television network concept for the Britannica Channel; global programming partnerships for the successful launch of the Discovery Health Channel, including a novel CME programming initiative and the Medical Honors live broadcast from Constitution Hall; and programming strategies for the creation of the first-ever IPTV network developed by Lockheed Martin.

Jeff was the co-creator of the *Science of the Olympic Winter Games* and the *Science of NFL Football* video series with NBC Sports, which won the 2010 Sports Emmy for best original sports programming, as well as *The Science of Speed*, a novel video series partnership with the NASCAR Media Group.

Jeff has also written more than 24 inspirational and commercially successful novels—including his latest blockbusters, *Jude*, *Peace*, *Oil*, and *The Books of El*—for publishing houses such as David C. Cook, Tyndale, Zondervan/Thomas Nelson/HarperCollins, WaterBrook/Random House, Victor Books, Hodder & Stoughton, Guideposts, and others.

Jeff is executive director of Climate Nexus and writes a weekly science column for *U.S. News & World Report* called At the Edge (www.usnews.com/news/blogs/at-the-edge).

Resources by Dr. Kevin Leman

Books for Adults

The Birth Order Book
Have a New Kid by Friday
Have a New Husband by Friday
Have a New Teenager by Friday
Have a New You by Friday
Have a Happy Family by Friday
Planet Middle School
The Way of the Wise
Be the Dad She Needs You to Be
What a Difference a Mom Makes
Parenting the Powerful Child
Under the Sheets
Sheet Music
Making Children Mind without Losing Yours
It's Your Kid, Not a Gerbil!

Born to Win

Sex Begins in the Kitchen

7 Things He'll Never Tell You . . . But You Need to Know

What Your Childhood Memories Say about You

Running the Rapids

The Way of the Shepherd (written with William Pentak)

Becoming the Parent God Wants You to Be

Becoming a Couple of Promise

A Chicken's Guide to Talking Turkey with Your Kids about Sex (written with Kathy Flores Bell)

First-Time Mom

Step-parenting 101

Living in a Stepfamily without Getting Stepped On

The Perfect Match

Be Your Own Shrink

Stopping Stress before It Stops You

Single Parenting That Works

Why Your Best Is Good Enough

Smart Women Know When to Say No

Books for Children, with Kevin Leman II

My Firstborn, There's No One Like You

My Middle Child, There's No One Like You

My Youngest, There's No One Like You

My Only Child, There's No One Like You

My Adopted Child, There's No One Like You

My Grandchild, There's No One Like You

DVD/Video Series for Group Use

Have a New Kid by Friday

Making Children Mind without Losing Yours (parenting edition)

Making Children Mind without Losing Yours (public school teacher edition)

Value-Packed Parenting

Making the Most of Marriage

Running the Rapids

Single Parenting That Works

Bringing Peace and Harmony to the Blended Family

DVDs for Home Use

Straight Talk on Parenting

Why You Are the Way You Are

Have a New Husband by Friday

Have a New You by Friday

Have a New Kid by Friday

Available at 1-800-770-3830 • www.birthorderguy.com • www.drleman.com

Connect with the Authors

DR. KEVIN LEMAN

DrLeman.com

Follow Dr. Leman on

Dr Kevin Leman | drleman

• • •

JEFF NESBIT

JeffNesbit.net

Follow Jeff on

jeffnesbit